A PONTIAC IN THE WOODS

Fred Misurella

Praise for *A Pontiac in the Woods*:

"Beautifully and empathically written, *A Pontiac in the Woods* is a brutal and brutally honest tale.... The characters are fascinating, the reality of Jamie's situation is starkly depicted, and Fred Misurella deserves a call from Hollywood for the movie rights." (Five Stars)
– IndieReader

"Jamie's story combines many of the everyday anxieties and experiences of growing up with others that are specific to her situation, and Misurella manages to find a compelling tale in the tension between the two. A rich … study of a troubled teen's life on the margins."
--Kirkus Reviews

"Fred Misurella creates a world that plies its own orbit, rending a contemporary coming-of-age fiction from a classical soul's journey piece in *A Pontiac in the Woods*. After a string of tragedy and disappointment with various family formations, the teenage Jamie Sasso takes up residence in a sleeping bag in the back seat of the titular symbol of American-freedom-on-wheels. The tension inherent in this survival, coupled with the grace in which Jamie grows into her own identity while a member of a forgotten underclass, would be an easy trope to fall into the sanctimonious, but Misurella excels at keeping the story both timeless and topical."
—Miette Gillette, publisher of Whiskey Tit

Fred Misurella

Praise:

"Through the novel's embrace of solitude, and Jamie's fierce independence, its readers find unexpected connections in a world that at first seems fraught with cruelty and misfortune. *A Pontiac in the Woods* is an important reminder that in the face of adversity, it only takes a little kindness to kindle the resiliency of hope."
—Jefferson Navicky, author of *The Book of Transparencies* and *The Paper Coast.*

"*A Pontiac in the Woods* is a compelling and deeply moving coming-of-age novel that explores the trauma of adolescent homelessness, interrogates ideas of home and identity, and highlights how both are integral to our sense of belonging and community. A raw and unapologetic portrayal of a life lived on the margins of society."
—Marco Rafalà, author of *How Fires End*

"… as compelling as it is heartbreaking, *A Pontiac in the Woods* feels authentic as if we've known Jamie all our lives, but only now are we hearing her story and we're better for it."
—Duncan B. Barlow, author of *A Dog Between Us* and *The City, Awake*

Also by Fred Misurella

Fiction:

A Summer of Good-Byes, a novel

Arrangement in Black and White, a novel

Only Sons, a novel

Lies to Live By, stories

Short Time, a novella

Non-fiction:

Understanding Milan Kundera:

Public Events, Private Affairs

A PONTIAC IN THE WOODS

Fred Misurella

Blue Triangle Press

#3

2020

Fred Misurella

Library of Congress Registration Number:

TXu- 2-207-047

The characters and events in this novel are fictitious. Any similarity to real persons, living or dead, is coincidental and not intended by the author.

Cover photograph by Anfiusa Eremina.

Author photograph by Filipka Misurella.

ISBN:

ISBN 13: 978-0-578-71792-0

For Kim, Alex, and Filipka, with love.

And for Wayne and Colleen Prophet,

wonderful people, loyal friends.

Fred Misurella

A NOTE FROM THE AUTHOR

No one has been more important to *A Pontiac in the Woods* than Jamie Sasso (not her real name), who has whispered her story in my ear during intense private conversations for several years, and who has allowed me to channel her voice in the form of this novel. Here are a couple of facts Jamie would like you to remember: According to the National Association to End Homelessness, a headcount in 2016 revealed that more than 550,000 people in the United States regularly experienced homelessness on any given night. Of those, more than a third lived in a place not meant for human habitation (a street, a car, or an abandoned building), and about 41,000 were unaccompanied children or young adults. This is the story of just one of them.

"The poverty of being unwanted, unloved and uncared
for is the greatest poverty."

—Mother Teresa

"'Home. . .'

'I should have called it

Something you somehow haven't to deserve.'"—

Robert Frost, "The Death of the Hired Man

PART ONE:

DANCE BEFORE YOU RUN

I.

Tough, I say. I never went to France, as Misha did, never to Provence or Paris, never to Tuscany or the Italian Riviera either. And I'm an Italian, just like him. *"Eye-talian American,"* as Dad used to say. Comically, of course.

We watched TV instead of travel—I followed the Yankees with my father, Lady Gaga and MTV with Mum—both of them sleeping in their recliners beside me, gorging on their nightly z's, along with music videos, umpires bellowing strikes, shrieking and giggling game shows, plus the occasional bouts of soap and schmaltz Mum liked to turn to before drifting off into her own secret happy-ever-after: a friendly, comfortable dream with two leather recliners not really needed.

Don't get me wrong. I loved them both, completely. Good, ordinary people, older than most parents of kids my age, yet special. They wished no harm to anyone (especially me), and did their best to avoid causing it by accident. Misha's parents are completely different: smart, educated, with lots of interests, a bit stand-offish at first and not really willing to let people know who, or what, they are. But they're always willing to help—or want to—with advice, opinion, even money. And you can always count on Misha's mom and dad to take you to really classy places: shows, museums, restaurants, New York. And yes, someday, maybe even Paris.

Ben, his father, loves Paris. He lived there decades ago, but looks on it, plainly, as his home, the best part of his life. "Boring," Misha says, mainly because he feels so displaced there, the way I do here. *Paree*. At the mention of the name, Misha raises his head, hunches his shoulders, and wriggles his wrists as if someone threw a pot of warmed-over stew—or sewage—on top of him. It makes him feel dirty most of the time, he told me. The language, the smells, the stiff, brusque movement of the people in the streets seem so different that he can't figure out who, or what, he is.

Again, my sentiments exactly—but here, in our little former farm community, where everything's turning highway or shopping center now, with large, expansive lawns held in check by bushes and fences so that the houses in the middle of all that grass remain protected. So much separation—isolation—when I, a young woman turning nineteen and ready for college soon, crave nothing so much as close friends and family, everyone piled together in a gathering of wooden houses on an old-fashioned neighborhood street with hardwood trees.

"Ah, the good old days," Dad used to say, walking me down a street somewhere in Newark, an old city block, maybe, with two- or three-floor wooden houses, where his grandmother and grandfather used to live. Or sometimes we'd enter an empty alleyway in the middle of another town—maybe near Philadelphia—where heat rose from the tar and dust as if we walked on the very lid of hell while still searching for paradise.

"We didn't have a lot of money when I was a kid," my dad used to tell me, "but we had spirit, and plenty of it, Jamie. People your age don't seem to have that anymore."

"Dad" was not my real father—not the one whose DNA I carry anyway. He was a sweet-tempered, older man, like an uncle who agreed, along with Mum, to adopt me when my real sperm-and-egg creators disappeared—in pursuit of a special, drug-induced, flying-carpet dream. "Good riddance, fuckers" is how I always thought of them, though it wasn't until much later that I learned about the really ugly details.

Anyway, "Dad" claimed to remember boyhood days when he had nothing to eat, when men arrived to take his family's furniture or car away, when his father spent nights in jail because he could not pay family bills. "We were not happy," he said. "But your grandparents had moxie, Jamie. They knew we deserved to eat; knew someone owed us a place to sleep—and to bathe. Be damned if my dad or mom would let them get away with denying it." So, they went out as a family, he said, shopping in the downtown markets, ordering veggies and meat, carrying home an occasional chair on the bus they went out in. "We didn't have a car then," he said. "That all came later, believe it or not, when things got really bad and salesmen needed a deal on their sheets to increase their take-home pay."

So they "bought" a car (he always put two fingers in the air, each side of his head), leaving a twenty-dollar deposit ("Lord knows where my father got that," he'd say), and drove home in style at last, parking the car on the street somewhere near the apartment they "rented" (again two fingers on each side of his grinning face). They lived "like real Americans" for a week or two, sometimes a month; then, without fail, the repo men came with an extra set of keys, entered the car and drove it away. Eventually, the landlord arrived with his toothpick-chomping enforcer, then the butcher (in his bloody white apron; "No meat cleaver though," my dad would say with a laugh) and the vegetable guy. After that, the police, or the sheriff, and even a priest who could speak Italian, "came to walk your grandpa off to jail for a week, sometimes more." Grandpa would smile, slip on his one clean pair of pants, a fedora hat, and a jacket, Dad told me. Then out with his wrists for the handcuffs, and off they'd go, down the front steps, along the sidewalk, and, somewhere at the end of the block, into a police car they had parked away from the house to avoid embarrassment—for themselves, as well as Grandpa.

"They knew we were human, and we had a right to be treated that way—though we were immigrants! It was the times, not a question of laziness or dishonesty, and they knew it."

"The times . . ." "Immigrants . . ." I have no idea what those two words *really* meant, especially in the 1930s, if I remember my history right. I've seen programs on the Learning Channel and public television at school, but everything looks remote, serious. Not at all like today. People dressed for picnics, smiled and acted polite (at least for the camera). Nobody scowled, flipped the bird, or struck a crazy pose. Nobody took selfies, drank too much, or took drugs. Well, I know people did some of those things, but apparently not for the camera. It was a part of their lives they kept private, a practice that fits my preferences to a tee. Misha's like that too. We both have hidden quirks and kinks, but we do our best to make them remain that way. No weird selfies with doctored faces, no biceps photos with painted tattoos, and definitely no sick rings glittering through ears, nose, dick or vulva.

Misha's dad tries to accept all this. "Tattoos are artistic," he says, shrugging. "Body decoration is as old as humanity."

We've gone out with them—Misha's parents— quite a few times, usually to one of the Asian or Indian restaurants in our town. We've also gone to movies and local art galleries, and about once or twice a month for a while, we took the car into New York and went our separate ways—lunch and a play for Mr. and Mrs. A; walking, window-shopping, and general sightseeing for me and Misha. I loved those New York visits, mainly because the streets vibrated wildly when we walked. I'd feel it from my soles through my ankles and thighs, and then up through the rest of me. I felt like some long-lost native dance was buried beneath the cement and macadam, and my feet tried to find it and dig it out. Misha and I pranced on the sidewalks and sometimes broke into a dance, or skipped down a block like a pair of ten-year-olds at a circus.

Once, we stopped at a corner, started a clap and rap beat out of the sounds of the city, and then I threw in a few vogue moves while we waited for the light to change. We were on the west side of Central Park, at 59th Street, I think, and just as we started to cross to the other side, a couple of young black kids came out of the park, joined us, and turned it into a breakdance routine as the cars, a horse and buggy, and a huge moving van lumbered past. I felt breathless when we stopped and walked to the other side. "Gotta loosen up, bro," one of

18

them said to Misha. "Move your legs more and show a little muscle. You," they both looked at me, "you skinny, but that's a black girl's ass. So loosen it, and swing with soul."

They rushed down Broadway from there, laughing and dancing, then smacking high fives. Misha and I stood looking at them, not sure if we had been insulted or not. "We have to practice," Misha said. "We wouldn't stand a chance trying to keep up with them in a contest."

We just smiled at each other and started toward Fifth Avenue.

***

II.

My dad died, two years after my mum. I got a job at the first Panera in our town, lived alone in our empty house for a couple months until it was sold by an older distant cousin who was supposed to take care of me but didn't. I received a very small amount of cash, which I put into a bank to keep for a day when I would absolutely need it. And after a couple failed attempts with foster families, I slept in the back seat of an abandoned car in the woods behind a neighborhood park. I went to school whenever I felt like it, really because I needed it for warmth and food. School lunches were awful but free, and I liked the gym classes a lot. Gym rat that I turned out to be, I actually loved working out on the weight machines, treadmills, and stationary bicycles until I built muscle and became what Misha still calls a pink-colored live extension cord with bulk. I'm a better lifter than him and a very good distance runner. In dancing, we're about equal and, with the body of a wiry 14-year-old, I could hop and *jeté* with the best of the dancers at the local dance studio and outlast most of the runners on our piss-poor boys track team. According to Misha, even now, more than four years later (he's a lot more muscular, I have to say), I make an easy lift and spin for him no matter what kind of music we dance to: jazz, rock and roll, show tunes—even his father's beloved Puccini.

Dancing keeps us close to this day. A fortunate hobby, you might say, two loner kids who fell into one another's arms at their high school's retro sock hop a little over four and a half years ago, not long after my dad died. Bill Haley and the Comets, Jerry Lee Lewis, Buddy Holly, and, of course, the King. "You Ain't Nothin' but a Hound Dog" brought us together the night we first met. Almost nobody attended the hop—word was the music wasn't "cool"—and those who did, at least the guys, didn't dance to the fast stuff. So you can say Misha and I had no choice but to face the music and each other, jiggle our butts and arms as an introduction, and try to outdo that skinny smiling opposite-sex stranger grinning stupidly right in front of us.

"Jamie Sasso," I said, slapping my ass and giving a little wiggle. He nodded his head but said nothing.

"What are you—a senior?"

"Junior," he replied. His eyes shone at me, although he pretended not to see the wiggle or even hear my name. He held his chin high, his nose pointed toward the lights in the gym ceiling, but as I turned away a second time and did a little voguing—arms, legs, belly, ass—I watched his head lower and his eyes follow with a hint of hunger. Of course, I gave another wiggle then a sudden bigger one, and, I hoped, a hotter sway. When I spun and faced him again, my hands rested on my scissoring thighs.

"You like this stuff?" he said.

He nodded to the music.

"I love to dance," I said. "Doesn't matter who or what's playing, as long as it's got a beat."

"Me too, I guess. Though I've never danced to this kind of music before. It's from my dad's time—or before, I think—and I'm surprised I like it. Kind of crazy."

"What's your name?" I asked. "I don't need to know your father's music because I'm not swinging my butt for him."

His eyes opened, but only slightly. "Misha Alto," he said. "What's yours?"

"Jamie," I repeated. "Sasso. And I like the music a lot. I'd call it bluesy."

He grinned. He had a shy smile most of the time, still does, but sometimes, lately, there's a glimmer, a little more certainty, as if he knows he's got the situation under control. Most of the time he doesn't, really, but that's Misha for you. A guy who, despite his looks (they're very good), doesn't really believe his own fortunate gifts.

"So, why'd you come?" I said, with another wiggle and spin, this time showing a little pelvic twist and thrust to rouse his interest. He shrugged and morphed into his own pelvic thrust, with a nice bit of grace, and spun away before coming full circle to face me again. *Nice cheeks*, I noted, front and back.

At that point "Hound Dog" gave way to something slower, moodier called "Who's Sorry Now?" which I'd also never heard before. I remember the song well, sung by a woman named Connie Francis. Misha smiled, stepped closer, held his left hand up and reached for my right, which was trying to figure out what to do with something (nothing) circling my right ear and making me feel itchy, and very uncomfortable. "I don't know this kind of stuff," I said. "It's a little bit slower than my feet are willing to go—most of the time."

He held my hand anyway, slipped his right arm around my back and, for one of the first times ever, I found myself close enough to a boy my age to feel something like—I don't know—not sexy, but nervous. He drew me and pushed me here and there, spinning us around during the heavier measures of the tune and, finally, bent me back and to the side so he could hold my waist and lean close while I got a good look past his hazel eyes toward the ceiling lights. "Hey, don't drop me," I giggled, more scared than I wanted to be. "And don't even think of putting your lips close to mine because it's not going to happen—tonight."

He straightened as the music thrummed to a quiet close, and then dropped his right hand, although he kept my right one in the other and started walking toward the out of bounds of the gym basketball court. "You dance really great," he said. "Even that slow one. You know, my father says he went to the same school as her—Connie Francis."

"Connie Francis... Wow. I don't even know who she is. Or was."

Misha looked at me and laughed. "You're not the only one. But my dad says she was big in his day—when he was in high school. She sang that song, a really huge hit."

"Oh... so?"

"So, she's the singer. That was her voice. She went to the same high school as my father."

"Wow. And he knows her, really?"

"Knew her. She's retired now. So is he. They were in a couple classes together, but she was absent a lot because she had TV appearances. Dick Clark's show, I think."

"Wow, I wouldn't mind getting off for TV appearances. I guess Miley Cyrus got off for that when she was in school—pre-twerking."

Misha shrugged. "They have private tutors now, I think, probably paid for by the TV people. My dad says Connie passed and graduated just like everyone else—cap and gown and the whole ceremony. Although she did sing the Star Spangled Banner when they began the program—to a rock and roll beat."

"Lucky girl. What happened to her?"

He shrugged again. "Sad life, according to my father. But she won some kind of honor at the White House. A medal of honor? I'm not sure, but my dad says she was a hot teenage star—movies and everything—whose life turned sour when she got older. Brother murdered. And I think she got attacked in some hotel."

"Jesus." I shook my head.

He held my hand and looked at me—a long time. I assumed he'd heard about me. All the kids had by then, I guess. I was living the silly fantasy life they dreamed for themselves when they weren't on Instagram or Facebook. You know, alone in a car, no limits to who you invite or what you do; no curfew to worry about when you're getting something on or concentrating on something—like a dick, an ab, or something pink and warm that somebody else might want to touch and hold. I couldn't afford Wi-Fi or a personal phone and, no, nobody wished me sweet dreams and a good night before I slept. But I was free, some of the stupider kids might say—whatever that means when you have to think about creeps crawling into your car in the middle of the night, a snowfall that might trap you in freezing cold for days, or even where the fuck I'm going to get some food when I run out of money. I wouldn't steal, I wouldn't let some pimp knock me around just to make himself feel like a king, and I sure as hell was not going to run down to county welfare and bellyache so they could *tch-tch* and try to set me up with another foster family. It didn't leave me much room to maneuver, I admit, but at least it gave me some strong guidelines about what I shouldn't let happen and what, maybe, I would die for instead of giving in.

"It's a bad place to be in," my dad used to tell me, though I never knew what place he meant, unless it was a state of mind. "Very few people in the world will help a loner, no matter how weak and deprived they are. Somehow, you do it all yourself. You have to be independent."

And so now, with Mum and then him gone so fast, I was—or tried my very best to be.

"Hey, you want to go down to Jimmy's for pizza?" Misha said. "I'll drive."

"I don't have any money," I said, lying, of course, because I had to watch my pennies.

"My treat. I just got paid, so I'm feeling very generous."

I stared at him, trying to figure out his motives. I didn't know a lot about boys—not my age anyhow—but I was also aware of all the possibilities. Books, movies, TV, and even school classrooms will do that for you. He seemed nice enough; a bit innocent, but I knew how fast that could disappear. I hadn't heard much about him, mainly because I didn't hang much with the other kids and didn't listen to their gossip when I did. As far as I knew, Misha Alto was a good kid, smart, a bit awkward (I guess I was, too), and timid, mainly because, like me, he didn't feel "normal" (yes, fingers winking beside my ears) but because his parents took him to operas, art museums and galleries, and yearly trips to Europe ("the Mediterranean," his father called it). He'd never seen a ballgame, never thrown a football; shot baskets in the stiffest, clumsiest possible way, and, for physical exercise, attended dance classes, ran a little around our school track, and worked out on a balancing bar from time to time. Somehow, as he would tell me later that week, none of it ever seemed sexy to the girls.

At the pizza place, "Jimmy's Wood-Burning Oven," as the sign still says, Sinatra was singing, filling the parking lot with noise—about life, how tough it's been—up and down and everywhere else, he sang— which made him very special—though to Misha and me he was just some bellyaching guy making the best of a lot of messed-up, sick experience. "Bad choices, pretty much like a drunk or whore," Misha said.

We nodded toward Jimmy when we entered. He stood behind the counter patting and spinning six-inch balls of dough that he turned into flying saucers and then caught as heavy, wet blankets before lovingly arranging them on the flour-covered counter and anointing them with sauce ("San Marzano tomatoes," he likes to brag). After crumbling on white mozzarella ("Fresh. Pure buffalo milk," he'll tell you), he lifts them from the counter with his wobbly pizza board and slides them onto the floor of a huge brick oven behind the counter— the wood for the fire burning in back and on the sides without reaching the board and, miraculously, I sometimes think, not charring the pie while it cooks.

"*Ciao*," Jimmy said, turning to Misha. "The usual for our future professor?"

Misha looked at me, as if I should know what either of those comments meant, and then surprised me with his courtesy. "Would you like the extra sauce?" he asked. "He's got a great recipe."

"Love it. That's always my favorite part."

Misha nodded to Jimmy again, asked about his wife, and then said he had seen his daughter, Kathy, at a mall somewhere near here. "She seems happy," Misha said, rolling his hand out from his chest down toward his lap. "Six months, right?"

Jimmy nodded, suddenly less smiley, and looking careworn but resilient, like Sinatra, I imagined. He took a ball of dough from a pot on the counter, slapped some flour on it, and began rolling it around. As Frankie crooned again, being a "poet, a pirate, a pawn, and a king," Jimmy nodded to the rhythm, tossed up a doughy platter, and caught it right to the beat. He slapped it on the counter, kneaded it a little more, turning it around like an old LP, then draped it in his hands, spinning and launching it into the air once more. Sinatra bellowed about falling flat on his face (happily, the pizza landed on Jimmy's fists), and the band began to swell, laying Frankie down to die while Jimmy poured tomatoes, cheese, and an extra ladle of sauce, before scooping up the pizza with his paddle. He consigned it to the flames and everything went silent, including Frankie and his band. Jimmy turned to a previous pie in the oven, inspecting the crust for proper browning, shoved it closer

27

to the wood-flames for about a minute, then pulled it toward the oven's mouth, lifting and slipping it into an open box with his paddle. He wrote something on the box, placing it above the warm oven, then checked our pie before turning to Misha and asking about his mom and dad.

"How's the old professor doing?" he said. "Enjoying retirement?"

Misha grinned, looking at me with a shame-faced squint before he nodded. "You know my father, Jimmy. Everything's fine, but not as good as it could, or should, be."

Jimmy shrugged, inclining his head a little to the side. I didn't know anything about Misha's family then, so I had no idea what any of this conversation meant. Jimmy checked our pizza, but then he turned toward us, coming closer to the counter. "Hey, Misha, he's a dad, yours. I know him. He's always going to want things better—for you, not himself."

Misha nodded, though very clearly he had some doubt. When Jimmy asked about his mom, he was much more relaxed, much more committed to everything being fine. Jimmy gave him a great big grin and said, as if it was the most ordinary thing in the world, that he still stared at the picture of his mother, Mama Lucia, that Mrs. Alto painted for him years ago. Jimmy turned to me, saw my puzzlement, and with his eyes wide pointed to a spot on the wall behind my head. "She was on that wall, behind you, young lady, for many years. When she passed, I had to bring her home to keep my wife, Tina, and my daughter company. Of course, I also like to see her on the wall near the table when I eat at home. This sauce is her recipe."

Misha grinned. I was about to say something totally stupid—I don't know, something like I'm sorry, but at the same time happy, that she still joined the family for dinner at home—but suddenly Jimmy gasped and turned to the oven where our pizza, we all saw, had turned into a gigantic burning cracker, maybe a Ritz. Jimmy pulled it from the fire with fluttering fingers, letting it simmer and cool on the brick edge of the oven. He immediately started another one for us. "Can't talk anymore," he said, smiling. "Costs too much money."

Misha went to the jukebox in the corner, swiped his card and picked out a few songs. I didn't know much about music at that time because the radio in my car wasn't working, and without Wi-Fi I didn't have much chance to listen to the cool stuff. I recognized U-2 at first, then maybe something by Beyoncé ("Single Ladies," I think), and something else by Lady Gaga and Tony Bennett, "I Can't Give You Anything but Love".

Jimmy said nothing, just paid close attention to our extra-sauce pizza in the oven, but he perked up when Tony shrieked an octave or two above Lady in the final chorus of their song. Jimmy shook his head and looked at me as if I had something to learn.

"That man knew how to sing from the time he was two," he said with a wink. "A Queens kid who made good—very good. I knew his family. This Gaga lady has got herself a very good teacher, the ultimate pro."

Misha nodded, staring at me in an attempt to keep my mouth shut, I think. Though I didn't have anything clear to say at the moment, his look didn't

29

make me want to keep it that way. "Well, maybe he wanted to learn something from her," I said. "His name's not selling the record. Hers is."

Jimmy turned to check the pizza. After a quick lift and delicate push toward the side flames, he returned to the counter. "Hey, maybe she's selling the record—to you kids—but she wouldn't have even had a chance to make it, not with those songs on it, if he wasn't singing with her."

He was right, of course, so I nodded, but not without throwing in another dollar's worth of wisdom. "She wants his audience, just as much as he wants hers."

Jimmy agreed, rubbing two fingers against his thumb and grinning. "*Soldi, soldi; fa girare il mondo.*"

He turned back to the oven, lifting and peering under our pizza as if it was a woman's skirt. He spun it one more time; then up with the board, under the pizza, he brought it to the counter to slide it on a round aluminum sheet. He cut it (eight slices), handing the platter to Misha, and the two of us walked to a table in the corner, as far away from the counter as we could.

"Professor, take a soda from the cooler. It's on the house."

With a smile, Misha stood and went to pick one out.

"Thanks," he said, holding up a liter of Sprite. He came back to the table with two plastic cups, sitting next to me as he put everything down.

"Napkins," Jimmy called, pushing a holder along the counter toward our corner. "And here's a couple paper plates."

This time I got up and walked to the counter, trying not to look at Jimmy. He handed me the plates, winked, and smiled as if he had something to tell me, but at that moment the door swung open with a ding, and he immediately turned to the new customer. *"Buon giorno! Come vai?"*

"Thanks," I whispered, and headed back to the corner table.

The pizza was good, very good. I watched my money a lot at that time, so it's safe to say I rarely bought anything at a restaurant. Canned and boxed foods were my specialties, hardly anything ever hot since the only time I could afford cooked stuff was when I ate my free meals at school. Every once in a while my distant prick of a cousin sent me care packages, as he called them, which I managed to heat up with a can of Sterno. Even less often one of the teachers at the school took pity on me and invited me home for dinner. High school kids—and their families— avoided me for the most part, and none of them saw me as a friend. Sometimes I wondered if I smelled (I didn't), had bad breath (nope), or somehow looked funny. But apart from my skinny, wiry body and my obviously practical Sally Ann jeans and shirts, I don't think I looked much different from any of them.

Still, I made them unsure. As Misha would tell me later, I just looked unattached, maybe a little wild, as if I didn't belong anywhere, or didn't want to, certainly not with upscale suburban high school kids from streets that used to be fields of corn. "Hey, I'm not a freak," I told him, "but my life is not a matter of choice." My parents, good and bad sets of them, happened to leave me this way—not necessarily of their choice either. "For some people, life sucks, Misha. Some people are lucky, most aren't."

His eyes dropped when I said that. For a brief moment I could see the guilt pull him away from me, as if he too saw me as a person who stank. I felt like doing something gross, farting in his face, maybe belching like the goons on the football team. But at the same time I wanted to run from him and whatever we were doing, shrink into a shell, and crawl into a corner hole where I could cover my head and scream. I admit I still feel that way sometimes, but especially then, in my rusty, freezing Pontiac at night when I actually wondered if I could make it through till morning. It was tough, but at the same time the pressure comforted me because I didn't feel like the other kids, didn't worry about my distant future, the boyfriend (or girlfriend), marriage, college, career, family. Not then. That stuff existed far out of my range of expectations, and I never imagined it in my likely future. So... no worries. Please, God, just get me through the next few hours. Let me see the sun shine in the morning, feel happy, and, maybe, buy some coffee with a donut before I run to school and wash my face.

Misha could tell his own sad story, of course, because he was adopted. But for now he lived a happy ending, which is why he felt guilty whenever I exposed my life to him. He shared what he had with me—invited me to his house often, introduced me to his parents, took food from their refrigerator and passed it on to me. At first I thought his parents didn't know what he was doing, but looking back now, my guess is they

32

encouraged him. Mr. A was stiff, Mrs. A a little distracted by her painting, but at bottom they had very good intentions—*heart*, as my good dad used to call it.

That's not to say they heard my story and immediately took me in. Certainly not that first night with Misha because, as usual, I cut that stuff off by keeping quiet about myself. So, he just offered to drive me home after we finished eating the pizza. He called out good night to Jimmy, smacked him a high five at the counter for the great meal, and as we walked to his car, he asked me where I lived. "Near the park," I answered evasively, though I assumed most kids knew about the Pontiac. "You can drop me at the corner—Oak and Chestnut. I'll jog the rest."

He stopped, looked at me, and tossed his keys into the air, catching them in his palm. "Um, you know, I'm not about to start anything—physical, I mean. You made the no-kissing part very clear during 'Who's Sorry Now?'"

"That's not what I meant," I said, trying for a warmer smile. "I just happen to like to run a little before bed. I sleep better."

He looked at the sky a few seconds: dark, clear, but with no moon and just a bunch of cold-looking, distant stars. They give me the jeebies sometimes, and I suppose he felt that too, because he said, "You feel comfortable running alone near the park on a night like this? I wouldn't. Who knows who's hanging out in there—or what they're hanging for?"

"I'll be alright," I say. "It's near the police station. I've done it thousands of times and never been bothered."

Which is a bit of a lie, I confess. I've been hassled there, but a dash to the police station kept me safe.

"I don't believe you. Besides, I'd like to know for sure where you live so I can pick you up sometime… You know, for a movie or something. Maybe for another dance."

Nice, right?—Super friendly. Stupid me, here's what I replied, "How do you know I'll want to go to a movie with you—or even another dance?"

His face dropped. He gave me one of those basic "What the fuck?" looks and started walking to his car. I caught up with him, put my arm around his shoulders, and, on tiptoe, kissed him—lightly—on the cheek. "Hey, I'm sorry. I didn't mean it the way that must have sounded. Sometimes I'm a bit of a jerk."

He pulled away, stumped for a second, and then continued toward the car. I ran ahead, stopped at the driver's door, and just stood there trying to think of something smartass to say. Stupid as I felt, I came up with nothing.

"Look," he said, "I'll drive you wherever you want. I just thought we were having a good time."

"We were," I said. "I mean, I *am*. I'm just not sure how much more I want—or can take."

Again, he showed me that look. My hands went up to my face, and I looked at him through the fingers. He seemed smaller that way, more petulant, as if I'd really hurt his feelings. I saw again, he wasn't as confident as he seemed, and I knew I'd really reached him. "Look, it's not pretty, Misha. I'm not sure what you know about me, but lots of it is not very good."

"I suppose I could say the same about myself, but I won't because it won't stop me from driving you home or picking you up some other night. So, what's your story? What makes it special? And so awful?"

I stared at him. Then I looked at my feet, trying to figure how much he needed to know. Am I ashamed of my life, who I am, the way I live, and *where*? You're damned straight I am! I see the other kids around me, their houses, their clothes, their comfortable world, then I look at myself, my rusty Pontiac in the woods, and I keep thinking that someone's cursed me, laid a dark, thick blanket of shit on my head and shoulders, and, worse, I deserve the whole awful, gloomy pile. I have no idea what I did, why I got dumped on and others didn't; but there it is, mist and doo-doo rising around me, pressing against my shoulders and neck, and most of the time, all I can do is look down at my feet to make sure I'm on firm ground before I start running.

"I have no special story," I told him, whispering. "I just like my time alone."

"Well. . ." He reached around me for the car door, but I nudged him away with my hip.

"But not when I'm with you!" I told him, trying to smile. "I had a really good time tonight. I mean, I'm *having* a good time."

He dropped his arm, straightened, and damned if I knew what to say next. My brain scrambled. My stomach churned, and the only thing I could do was put one hand on each of his shoulders and sort of hold him away at the same time I wouldn't let him go. He had that look on his face again that said, "What the fuck am I getting into?" or, "How do I climb out of this shit-filled hole she's digging?" But I could see for the first time he didn't really want to leave.

"I live like a tramp, Misha. Plain as that. There's nothing in my life you want to know."

"A tramp? You mean. . ."

"I live in a fucking car, a rust-covered Pontiac that doesn't move. It's a mess, but it's my house, my home, and I sleep there—by myself—every night. I have to shit and pee in the woods nearby."

His eyes narrowed, as if I'd said something he couldn't possibly understand, but he was giving it maximum effort. "Jesus," he said at last. He lifted his hands to cup my elbows in his palms. "I've heard some stories, but Jesus. . . They're true?"

I nodded and looked down at my shoes, ashamed and maybe a touch relieved. I began to leave.

"I never really believed them," he said, holding on to me. "I figured they wouldn't let it happen. The school, or state, or county would have to put you up with somebody—a family."

I shook my head. "County services tried, but nothing worked out. I didn't really like any of the foster families they put me in, so they gave me some money and let me take care of myself—as long as I report to a county social worker every week or so."

"Wow."

I smiled—I'm not sure why. He did, too, at his own surprise, I think, and I began to tell him the stories of my two sets of parents—the ones who bore me and disappeared, the ones who cared for me and died too soon. Misha listened—attentive, I have to say—but I still saw a look of something in his eyes I assumed was disbelief.

"Misha, this is not made up. None of it. I know it doesn't seem real, but I'm living in this shitty dream every day, and it's not easy to get out of it."

He nodded. "I believe you. No question there. But the people in school—the principal, the guidance counselors—why did they let it happen? How could they?"

"They just did. I mean, they just do. As long as I don't have trouble and tell them I don't want to be with anybody, they leave me alone. Good or fucking bad."

Shaking his head, he reached for the door again. Pulling it open, he began to slide into the front seat. I gripped his arm with both my hands. "Are you pissed—at me, I mean? Why?"

He sat back, one leg dangling out the car, as he hung onto the wheel. We were not shoving or pulling, neither one swinging or twisting, but inside us both a real wrestling match went on. I felt my fingers squeeze harder on his upper arm; I saw his left leg strain to lift his boot from the ground.

"Jamie, you just said it yourself. You don't want to be with anybody."

"What?"

He nodded. "And so I'm leaving you alone."

"What? You can't. I won't let you."

He stared at me. Not smiling, but surprised, and I wondered if he could see the same surprise in me. Because I was surprised—shocked even—at everything happening. I was in one of those places that Dad used to talk about: *You know where you are, you know where you don't want to be, but with no clear idea where the hell you want to go—or have to.* "Life," he used to tell me, "at its most crucial moments."

"So this is a crucial moment?" I wanted to ask him, but obviously Dad wasn't there to answer. And the guy who was, young Misha Alto, looked even more puzzled and clueless than I was. He sat in his seat, one cheek and leg hanging out, but I noticed he wasn't straining to get that boot off the ground anymore. Well, it must be a crucial moment, I figured, so let's take advantage of it with a stream of horseshit that may just change his mind.

"Just give me a little space," I told him. "It has nothing to do with you. Really. I just need to breathe a little. I need to think."

He laughed but said nothing. I saw real doubt on Misha's face, as if the whole night between us was just a horrible Disneyland dream, and we were trying to entertain ourselves like a pair of technicolor kids.

"I can see you after school next week," I said. "We can meet in the Sugar Bowl."

He laughed again, not happily. "You're serious—with all the jocks and cheerleaders? Do you hang out there often?"

I lowered my head and dropped my hands to my sides. "I've never been in it. I've just heard people talk."

"You probably ought to keep it that way. Why don't I meet you on the corner beyond the park? Tuesday. I'll walk you home, if you want to show me your place—whatever it is. Or maybe I can take you to my house, where we can dance."

"Perfect," I told him. "I really like the dancing idea."

"Okay," Misha said, smiling. "I'll run it by the old people. They'll be ecstatic."

The boot finally slid into his car. Cute cheeks adjusted, and the seatbelt clicked closed. After kissing his forehead, I shut the car door and waved as he drove off into the night.

***

III.

So that was our first date—at last with a guy I could stand. After he drove away that night, I walked home from Jimmy's parking lot without the slightest fear—unusual in my recent life. I just felt that something wonderful had finally happened, and that even the sleepy monsters running the show from up in the sky, at least when they thought about it, wouldn't ("couldn't" is a more hopeful word) do anything to ruin it for me. I look back now and see how stupid all that was, but as Dad used to say, sometimes idiots are lucky. It just worked out fine. I walked back to the school grounds on Main Street, and then, as I often do when it's dark, took the long, slow trek past the police station at the opposite end of the park just so I could keep myself under street lights. I walked the center of the street most nights, figuring people could see me from their windows, if they happened to look out, and the creeps hiding in shadows or an alley someplace along the way would have farther to go and give me a chance to run.

Oh, yes, I had to run quite a few times, even on Main Street. But I've always been a fast mover—still am—especially with a comfortable lead, and so I felt confident I could always get away, at least as far as the police station before anyone could catch me. So, I wore running shoes every day, not as a style thing like most kids my age, but for the traction and sprint-speed I might need to generate. I actually had six pairs of black New Balances lined up in the backseat shelf of the Pontiac, and I wore a different pair every day to keep them fresh. I walked a lot, as you can imagine, because buses—and most moving vehicles—made me nervous. Misha's old Honda was the first car I'd ridden in for more than a year. No comfy daily drives in an SUV or van; and of course, I didn't take cabs because I couldn't afford them. So, my New Balances ("nimble NBs," I called them) did my traveling for me.

I don't know where I got the habit from. Dad used to talk about walking for many miles to school every winter morning, and though I never really believed him (he was a city boy, Mum told me), I always felt or saw this image of a young Dad with cold, wet snow hitting his face as a kind of exaggerated model of the good American country life. "It was a struggle," he'd tell me, "but I never missed a school day from kindergarten through the end of twelfth grade." He even went when they canceled for lousy weather a couple of times because he left his house before the announcement came. "My one academic achievement," Dad used to say. "At graduation I received a plaque to reward my hundred percent attendance. They called it the 'Faith Award'— Just being there."

That was Dad for you. And, I have to say, Misha is the same, somebody you can count on to be there. We got together the following Tuesday, as promised, a block or two beyond the park where there were no other kids to stare and make comments. I saw him standing at the corner waiting, while I jogged up the sidewalk from the school, where I had showered very thoroughly after cross-country practice. He looked comfortable standing there, and *really* happy when he saw me running across the street. I was happy to see him too, of course, but at the same time I had no idea what we would do, or worse,

41

what we would talk about. I thought of Misha as a loner, like me in lots of ways, a guy who didn't quite fit in with any school group and who somehow felt at fault because of it. He didn't hang out with anyone—neither jocks nor the fratty, bookish guys who always worried about their grades—and I never saw him with a girl either, socially or in the library. He always stood alone, separate, talking to kids or teachers here and there, but never for more than five, maybe ten, minutes. Just enough to get an assignment straightened out or to clarify some idea about a topic, a class, or, maybe, another kid. As you can imagine, I wondered how this afternoon would end.

"Hey, Jamie! Hi!" He spread his arms as I trotted up to him, and, cheesy me, I had zero idea about how I should respond. Confused, blinking, I ran right between his fingers and hands, slammed into his chest, and, to my everlasting embarrassment, almost knocked him over!

"Woah, Jesus," I said. "I'm really sorry." I caught him by the shoulders as he stumbled backward, smiling, almost taking us both to the ground beside a streetlight pole. Finally, we steadied ourselves, and without looking at his face I just dropped my hands, stared at my feet, and, feeling my cheeks flush, turned to go.

"Wait," he said, still smiling. "Where you going?"

"Home," I said, though at the same time I felt how stupid it was to use such a word for a rusty piece of metal, glass, and plastic.

"Hey, you just got here. I'm okay. Nothing's broken, but I need somebody to tell me if I'm bleeding."

"You're not bleeding," I said, more to my NBs than him, but out of the corner of my eye I saw that he was covering up a laugh. I looked up, made a face, and, embarrassed or not, started laughing with him. "Boy, you got some hick of a farmer girl to be with today."

It was something Dad, or even Mum, might have said, with a blushing grin whenever one of them did something foolish. Misha just laughed and held out his arms again, and with my head a little clearer I stepped between them, snuggling up close, although I didn't offer to kiss. He took a step or two back and to the left, and then spun us around the lamp pole, humming as if we were in some technicolor musical. I think you may have guessed this, but that's exactly what Dad would do with Mum whenever they felt silly. Once or twice when we were alone, he did it with me too. "We all need romance," Dad would tell me. "The whole world needs it. We're getting too damn serious about everything, especially ourselves."

Of course, Misha wouldn't say that, but I could feel his emotional attempt to lift us off the ground, maybe relax us both a little so the afternoon could be fun. I felt his good heart right away—that he wanted to make me happy—and so I didn't fight him at all, just let myself go and for the few seconds of that little movie dance trusted him and life and whatever the day had to bring us together.

He dropped his arms after a few spins, stopped dancing, and with a deep blush took my hand in his. We started down the block toward the police station, and he asked me to take him to my "home". Of course, I said no.

"I want to see how you live," he said, seeing me shake my head. "You've got more guts and independence than I could ever have."

"*Guts* isn't the right word, Misha. I have no choice; it's a necessity."

"From what you told me at the dance, you do have a choice, and you're brave enough to follow through on it."

I shrugged my shoulders. Whenever people said I had courage for living in a car, I often reminded myself that courage was just another form of stupidity—the kind that people praised. There was some truth in that, I suppose, but as far as I was concerned there was nothing else for me to do. I didn't want to live in a foster family—with strangers. Again, "couldn't live with them" would probably be more accurate. And since my older, very distant shit of a cousin didn't give a damn about me or my future once he got his money from our house, I just flat out had to do it on my own. Then because the social worker on my case, a nice guy named Dominic Santa, reluctantly agreed that I could live alone if I visited him in his office bi-weekly, both the state and the county dumped some money in my bank account each month to make up for my distant relation. Mr. Santa sent him regular reports, but the shithead never responded— not even once. "Bad luck," Mr. Santa called it, but I just looked him in the eye, raised my hand with the pinky and forefinger up, and pointed it somewhere toward the western part of our county as if I was sending the evil eye.

"Fuck him and his money," I said. "I wouldn't want to live with that fuckhead anyway, even if he begged me."

Oh yes, I said that. And with all that mental baggage I still took Misha into the woods across from the station to see my car that night. It was a 1960 Bonneville that, I'm sure, had once been metallic blue, but with most of the paint gone now, just looked like a rusty brown tank abandoned under some menacing trees. The seats were torn and loose, tires flat and obviously deteriorated, but the windows, miraculously, were left intact though pock-marked, letting in just enough light for a grimy, depressing glow. As I told Mr. Santa once, I spent my entire life there as if it were five o'clock on a graying winter afternoon. Bed was the mangled, spring-exposed seat in back, and a brown army blanket, with as many coats and pants as I could pile together, kept me warm in fall and winter. For hot days, I'd slip under the steering wheel in front and scrunch down very low because there was a hole in the floor above the front left tire that would let in moist, mostly cool air. I covered the hole with a tarp and some stolen blankets during the dark days, but I found the damp ground and whatever fresh air a breeze could bring relieved almost any heat I felt during summer.

"Very cool," my beaming Misha said as we came around a fat forest oak and saw the Bonneville waiting behind a tuft of tall grass beside a dark rock. He walked ahead of me, circled the rusty beast, and came back toward me with a huge grin on his face. "Jeez, my dad used to have one of these. He said he learned to drive in it and didn't want to let it go. Finally, it died and he just junked it. I'm sure it wasn't this one, though, cause I've seen the pictures. His was a very bright yellow."

I pulled open the driver's door. The screech of rusty hinges made us both cringe. I slid in across to the passenger's side on the blackened slate-blue couch seat, and Misha sat behind the steering wheel. "Wow, I feel like I'm piloting the *Queen Mary*," he said, making as if to steer. The wheel, basically frozen in place, turned just an inch, maybe a fraction more. "Whoa, no more power steering here," he said. He turned to look in the back, where, beside the six pairs of NBs, I had a stash of canned food, mainly vegetables and a little meat and fish. From there he peered through the grimy scratch of my windows to surrounding bush, grass, and trees. "Pretty private," Misha said. "You could do some pretty wild stuff here."

I gave him a hard stare, but he was just trying to be nice, I figured, so I didn't try to make much of it.

"I'll trade any time you want," I said finally, smiling, "your room and family for this house."

My fingers semaphored around "house", of course. But then I let my fingers drop, and we spent a few embarrassed minutes just looking around so we wouldn't have to stare at each other or say something stupid. With Misha there, my abandonment was painfully obvious, not only because of the old, fucked-up blue car, but also my fucked-up blue life. I knew it had to lower me in his eyes—maybe in a kind way, maybe not. But I mostly knew it had to make any life between us very short.

"Well, we should do something," Misha said. "We can't drive this thing, but we sure as hell can walk.

You want to go someplace for coffee? Even the Sugar Bowl?"

I reluctantly nodded my head. "Ice cream is good for me. At least it's homemade there, I hear, and I'm a little hungry after practice."

So we left my "house" (semaphores again), walked past the police station, back to the school, and into town. The Sugar Bowl was a block or so beyond the high school, on a corner where there was an old-fashioned barber shop with a barber's pole outside. Across the street stood a woman's clothing store and next to that a Turkish falafel place, where on Saturday nights you could see a blonde belly dancer strut her stuff. In the Sugar Bowl we sat at the counter and waited for one of the college girls who worked there to serve us. A dark-haired, blue-eyed one came over, checked Misha out, and asked what we wanted. Misha looked at me and widened his eyes. I looked at him and shrugged. The college girl stood there, her baby blues darting from him to me and back again. "A soft vanilla freeze," I said, "large." Misha looked at her and raised two fingers. She went to get the two ice creams, and when she returned she glanced at Misha again.

"You're Professor Alto's son, aren't you?"

Misha nodded.

"I remember you used to come to his class sometimes when you were out of school. Dmitry's the name, right?"

"Misha," he said. "The other's a bit too formal for my taste. And Russian."

"Yeah. Misha's cooler. I used to watch you playing games on your phone, and I wondered how your dad would take it. You know, he always hated when we had ours on the desk."

Misha laughed. "He took it alright. He just wanted to keep me quiet and in the classroom."

"Yeah. 'This is about art,' he'd say, 'with a capital A. You can't be texting and friending in the company of the greats.' He'd laugh like it was a joke when he said it, but most of us thought he really believed that, too."

Misha nodded. "Oh, I'm sure he believes it. Dad thinks there's a special class of men—and women, too," he added, looking at me. "They carry the rest of us along. We've got to pay them attention."

The college girl looked from him to me and revved up a spectacular smile. She handed us our ice creams, took Misha's bill and gave him change. As we started to leave, she said, "It's got to be hard," she said. "I'll bet he wants you to be one of them. But look, what does an art school education get you?" She motioned around the room.

"Communing with the greats? No profit in that."

Misha grinned, licked his ice cream, and held open the door for me. We walked back toward the high school and didn't talk much. It was nice just being together without having to say anything bright or humorous, or even serious. "Just being," Mr. Santa would call it when we talked about my lack of friends. He thought I should just find people who I enjoyed hanging with and not worry about the shame of the Bonneville and the way people thought of it—or me. Which, I suppose, is why I started running seriously, and why I enjoyed the cross-country team, even though I was

48

not allowed to run any school races. It gave me a place and a group to go to every morning. It gave me a bunch of guys who grew very protective and friendly, even though some of them referred to me as their "pretty little mascot." And it gave me people to sit with at lunch and study hall if no one else would make room at a table.

I never dated any of the guys, but because no one had ever asked. Coach Span had clued the team in on who I was and why he wanted me to run with them, and he made a point of warning them to be friendly, yet not too social. "I don't want fights in here," I heard him tell them once. "I want the competition to be about running, not about who's riding in the Pontiac."

Everyone but me had a good laugh about that, of course. But good-natured though it was I can't deny it pissed me off. Mr. Span had been helpful to me as a runner—and a person, I guess—but his good old boys joke lowered him in my eyes, just as I'm sure it sank me before the team. I became the "Bonneville Girl" at the high school, a freakish girl who everyone either felt sorry for or laughed at. Team mothers invited me home for dinner sometimes, teachers took me out to lunch, and two of the cops who were fathers to a couple of the runners made sure to check on me in the woods before going home from their shifts at night. It was all good-natured, sympathetic, and fun, but sickening at the same time because no one, before Misha anyhow, even made a pretense at friendship. I mean the real, lasting kind where you can count on somebody if you need to.

Misha always said he understood what I was feeling, felt it himself in fact. He knew how anxious I was for friends, how positive, and yet how fucked up. He

49

said he'd seen me running around the school grounds, laughing and trying to smile at everybody I passed, but he also noticed I was always alone when I stood still. I pulled away from people, especially the bozos, as he called them, on the cross-country team. "You may run and, occasionally, have lunch with them," he told me once, "but I'm damn sure you don't feel like you're part of the team."

He was right, of course, but I never felt part of anybody but Mum and Dad. How could I, especially after they had passed? Why Dad thought his shithead cousin would take care of me I'll never know, but my guess is he had no other choice. The lawyer who had written his will assured me I had no other living relatives, and though Dad didn't know him well he figured that family (by law, not by blood, remember) would gladly take on the responsibility. "Not," is all I can say about that figuring. Dad saw bad luck and evil as inevitable in this life, but he also thought human beings individually worked against those forces. "No one," he told me shortly before he died, "is going to see a beautiful young girl like you alone in the world and leave you there. Humans are not built that way."

Maybe so, Dad, but from what I see today, I would only reply that not all human beings are completely human—especially your shithead cousin.

Anyway, by the time we finished our ice creams, Misha and I were walking in the park, and after a few steps, entering the woods to go back to the car. I didn't want to bring Misha back again because I had no idea what we would do except talk about how pathetic everything was. When we crossed the field and started toward the hardwood trees, Misha stopped, put his hand on my shoulder, and looked into my eyes. The pale green in his struck me as amazing. I think I may have blushed.

"Jamie, why don't you come to my house instead?" he said. "We can dance in the basement or just hang out and watch TV." He grinned, stupidly from embarrassment at that moment, but maybe I was just as stupid looking to him. I felt relieved, but at the same time I wanted to seem disappointed.

"You're sure your parents won't mind?" I asked. He shook his head. I nodded, with real reluctance now because, I have to say, I had no idea how to talk to a parent or professor—especially an artistic one.

"They always want me to bring friends home," Misha said. "So why not bring you?" I laughed, looking down at the grass. "A broken down car as a home would be a very good reason."

He reached around my shoulders, hugged me, and slowly turned us around toward the street. "Ben and Lee Alto are not snot-nosed," he said. "In fact, I think they're pretty nice."

Shaking my head, I followed him as he led me out of the park, past the police station and the Sugar Bowl, and, finally, toward the county bus stop. To my surprise we didn't take a bus. Instead, we walked by the station, out to a county road with no sidewalks. We trudged on the berm against traffic for about a mile, and then, after a stand of evergreens with a scattering of young maple and oak among them, we turned down a narrow road with nice houses, big gardens, and plenty of bushes. Still no sidewalks because . . . "Nobody runs around here," Misha told me. "Everybody drives."

He double-timed ahead a few steps, then turned and smiled. "We're down here a bit. Just a few more houses."

We turned a sharp bend, stumbled down a rocky hill of grass and weed, and then, in a little valley with an even sharper bend to it, crossed the road before entering a driveway. "Chez Alto," Misha whispered. He was grinning, though his eyes told me he felt as nervous as I did. "Mom'll be home—painting. I'm not sure about my dad."

We went around the side of the house and entered through the garage door where I saw a yellow VW Bug on one side of the garage. The side we entered was empty. Misha opened the house door with a key, and I followed him in, taking a deep breath. No one greeted us, but we heard a small voice from upstairs breaking the silence. Misha walked ahead quickly to call to his mother on the second floor.

"It's me, Mom. I have a friend with me. We'll be downstairs listening to music." He opened another door and motioned me to follow him.

The stairs were bleak, unfinished, but the basement itself had been turned into a comfortable playroom or, maybe, den. I saw a couch against the far wall, a TV screen diagonally across from it, and what looked like a very good sound system with standalone speakers beside the TV. Four or five landscapes with the Delaware Water Gap featured in them for different seasons lined one side and a large wood desk stood at the wall nearer to us. Four sections of floor-to-ceiling bookshelves hung next to it.

"Shit!" I said, looking at the bookshelves. "Somebody's a reader. Are these your father's?"

"Professor Alto's study library," Misha answered. His blue-green eyes twinkled, though his voice sounded very serious. I couldn't look at them, not the shelves, not the books or the paintings, especially not his eyes; though I have to say I was impressed. How could anybody read so many books or do such intricate paintings?

"Has he opened them?" I said, pointing toward the books. "All of them?"

Misha shrugged, smiling. "He reads a lot. He wants to leave them to me when he dies."

I laughed. "What are you going to do—digitize them? You're going to have to open a store—or burn them. It's all on the internet anyway."

Misha nodded. "One of my Dad's great regrets. His legacy has been taken over by Google."

"Gee. My dad's cousin complained he had to throw away all Mum and Dad's stuff to clean up the house before selling it. Even the Sinatra records, from way, way back. What would he have done about these— or the paintings?"

"You had records? You mean antiques? My dad says there's a lot of money in that."

I shrugged. "My cousin took everything—all the money, except for what Dad left me in his will."

Misha frowned, genuinely sad for a few seconds, but then his face brightened. "I guess it keeps you moving." He looked me up and down. "You're skinny, but you have a lot more energy than I ever have. Maybe muscle strength, too."

He turned to the sound system, punched a button on the tuner, and the room—I should probably say the house—filled with booming sound. Some group I never heard before came on and, with screaming electric strings and thumping drums and bass, made the walls around us vibrate. I expected Misha's mom to come yelling down the stairs right away, but as he took my two hands and started moving, I was pleased not to hear her steps or her voice.

"Let's do it," Misha said. And before the song ended the two of us were bouncing and smacking our hands and hips, sweating as if we'd been dancing for hours.

As soon as it ended, another boomer began, and this time I took the lead from him, swinging and winging us around the room as if we had lost our minds—which, for a moment, I guess we did. Dad used to call me a Dervish when I danced in our house, and before she got sick, Mum used to dance with me, too. It was fun, probably the nicest memories I have of my time with them—Dad, on the couch, keeping time with his hands and feet, Mum and me spinning round and round, hands together or separate. Occasionally, we'd do something more classical, a tune from a Tchaikovsky ballet, the Nutcracker or Swan Lake, or sometimes some very cool jazz with muted trumpets and a whispering sax, which Dad loved to listen to after dinner at night, if we didn't watch TV. He loved to listen to this stuff on vinyl—big ten- or twelve-inch discs that looked like you could play Frisbee with them. He claimed the music on them was sweeter, clearer, and more mellow than CD or streaming stuff, and he refused to buy a player for digital tunes. He loved our turntable (his, really; a birthday present from Mum) and guarded his record collection, a couple hundred of them, along with dozens of big-holed forty-fives and a crate full of older shiny slate ones that he called treasures. He'd play the treasures on special occasions only, handling them carefully while telling me about the old-time singers and musicians. A few—from Sinatra, I remember—had no music behind the singing because of a musicians' strike "back in the day," as Dad called it. "Jamie, can you imagine anyone today listening without those awful electric sounds behind the voice to blot out missed notes and lousy diction? People don't want beautiful singing anymore. Just noise, with lots of whining and screaming."

I guess that's true, though I don't think about it very much when I'm dancing. The music just lets my body go free, like a bird riding the wind, its wings floating on vibrations. Thinking about it now, I can only say that Misha was like that too, which is why I was so completely ready for his friendship. He seemed so comfortable with himself, at least when he was with me. His Dad wanted him to excel, be a super student and also a star jock. His Mom wanted him to develop artistic sensibility and talent (she kept telling him he had great hands and a wonderful eye for color). But he, like me, had no clue about what he wanted to do or could become. He made fun of the urge to be important—as an artist, a writer, or anything else. He just wanted to live his life, clowning around or dancing, occasionally, but primarily working through each day.

"No money? No fame?"

He shook his head. "Respect . . . I just want people to like me as I am."

"Well, I do too, of course. But I can't speak for everyone else around here. Most of the time they think I smell."

His face dropped—but I'm sorry to say it was true, mostly. People wondered if, or how, I kept clean, and I just gave it my best shot. One of the main reasons I ran with the cross-country guys was the daily shower. I got to bathe and brush my teeth in the gym every school day morning and never had to worry about stinking out the classroom. I'm happy to say that although I took plenty of flak from the other kids, no one ever dared to say to my face that I smelled. First, people knew I didn't give a shit what they thought; second, maybe more important, I had very little to lose and was happy to start swinging, kicking, and biting after the slightest hint of an insult. They probably also guessed—incorrectly—that some of the guys on cross-country would back me, unless I fought a girlfriend. Yes, Misha's right. I am skinny, but occasionally—just occasionally—I could be one of the guys, wearing team colors, running team splits, leading cheers when we had our meets. Like everyone else in school, the team thought of me as strange, but I could outsprint quite a few of them, and so they respected me—despite Mr. Span's little joke about the Pontiac.

Still, none of them were real friends. Maybe it was Mr. Span's dumb joke, maybe it was other stuff I don't need to mention, but I never felt I could just sit and talk to any of them alone. Either they didn't seem interested or their interest filled me with suspicion:

groping hands and other body parts moving toward my boobs and crotch. One guy—not a great runner—walked me to the mall one afternoon that year so we could share a Big Mac lunch. In the middle of it, he asked me what kind of sex I liked best, "sucking or fucking?" Another, better runner took me to a movie that I didn't want to see but went to anyway, just for the company. Here's what he said: "Where do you fuck—front or back—when you have a guy over?"

"Nothing weird or fancy," I said, "as long as there's a clean mouth involved." Then I dumped the bag of popcorn in his lap and left.

Most of the time I tried. I asked about their lives, their families, their hopes for the future. But what could I say about my own life, my own future?—"Oh, yes, I'm really looking forward to summer—when mosquitoes fill the woods and drain my blood if I happen to want some air at night?" Or, "Oh, no, not college. I'm tired of school. After we graduate I'm looking forward to opening a business right here in town—in the back seat of my car, in fact. Would you like a free sample?"

Yes, I tried, and I guess some of the cross-country guys did, too. But there was a wall between us, and I imagine that except on the track, I will not be among their most memorable high school friends or experiences. I'm pretty sure I'll be looked on as weird or freakish, and at some future reunion they'll drink beer and tell each other lies about fucking me dozens of times in the back of the Bonneville. Dad and Mum would have told me not to worry, that I should do good and think about my own memories, not the team's. But of course they would never have imagined that my most unforgettable high school experience would be of cold, dark nights in a rusty, motor-less piece of junk that couldn't go anywhere. Just like me.

Then Misha Alto entered my life. I don't know how he managed it, but he certainly made an impression. In fact, he made me happy. I often think about that dance, which I almost didn't go to because I felt so shitty having nobody to go with, and I wonder if there was some other way I could have met him. Not likely. He wasn't a jock, had no interest in running cross-country or track, and followed a different set of teachers and courses from me. He didn't know any of the runners on the team, and they had never even heard of him since he did nothing—good or bad— to call attention to himself at school. His clothes were ordinary, maybe a little less sloppy than other kids', and maybe he showed a bit more color. In any case, he wore no witch's hat, no wizard's cape, and revealed no sinister eyes or ghostly cackle in the hallway. He carried books in a backpack slung over his right shoulder, wore granny glasses that turned dark in the sun, and always wore a pair of black New Balance cross trainers, though he seldom ever trained. I must have passed him on the way to class more than a few times before that dance but never noticed him, probably because I was so tuned to my own shamefulness and needs—no friends, no family; no possible, realistic dream of happiness.

I went to the dance that night because at practice in the morning two or three of the guys said they were going and, without a giggle, hinted that they would dance with me if I dared to show up in something other than a track suit. Something about the way they said it—

not delighted, more like "Why not? It won't cost anything"—made me go just for the opportunity to blow them off when they asked. But then retro-Presley boomed off the bleachers and walls; the hardwood floor vibrated beneath my stockinged feet. And, lo and behold, I met this dark-brown-haired, incredibly hazel-eyed boy with funny glasses, and the night became something more important than saying no.

***

IV.

We became a number, in our own goofy way, almost immediately. I don't know how Misha endured the sudden descent into notoriety. After that day, when we walked together from the Bonneville to dance at his house, we saw each other almost every afternoon after practice. People saw us—really, people stared; but no one said a word. At first we always met at that same corner (Oak and Chestnut, though I didn't repeat the mistake of running into him at full speed), but gradually he started waiting for me closer to school, and then finally outside the gym's locker room door. We didn't do much physical stuff in those days, just high fives when we got close, and then gradually we built up to walking hand in hand (with an occasional kiss on the cheek) wherever we went. It was a sensation I still can't describe without some exaggeration. His hand was large, strong, yet delicate despite its fleshy feeling. It sent warm shivers from head to toes whenever he twined his long fingers in mine. We walked everywhere like that, except in the school hallway, I should say, partly because there was a rule against it, but mostly because I preferred space between us among the other kids. I just feared that the two of us would make easy targets, whether by some of the cross-country runners or the bitchy girls (and guys) who built themselves up by slapping down others.

Misha didn't feel that way; I'm not sure why. He clearly wasn't the swaggering type, and more than likely didn't notice or just didn't care. I would have been the one to start swinging if somebody said something snarky, while he would have nodded, maybe made a quiet self-deprecating joke, and walked away. Mainly, he just smiled whenever we walked together—down the hall, outside of school, holding hands or not—completely comfortable with what we did. He said he just wanted to make me happy, and since I held a weaker position in the hallway rating game and street-level gossip mills, he followed my lead. "Sounds tacky," he said to me early on, "but I'm happy to know you're satisfied. With me and us. I don't need anything more."

He meant it, I'm sure, and in those days I already knew it showed inner strength—because it reminded me of Dad. But every once in a while a bratty bitch or some underhung jock would come up to me in the halls or out on the street and, grinning like a moronic jerk, ask me about my *"widdle* puppy dog".

"Where's the obedient pooch today? I don't see him piddling at your feet."

I was shocked and silenced the first time that happened. But I felt responsible, and after that my fists and feet went flying. Though I got a week's detention and a two-week suspension from cross-country practices for it, there were no other incidents to worry about for a long, long while. Misha waited for me on the detention afternoons and walked me back to the Pontiac, even in the very hard rain during two of those nights. "Look," he told me, "I hear what they say, but I don't want you to fight my fights. I know who it's coming from and a little of the why. I just don't care."

I nodded. "Well, maybe one of the cross-country guys puts them up to it," I said. "A couple of them like to get on my case since I don't think they're pricks come from God."

Misha laughed at that, though he did say he thought most of the guys were probably pretty decent. But he followed my lead about the team, limiting our hand holding (and the friendly kisses) around them, and soon the team and the school began to get used to us as a couple—a pair of independent geeks who were a little more than best friends. When we started dancing together in talent shows, then won a prize or two in some county competitions, notoriety eventually turned to respect—grudging, but real—that made me happy about my life for the first time since Mum and Dad passed away.

I started to spend almost every afternoon and many evenings at Misha's house—especially in the basement. Most of the time we made out while listening to music. He liked my legs and chest ("boobs" would be too exaggerated), and I just loved the warmth of his arms and shoulders while I melted in the hot stare of his aquamarines. We danced, of course, but occasionally we'd log on to his father's laptop and watch a film. The only really wild thing was that sometimes he read to me from a book on his father's shelves. He liked poetry, especially reading it out loud, and he had a quiet, solemn tone that made poems by writers he liked come to life— almost as if the writer was doing the reading. His favorite was an Irishman named Yeats, and he often read aloud his poems about dancers because, Misha said, they represented the human soul in action. He was serious about this, and one afternoon, when I twerked against his dick and asked what kind of action our souls were taking, Misha just looked at me and blushed. I felt embarrassed and came very close to apologizing. But then his face lit up, and he laughed before I could say anything. "Well, whatever keeps you going," he told me.

One day he opened a book to a poem by Yeats called "Among School Children," and read it to me, making his voice sound tired and wizened, portraying himself as an old man visiting a first or second grade classroom. I don't remember many of the lines—except the last couple, which showed an amazing leap in Irish logic that none of our English teachers would have accepted if we wrote like that. But I do remember the part about girls growing up to look like paintings and boys mourned by mothers after growing old and, eventually, dying. Then, suddenly—and this is the amazing leap I'm talking about—everything in the poem became a monster chestnut tree, and the old man in the classroom talked to it as if it was human, wondering, I think, what it really was—the leaf, the flower, or the trunk itself, which the poem refers to as a "bole".

Strange writing, I thought, at least in that part. But then the last two lines leaped again and, for some weird reason, maybe the way Misha read them—not with his tired, old man's voice, but like a magician or a priest peering and shouting into the future—the words took my breath away:

O body swayed to music, O brightening glance,
How can we know the dancer from the dance?

My stomach turned when he read that, and I started to cry. Misha had some slow, classical music playing as a background, and until it ended with a quiet run of piano keys and soft strings, I just sat there,

63

sobbing, tears rolling down my cheeks onto my t-shirt. Misha sat facing me, quietly choking and looking at me as if he was afraid I would die. He didn't cry or say anything out loud, but I could see my tears flowed right into his own deep sadness. He squinted and pressed his lips together.

"Jesus," I said, finally, "I have no idea why I'm doing this. Bawling—like a baby—but I have no idea what it means."

Misha nodded, smiling. "You're a dancer. Maybe you feel the sadness in your feet."

I laughed and, wiping something from his eye, he got off the couch and played something livelier on the system. We bounced around a bit—to Miley Cyrus and then a little bit of Adele, who was very hot at that time, and then, while we were working on some moves to an old Elton John song, we heard the door upstairs open and quiet footsteps coming down the stairs. First was a dog, a golden retriever they called Vincent Two, then Mrs. Alto came after him. She was slim, a little short, but had a very powerful appearance. She wore jeans and had long black hair down to her shoulders, with a wisp or two of white and gray around her ears. She carried a tray with some drinks and snacks on it, setting it down on a table near the couch. Vincent Two waddled over, sniffing and wagging his tail, but Mrs. Alto waved him away and threw him a doggie treat. He scarfed it up and lay down in front of the sound system speakers to chew it.

I had met Misha's parents a couple of times—his mom the first day he brought me to their house, and his dad almost a week later on another after-school visit. They were nice, but I could see they were not used to visits from Misha's friends. They were polite, a little formal, with no easy chatter for me or Misha. Mrs. Alto brought food and drinks to the basement, but apart from asking how, or what, I was doing, she didn't talk about anything, except once, some ancient music by Joni Mitchell or Tom Rush that Misha happened to put on for fun. She watched us dance a few minutes that first day, told me there was more to eat if I wanted it, and then, basically, left—either to paint or start dinner, which she invited me to, although I declined out of embarrassment.

Mr. Alto was another story—completely. He was friendly, or at least tried to be. But he loved to talk, usually about stuff that meant nothing to Misha or me. He reminisced about music in high school—Presley, Little Richard, Fats Domino, and some others—and very quickly led up to jazz in college and, finally, the three B's of classical music after he started teaching. He loved the French Impressionists, he told me, and so with everything else, Debussy and Ravel had become his favorite modern composers.

Music—except for what I heard in snatches from passing car radios, the hallways at school, and the loudspeakers at cross-country meets—was so far from my daily life at the time that I had no idea who most of those people were, except for Elvis Presley, of course. Dad played 40s and 50s stuff on his old vinyl records, an occasional classic like the Nutcracker or, probably, the three B's, but he never considered rock and roll as music. So I knew plenty of performers and bands from the days of black and white movies, but, except for the Beatles and Stones, I heard none of the sounds that came in multiple colors. Laughing, Misha called me a musical virgin, although he apologized for his dad whenever he got into one of his serious rants. "He didn't intend to make you feel stupid," he said. "He just assumes what interests him interests everyone else, which in his case is usually not true."

I laughed. I mean, who else would read a poem about an old man to a girl he's brought to the basement to, maybe, undress?

Which, despite the dance, the poem, and the very breathless minute or two that followed, probably wasn't true. His mother—and Vincent Two—were always there and came downstairs without any announcement except the sound of footsteps. He would have been smarter to walk with me to the Bonneville in the woods if undressing was his only purpose. I also think he genuinely wanted to have a friend—male or female— and probably knew that ultimately sex would throw that out the window. Still, I have to admit it was often on my mind, at least as a firm possibility, and I wanted to see how he would react to the idea. But the poem and the blush were all I got for an answer that afternoon, and I had no idea what that meant. Embarrassment, but over what? That I knew what he was thinking? Or had the same idea? I talked to him about it later that week but still learned nothing. He sounded genuinely surprised when I brought it up while we walked back to his house one day. He had no strategy, he said, either about the poem and blush or the possible sex. "I just thought the poem was cool."

So, I'd be lying if I said I got to know him better after we talked. Misha could be one cool customer about romance. I'm not sure if he was always like that, or just became that way with me. He just liked to keep things inside, "for neatness," he told me. Occasionally, you could see flashes of emotion in him, but if you weren't looking closely at a particular flash-filled moment, it would be gone—like his blush that afternoon. "I feel things, a lot," he told me. "I just don't feel the urge to bring them out into the world."

"Or scream them, the way I do. And certainly not cry."

"I repeat: I feel things, and I do cry. It just takes a little more for me to let it out."

"Does that make you stronger? I seriously doubt it."

He laughed. "I doubt it, too. That's why I always look for slow stuff to play when we dance."

That's Misha for you. There's usually some kind of off-the-board maneuver he'll try to pull, an idea slipping out of nowhere that keeps me from pinning him down, or guessing what comes next. Yet he'll look at me, all serious, and make some pretty accurate comments about how I'm feeling or, sometimes even, what I'm thinking. Sometimes I get the creeps.

"How the fuck do you know this?" I'll say. "You just saw me walk out the door."

"Body language," he'll say, holding back a smile. "Head's down, but your shoulders look like they want to kick butt."

Really. This one afternoon we met just outside the gym locker room after practice. I had just overheard Mr. Span make another bad joke in his office—about me. "The rabbit," he called me, "whose tail you guys are still too slow to catch."

I wanted to scream. But as I stood outside the locker room door near his office, I thought how much I wanted to run with the team and how generous Mr. Span was in giving me tips for improving my time. So, pussy that I was, I just swallowed and turned toward the exit door, shoving the panic bar with my hip, and stomping out ready to explode. My ears buzzed, my skinny chest just about popped the buttons on my shirt, and my mouth hung open, gulping in air. When I think about it, I'm sure a two-year-old could have told I was pissed, but then Misha—sensitive, always attentive Misha—had to enter the drama and open his overly careful mouth.

"Uh, oh. Something happened. You're not looking like the happy camper I know."

"Fuck you, happy camper," I said. I flipped him the bird, middle finger directly under his nose. Then, seeing his eyes twitching on his suddenly red and embarrassed face, I turned back to the gym, pulled open the door, and headed right to the coaches' office. He wasn't there, so I turned toward the boys' locker room and entered, slamming open the door without knocking or announcing. I raised my hand and middle finger and marched down the aisle, panels of open lockers and naked boys on either side. "I resent this fucking shit," I shouted. "I am not a rabbit, I am not a tail these jack-offs are chasing, and I am not something to ride inside a rusty fucking Pontiac sitting in the woods."

I was about to say something even more pointed, when I looked around and saw those naked boys—about a dozen of them—standing in the rows of lockers with towels bunched in front of their dicks. What a sight! I almost laughed, but then Mr. Span, more red-faced than

Misha could ever be, stepped in front of me, looking as if he had been prodded with an electric pole rather than my finger. He was fully dressed, but there was something naked in his expression, so I just stepped closer and, with my fists down, leaned into his jowly, beef-red face.

"You have no right to say those things about me," I shouted, "here or anyplace else. I am not a piece of meat. I am not an animal to be hunted. You should know better."

I grabbed his arm, but he pulled it away and started down the aisle for the exit without a word. I followed him into the hall and ran to stand in front of him as he headed toward his office.

"Jamie," he mumbled, but with a look of real menace in his dark brown eyes, "you've gone too far this time. I've enjoyed letting you run with us, but I can't tolerate this sort of behavior, especially in the locker room."

"Fuck this behavior!" I shouted. "What about yours? I heard what you said in there. I won't take it."

He stepped around me and opened his office door. Then he slid behind the desk without sitting down, and I suppose the power that desk gave him made me stop. I stood inside the office door, and in those few moments lost everything I had in mind to say. We just stood and stared at each other, and after what seemed like a dozen years I became aware that Misha hovered beside me. He said nothing. I said nothing. We both stared at Mr. Span, who also said nothing, although his face rapidly fluctuated between tomato red and a particularly putrid shade of mustard. I slammed my fists into my thighs and turned to leave. Misha muttered something behind me as I entered the hall, and then I felt him trotting and walking by my side.

"What a jerk. He may be letting you run, which is good. But he's still a piece of shit as a man."

We walked out of the parking lot, off the school grounds, and—still wordless—headed down Main Street with some kind of rage-fueled, foot stomping speed. It was getting dark, I remember, one of those gloomy gray sunsets we get in late fall, and it just added to the weight on my skinny shoulders. "The bastard!" I shouted. "How could he say those things about me? I run faster than more than half the assholes he coaches, but most of the time I end up carrying equipment for them—because I'm a girl!"

"I told him I heard him. That I could be a witness. I also told him he'll hear from my parents. My mother will be happy to take a palette knife to his balls."

We were heading toward the Sugar Bowl again, mainly because we usually went that way to get to Misha's house. But I certainly wasn't in any mood for dancing or talking politely to his mother. When we got near the coffee shop, I pulled him across the street to a falafel place called the Cedars of Lebanon and went inside for a little anonymous quiet. We ordered a pita sandwich with grilled eggplant and sesame tahini and shared it with a couple glasses of sweet mint tea. I must say it calmed me, especially the tea, and I felt grateful to Misha for coming in there with me. Most of the high school kids avoided it because it was foreign. When a barefoot blonde came out of the back room wearing a sparkly gold halter and a pale green skirt that showed all kinds of leg muscle from knee to hip, we both stopped eating and looked at her. "You want me to dance?" she asked, without the slightest mid-Eastern accent. Misha nodded toward me. I shook my head, and we both giggled. The girl shrugged and walked to a table near the window. She stopped at the counter to order tea, and when she sat again, she pulled out a pack of cigarettes from inside her halter. "You mind?" she asked, waving the cigarettes at us. We both shrugged, but as soon as she lit up I knew I had to get out of the restaurant. The smell, plus the grease from the fried falafel, went right up my nose and seemed to clog my brain.

"Sorry," Misha said as we passed near the blonde. "We're in a hurry." She nodded, blowing out a cloud of smoke with an embarrassed smile. I pushed open the door and gulped some cool air before turning back toward the school. Misha caught up with me again and invited me to his house for the afternoon. "And, maybe," he said, "for dinner."

I shook my head.

"Please, just leave me alone. I'll go home by myself," I said.

"No! That would be horrible, especially tonight. Come to my house and stay overnight. My parents won't mind—they'll love it."

"Misha . . ." I looked at him and saw such a good-hearted, sad confusion on his face that I knew I would hurt him if I refused. Still . . . I really just wanted to go back to that car and wallow in my misery. "I can't. I just can't," I said. "And I wouldn't want to embarrass you in front of your mom and dad."

"I'm sure they won't mind. They've already told me to invite you to stay over. Many times."

"Another night, please." Then, without thinking, I broke into a run and, even with a backpack of books and cross-country gear pounding on my shoulders, left him behind pretty quickly. He had started after me, of course, but I ran faster, and he couldn't—not by a longshot— keep up. By the time I reached the school again, I stopped and turned, but didn't see him anymore.

I ran on anyway, slowing to an easy jog at first, loving the feel of the ground against my shoes, the wind gushing into my mouth, and the blood rushing urgently through my ears. It was well past sundown when I got to the park, and so I ran beyond it to the police station and entered the woods through a stand of maples, oaks, and softwoods along the road. It was quiet in there—as usual, just an occasional car going by at reasonable speed because of the police station nearby and, of course, the sirens, which screamed out any time of day or night but somehow comforted me because they meant the danger was somewhere else and there were people on the way to control it.

I slowed as soon as I reached the softwoods, working my way through scrub brush and pine, with an occasional mountain laurel or blueberry bush mucking up my path. I reached an open field of grass and ivy, headed toward the boulder that hid the Pontiac from the road, and went around it to my "home". It looked peaceful back there, with nothing unusual in sight or sound, but edgy as I felt, I was sure that someone, or something, lay in wait. Night sounds started building—a creak of a tree limb I had heard hundreds of times before, then a wind-blown rustle of leaves and bush that *had* to be footsteps followed by the plop of something on the moist ground that could have been a heavy weapon. I heard these noises every night, of course, but tonight I felt more reason to worry. I grabbed a flashlight from my backpack and held it high above my head to make me look really tall. I shined it around the car, at my feet, and through the surrounding trees and bush. Nothing moved. I went straight to the Bonneville, opened the door with a sigh of relief, and threw my backpack into the passenger's seat. I was just about to slide behind the wheel myself, when I heard a rustle to my left and, before I could get in and quickly lock the door, I saw Mr. Span standing in front of me, holding the outside handle.

"Jamie, what's this about?"

"You fucking well know," I said. "You bastard."

"I thought we had an understanding. You're not abiding by it."

My throat tensed. I actually gasped for air and couldn't make my mouth form any words, especially confident ones. I couldn't even look at his face. Instead, I stared at his belt-buckle, the little paunch of his stomach hanging over it, and the weird pumpkin color of the jacket he was wearing.

"I'm sorry for what I said. I mean it. I wasn't trying to cheapen you. I was just trying to motivate the team, and so I had to speak their language."

"Their language?! I am not a tail, I am not a cunt, I am not a piece of ass for them—or you—to chase around the track. I can outrun most of them, and I sure as fuck know I can outrun you, even while carrying this rusty piece of shit on my back. You have no right to try to use me that way—for motivation or anything else!"

My anger freed me, I guess, at least for that moment, because now I stared straight at his face and into those beady brown eyes as if they had no business looking back. My hands trembled, but my feet held firm as I stood tall in front of him. He didn't change his expression for a few seconds, but then he just shook his head and turned from the car.

"Their language!" I repeated. "That's all bullshit, and you know it!"

I heard him push through the brush and pine branches. After a few more minutes, I heard a car start down by the police station. I began breathing more normally when it pulled away.

***

V.

Next day I didn't go to practice or school; I just couldn't bring myself to face it all, Misha included. Instead, I went to see Mr. Santa in the county social services office. If nothing else, I figured, at least I would get some hot coffee. He greeted me the way he always does, with a tired smile, feet on the desk, and a busy wave to sit in the chair facing him while he leaned over a stack of papers. I sighed, looked out the window, and tried to fight off an awful feeling of failure and loneliness. He had a large ballpoint pen in his hand and beside the pile of papers a green tennis ball that I knew, from previous visits, he would regularly pick up and squeeze a dozen or more times for exercise.

He's a short, athletic guy who loves sports, especially tennis, golf, and running, and it's because of him that Mr. Span let me work out with the cross-country team every morning. They were tennis buddies, according to Mr. Santa, and he had mentioned me to Mr. Span one day after a tennis match. We had run together a couple times during the summer. Mr. Santa thought I could run with the high school team if I wanted, but the coach of the women's track team didn't like me very much because I had fought with a few of her girls one day in school and one of them ended up with a badly bruised thigh and a pulled muscle in her groin that kept her out of meets for most of the season.

As Mr. Santa put it, I probably wouldn't be a "good fit" for the girls' team, so he talked to Mr. Span about cross-country. There was no girls' cross-country team, as I already knew, but Mr. Santa hoped that would be a good reason to let a girl "who runs extremely well" try to compete with boys in races. Mr. Span didn't like the idea, nor did the state or the region's high school athletic associations, so Mr. Santa pressed for a deal where I could work out with the team, even accompany them to meets, although I would never really compete. "For fear," Mr. Santa said in his gloomiest, angriest voice, when he told me about the decision. "Fear that a girl would embarrass the boys by beating one or more of them in a race."

"I'd beat most of them on this school's team," I told him.

I started working out with them that spring, late in my freshman year. For the first two or three weeks, Mr. Santa picked me up in front of the police station at about six o'clock in the morning and drove me to school, accompanying me into the gym and waiting with me while the team gathered out on the track. Then he'd stand talking with Mr. Span or a few of the boys through our first two or three laps around the school grounds, and he'd wave goodbye and leave when we started out into the streets to extend our morning run. After a few weeks he said the boys and I had adjusted to each other, and so he gradually cut back on driving me in. About a month after I started, he thought I was ready to go it alone. And I thought so, too.

"How many times did this happen before you blew your fuse?" Mr. Santa asked me after I told him about my flare up in the locker room. I had just poured myself a cup of coffee from his Cuisinart and was in the middle of my first sip when he dropped his papers on the desk and started listening. I shrugged, trying to hold back tears as he looked at me.

"A couple," I said. "The first time I thought it was harmless. But I just don't like those kinds of jokes—about me or anyone else. I'm not a fucking piece of meat."

He nodded. "You shouldn't like them. No one should. I'm surprised Craig would say such a thing."

"He didn't think I would hear. I'll give him that. But I was standing outside the boys' locker room near his office, and I couldn't help hearing. He's got a loud voice."

Mr. Santa nodded. "Very loud at times. But I'm still surprised he said it. He's not that kind of guy."

I laughed. "Not with you, maybe. But I know I wasn't hearing things. The team wasn't very serious during practice yesterday. Guys were limping around the track, faking injuries, and a couple of them didn't even show up. When we ran quarters as a team, I ended up beating every one of them by the time we got into the second mile. I think he was pissed about that."

Mr. Santa's feet dropped to the floor. "Pissed that you beat them?"

I shrugged again and shook my head while I took a sip of the coffee.

"More likely he was pissed that they didn't beat you, and he said that stuff to motivate them to work harder."

Which seems reasonable to me right now, I have to admit, although that day I didn't want to give in to anybody—reasonable or not. "I don't run or fuck like a rabbit. I won't let anybody talk about me like that."

Mr. Santa raised his eyebrows—at the language, I think— and put his feet back on the desk. He leaned back in his chair, folding his hands together with his elbows resting on the arms. "Look, I don't blame you, Jamie, but you have to admit that working out with the team has been good for you. Last I heard, Craig Span thought it was good for the team too. I wouldn't want you to let that go."

"I can't go back there. I'm sorry. I can't go back to school either. I just wanted to let you know—in case you heard something."

Neither of us said anything for a while, but of course he didn't like it. I took another long sip of coffee while Mr. Santa stared out the window beside his desk. Finally, he dropped his shoes to the floor and leaned forward in his chair, his arms dangling between his legs.

"Listen. Don't quit now, at least not definitively. And please keep going to school. Maybe after things cool down, you and Mr. Span can work this out. It'll be good for you and for the team."

I shook my head because I didn't know what to say. All I really knew was that I didn't want to speak to Craig Span ever again. I didn't want to see him or anyone on the team. And I was very committed to leaving school, although Mr. Santa wouldn't like it.

"Well, I'll give him a call and see what he has to say about all of this. He's really not a bad guy, I'm sure of that. Maybe a little loose with his tongue . . ."

At that point I stood up and brought my empty cup to the Cuisinart. I put it down—hard—beside the machine and came back to the chair. But didn't sit. Instead, I just stared at Mr. Santa with what I hoped was

78

a look of complete disgust. "I don't see how you can excuse him, even if he is a friend. If he said this stuff about your daughter, I'll bet you'd go down to his office ready to have him fired—or knock off his head."

Mr. Santa frowned, nodding. After a few seconds he said, "For sure I'd let him know, but I like to think I wouldn't be that violent."

I left his office soon after and spent the day wandering through town—but nowhere near the school. I went to the park, napped in the car, and at the neighborhood church, St. Anthony's, sat and prayed for a while, enjoying the quiet and the gloom. By early afternoon I could think of nothing better than going to the town mall. I knew I'd see kids there as soon as school ended, so I couldn't go to a movie. But I had at least an hour, maybe two, before they'd flood the stores and fast food shops, so I bought a couple slices of pizza and a large Pepsi. After eating the pizza out on the dining terrace, I went to the New Balance store to check out running shoes. I couldn't afford to buy new ones right away because I wouldn't get a county relief check for almost a month. I tried a few pairs on anyway and looked at some leather dancing slides they had on special. Thinking of Misha I came very close to splurging on a pair. But new socks were good enough, I decided, especially since buying food was obviously much more important.

I left the store and walked down the main hallway toward the Cineplex when I saw a couple kids I knew coming in the doors at the other end. They were problem kids—like me, I guess you'd say—so for whatever reason, they probably hadn't gone to school that day either. I turned around, went into a Kohl's next to the New Balance store, and walked as quickly as I could toward an exit. I crossed the parking lot outside and, on the run, hurried down the drive to the highway, where I waited for a bus to take me across town to the police station and the car. No one else that I recognized passed by, so when the bus came I hopped on and sat in the back seat where I could scrunch up and hide behind the tall chair backs.

I felt spooked. I'm not sure why, because the ride across town was quiet, completely uneventful. Along the road a few old ladies and a couple old men huffed and puffed up the two bus steps then struggled down the aisle to their seats when the driver took off again. They talked loud at first, crying out when the bus's motion threw them into their seats, but didn't even look to the back to see whose feet were sprawled out on the bench seat. They got off near the school, but I stayed on the bus till we reached the park. I went in, walked behind some bushes on the perimeter until I got to the hardwood trees that I used as a marker. From there I cut behind the fat trunk of an old oak to enter the softwoods where my Bonneville waited. I took my usual shortcut, went behind the large rock that hid the car, and the first thing I saw behind there was a boy, Misha, sitting on the hood. He stood up and started toward me.

"I don't want to talk," I shouted. "Not today anyway. Go home."

I wanted him gone, right away. Again, I don't know why. When he didn't leave, I turned, starting to run, certain he would never catch up to me. But he called out, saying he had news and had to talk to me. I hesitated and, after a few steps, stopped, trying not to be too agitated while waiting. From the look on his face I could see the news he had was not good—not likely to make me happy. I almost started to run again, but he looked so earnest—and pale, sickly even—that I just couldn't leave him behind. Somebody in his family must have died, I thought, and then (with mixed emotions, I should say) I thought it might be Craig Span. I couldn't get my mind around any of that, especially Mr. Span.

"What's up?" I asked him. "Did somebody realize I'm getting fucked?"

His jaw dropped. He stopped to stare at me, as if he couldn't figure out what I had just said. I began to say it again, thinking to put more nastiness in my f-word, but I knew he must have heard me, so I just stood and waited some more.

Shamefaced and resolved, Misha stopped before me. He didn't smile or talk at first, but he stood very close, his hands soft on my shoulders, and looked very carefully into my eyes. Then he hugged me. "I'm so sorry, Jamie. I don't know exactly what happened in that locker room, but you must feel awful. I missed seeing you in school today."

"Well, you're probably never going to see me there again," I said. "I've had it. Up to here. They're a fucking bunch of hypocrites—especially Mr. Span. I don't want to walk down the hallway, let alone run or go to classes."

He stepped back and looked at my feet. He lifted his head and stared directly into my eyes again. His were greenish-greenish blue that day—very intense. When Misha looked at you, you had the sense (at least I did) that he looked through you to someplace beyond, maybe to another dimension—a place you should be at or, maybe, were going to. He could rattle me because of that, and he often made me feel confused. "What are you going to do," he asked, stepping close again, "stay here, in the car, all day? All year? Snow, wind, rain, and all the climate change? What kind of life is that? You'll turn into a cold piece of metal, like the rest of this."

"I don't want to go back to that school, Misha. I can't stand the people—the kids or the teachers. I don't even want to think about the shit they must be passing about me in the halls right now."

He nodded grimly, looking down at the ground. "You've got to go to school, Jamie. You're too smart to let it go away. You can go to college. You *should* go to college. There's so much that you can do."

I laughed. Sure, I was flattered—because I liked Misha, a lot. He was smart, and I was happy he thought I had brains too. But he had no idea of how I really lived my life. *Had* to live it.

"Sure," I said, "I could do a lot. I could be a stripper, if I wanted, or a belly dancer, like that poor girl in Cedars. And, oh yes, of course, I could also be a whore. Think of that—lots of sex and all the dirty money I could shove up my ass. Maybe a sugar daddy will take me to Acapulco to fuck me in the winter."

He shook his head, saying nothing. I knew I had gone too far. I also knew he meant well and wanted to give me hope. But at the same time he hadn't sat in that fucking car in the freezing cold and stared out the filthy windshield at the stars and moon, trying to read them to find his future. Mr. Santa was nice, Mr. Span had been nice—but what were they going to get me other than a high school diploma? It was pointless, as far as I was concerned. I already received money from the state; I wasn't proud of that. And I knew that at some point I'd have to find a job and pay bills myself if I was ever really going to have a life, no matter how pitiful. How did going to college fit in? It couldn't.

"Well . . ." Misha said, but then he stopped and closed his eyes. He stood with his hands folded before him at his belt-buckle and just breathed, quietly, for a few seconds, his lips tight, as if he was gathering his thoughts. I thought he was going to cry for a minute, but then he looked into my eyes again. "Jamie, it's your call. But I know I'll miss you if you don't come back to school. I . . . ." He stopped again, and while I looked straight at his face I felt too embarrassed to say anything. "I know we've been together just a few times, but I also feel closer to you than . . . than anyone else at the school. Maybe anyone in my life."

I shook my head. I felt my face suddenly grow hot, but not with pleasure or happiness. Oddly enough, I knew it wasn't just embarrassment either. I was about to say something stupid and off-putting just to get rid of it, but then I looked more carefully in Misha's eyes and saw real—I would almost say awful—suffering in them. Was this his declaration of love? For some dumb reason I bit my lips, turned without saying anything at all and, as he stammered and stumbled over words I could only imagine, ran.

***

To be honest, that was one of the most cowardly things I've done in my life, I have to admit. As I think back on it, I honestly don't know why I ran. It seemed to be the only thing to do because at that moment anything I said would be impossible. And I felt I couldn't bear whatever Misha had in mind. Dad would have told me that was a key life moment, and I had hurt myself (and Misha) by running from it—no matter what "it" happened to be. Of course, I knew he wanted to tell me he liked me, maybe even loved me, whatever that might mean at our stage of life. But other than blushing and stumbling, or laughing and crying, maybe even screaming out loud a warning not to complicate my already fucked-up and complicated life, I was just afraid of what I'd have to do with the information.

So, I was halfway across town, beyond the school, beyond Main Street, before the yips were gone. When I stopped running, I found myself behind a bunch of kids heading for the mall. They didn't notice me at first, but a couple girls in the rear must have heard my heavy breathing because they looked back, did a quick, half-hidden second look, and then said something to one of the girls in front of them. I turned around, of course, crossed to the other side of the street, and headed back toward the Cedars of Lebanon. When I reached the opposite curb, I heard somebody call my name, but I pretended not to hear and just kept walking. Then I heard a second voice—*Jamie!*—that sounded very earnest. It was a girl I knew slightly, named Michele. She was in my math class and went out with one of the cuter guys on cross-country. She let a couple cars and a yellow school bus pass and then jogged across the street toward me.

"Hi!" she said, as if to begin a normal, friendly conversation. I actually smiled and said "Hi" right back. But I saw that across the street the whole group of kids she was walking with had stopped and were staring at us. My smile froze; I saw her face go stiff, too.

"I heard about it," she said. "I'm sorry. Really. You must feel awful."

I looked from her to the staring crowd across the street and could think of nothing to say except, "I do. Thanks."

"The guys don't all agree," she said, "but Jody (her boyfriend) thinks Mr. Span was terrible. He went too far, though he also said the team hasn't been working very hard."

I shrugged. "'Dickhead' is how I would describe him—and all the rest."

Michele winced and closed her eyes. "Jody thinks you were good for the team. You made the guys work harder, he says. They just don't like it when you show them up."

I shrugged again. For the life of me I had no idea what to think about any of that. I knew I had been used, but I also knew I liked being used—at least in the way they were using me. But the team liked Mr. Span a lot, and they probably figured that what he had said was completely innocent, motivation, as Mr. Santa said, by saying a girl could run faster—longer.

"Well, I didn't show them up. I just paced them, and they didn't feel like working," I said. "So fuck them and their coach."

Michele winced again, but this time she kept her eyes on my face. "Well, some of them are saying things—bad things—about you. Jody says they're trying to protect Mr. Span."

"I don't give a fuck," I said. "I'm done with them." Before she could reply, I turned away and started toward the Cedars of Lebanon again.

"Be careful, Jamie" she called. "Jody thinks you better watch your back."

When I reached the Cedars of Lebanon, I glanced through the window, saw the blonde girl behind the sandwich counter, and decided to go inside. She smiled at me, a little shamefaced, I thought, then turned back to the sandwich she was making. Today she wore a plaid flannel shirt and jeans and had her hair back in a net.

"You make sandwiches, too, I guess."

She laughed, grimly. "My main job," she said without a smile. "When the owner's here to make them, I dance."

"Not an awful job, I guess. Are you doing this while you're at school?"

She stood up straight and glanced over my head. On her shirt I saw a tag with the name "Ciara" printed in white letters. "This is my regular job. I don't go to school," she said. "It isn't too bad, but it doesn't pay much. I have to do other work on weekends."

I nodded. Behind her I saw pots and dishes piled in a sink. I also saw jars and cans of what I imagined were the makings of salads and sandwiches. There was a big pot over a small flame on the stove, and I remembered that was where the owner threw the falafel last time before we had our sandwiches.

"Do you get to dance very much?" I asked. "Or are you mostly making the food?"

"I don't dance very much here," she said. "I make the sandwiches. But I get to turn it loose on weekends—in other places."

"Belly-dancing?"

She grinned, laughing as if I were a sweet little girl.

"Hardly. Although sometimes they like it as part of an act."

I nodded, but I really didn't understand. I had images of go-go dancers or strippers in my head, but somehow she didn't seem hard or sleazy enough. She laughed at me again, but I could see it was more good nature than snobbery. "I like ballet, believe it or not, and modern dance. I teach them at the community college on weekends, and sometimes I'll get in the chorus line of a show. Once I danced in a Fosse musical in New York. Tap, of course."

"New York? You danced in a Broadway musical?"

"In the chorus," Ciara said. "*Chicago*. I played one of the trampy molls. You know, black net stockings and plenty of cheek, but just for ten days. Some kind of a bug had hit the chorus, and they were short on replacements."

I nodded, but all I could think of was "*Wow.*" Of course, I didn't say it. But I did say, "Even so. You must be very proud."

She smiled, a little bashful. "I'm still making sandwiches. Dancing's not an easy life, you know. You get old very fast. Like me."

I felt bad for her, and I felt especially bad because Misha and I had turned down a chance to see her perform, mainly because I couldn't stand the smell of her cigarettes and the cooking oil. I asked her for a bottle of Deer Park water, which they take from the ground somewhere near here, I think, and sat at a table to drink it while she continued to make the sandwich. It was a take-out, I guessed, and maybe she had to make more than one. So I didn't say much because I didn't want to slow her down. I watched her drop a couple more falafel balls into the pot of oil and then come back to the counter to break open several pita rolls and stuff them with lettuce and tomatoes.

"So, you like to dance?" she asked.

I shrugged, looking down at my shoes. "I'm a runner, really. Or was. Where am I going to get with that? Right now I'm just trying to figure certain things out."

She grinned—again as if I was a kid. "Boy things, I'll bet. That guy you came in here with last time—he's cute. Is he special?"

I looked down and shook my head. "Not that way. He's just a good friend. And he likes to dance."

She scooped two falafel balls—now golden brown and shiny—out of the oil with a skimmer and brought them to the counter on a plate. She placed each very carefully into a pita roll already half-filled with lettuce and tomatoes and spooned creamy-looking tahini on top of them. "Here. Take one of these," she said. "No charge. I'm making these for an early dinner."

I told her I had eaten already, which was not true, at least not about dinner, but she just carried two paper plates around the counter and placed them on the table in front of me. She went back to the counter for a bottle of Deer Park and came back to sit at the table. "Come on. Join me," she said. "There's nothing I like less than eating alone."

I shrugged, took a small bite of the sandwich, and sat back to watch her eat. I noticed that she was a lot older than I would have guessed at first, and now I wondered about the rest of her life.

"Are you married? Do you have a family?"

"No." She grinned and bit into her sandwich. "I have a daughter though, just about your age. She's living with her father."

"Wow, her father. And that doesn't make you sad—or angry?"

"Not anymore." She sighed. "I guess I realized I'm not a good mother. It's pretty hard when you want to make it on the stage. Besides, her father's much better at family stuff, especially now that he's got himself a new girlfriend."

Ciara smiled, as if she didn't care about that, but I felt pretty sure I was seeing her pain. I picked up the falafel and took another bite—a larger one—as if that would make her feel better. The tahini dribbled from the corners of my mouth, and Ciara jumped up for paper napkins from the counter. "Here," she said, putting one to my lips and cheeks and wiping them. I thanked her and took a long drink of the Deer Park before picking up the sandwich again.

"So, you like to dance with this guy?" she said when she sat again. "He looks pretty limber."

I shrugged. "It's fun. I just don't know where it can go."

"You mean with him?"

She grinned again and drank her water. I began to feel a little tired of that cutesy smile, so I got up and looked out the window. A bunch of kids just left the Sugar Bowl, and I watched them mill around before heading down the street toward the mall.

"Well, where do you want it to go?" Ciara asked. "I mean with this guy? Is it showbiz or some kind of a real romance?"

"For me it's neither. For him, I'm not so sure." I shrugged.

"Believe me . . . What's your name again?"

"I never told you—Jamie."

"Well, believe me, Jamie. It's not bad to have a guy gaga over you—for dancing or anything else. It makes you feel good—secure—and if it gets serious, you won't have to worry about making sandwiches for strangers."

I stared at her, a little surprised myself. I think I flashed her the look that she had given me earlier—like she was an innocent kid who still had a lot to learn.

"What if I want to dance on Broadway?" I said. "Or in the movies?"

"Three words," she said, smiling, with three fingers before her face as she ticked them off. "Don't. Get. Old. Or pregnant, though that makes four."

I was about to answer with another shrug, but the bell tied to the front door rang and what looked like a family of three entered and just about ended the conversation. It was a man and woman, about Ciara's age, I thought, with dark eyes and amber skin and a child with darker hair and eyes than theirs, although her skin looked much lighter. They ordered falafel sandwiches along with three Greek salads and a large bottle of lemon iced tea. Ciara retrieved the tea from a cooler, placed it on the counter, and handed the mother three plastic cups to drink from. They took a table across the room near the door and sat down to watch people walk by. I watched Ciara scoop up three balls of dough and drop them in the heated oil before starting on the pita rolls at the counter. She winked at me as I sat and ate my sandwich along with sips of water. She brought the sandwiches to the family and was about to turn back to me, but I stood up to go before she took a step.

"Somebody's waiting," she said. "The cute dancer?"

I shook my head. "I have work. I've got to get to the library for some books."

"Oh yes, research. Remember that from long ago. Come in again when you have more time."

I thanked her and left, feeling pissed and a little guilty at the same time. I wanted to run, I wanted to dance, but I did not even want to think about babies— especially my own. She didn't either, I figured, at least not when she was my age. So why not find something else to talk about? I walked as fast as I could, then jogged a bit until I reached the county's public library a couple blocks beyond the high school. I walked in, wandered among the stacks for a while, and then I settled down with an illustrated book about modern dancers. I loved the clean lines and the muscular looks of their bodies, which, I must say, made me want to be among them. They were like marble sculptures I had seen photos of—only they were fluid, never meant to be frozen in time or motion. It was a way I hoped to be and, I gathered, Ciara never was—or at least wasn't allowed to be.

I checked out the book and left the library to head back toward the Bonneville. By this time, I was sure, Misha would be gone, and I'd be able to spend the night on my own, reading about dancers' lives and, maybe, figuring out the next step in my own career. It was getting dark, so I walked down the middle of the street past the police station and then slipped into the woods by the maple trees and brush. I found the trail, peered around the huge brown rock and saw no one behind it near the car. I walked over, opened up the door, and leaped back immediately—screeching. The smell hit me first, followed by the awful sight. On the worn-down vinyl front seat, just beneath the steering wheel, rested a brown pile of freshly minted shit.

***

PART TWO:

FAMILIES

VI.

I can laugh at it now—especially that shrill screech—but I must admit, that evening I felt terrified. I knew that someone from the team had done it, of course—or maybe, some of the team's friends (girlfriends)—but I didn't know what they would do, or how far they would go afterward. I'd lived in the car for a little over a year by then, and the worst that had happened was when people walked by—on purpose or by accident— and saw me sitting behind the wheel with a book or a notebook in my hand. I felt exposed and foolish, I guess—like somebody caught naked in the bath—but no one ever said or did anything to make me feel worse. Occasionally, they'd nod or smile, but apart from that not one bad word or remark followed. They just seemed to slink away out of the woods again as if they had intruded. After a while, it gave me more confidence in people. I'd just smile or nod, as if I lived in a glass house, and go on with whatever I was doing. But this was another kind of intrusion, a particularly nasty one, and I wondered what would come at me next.

I didn't go back to school or cross-country practice for the rest of the week, but on Friday Mr. Santa came to the car in the morning and knocked on the back bumper while I was reading that book about dancers. I looked in the mirror, saw him grinning through the back window, and then opened the driver's door to greet him.

"Hey, pretty studious in there," he said, a big (I should say phony) smile on his face. "It's nice to know you're making up for missed classes."

I shook my head. "Well, they're missed forever, Mr. Santa. I'm not going back to that place."

He walked up to me and leaned on the open door. "Jamie . . . "

"You know what happened. But you don't know what happened when I came back here the other night."

His arms dropped to his side, and he stood up straight. I knew that look on his face; he wore it when he heard of somebody getting abused. "Did somebody hurt you?" he asked, his fists clenched at his side. "I guarantee you—it won't be allowed. Even Craig . . ."

"Mr. Santa, no one hurt me, not on my body. I was just given a message about what someone thought—about me."

"What are you talking about—a note?"

I laughed. His hands relaxed, and his face softened into what I used to think of as a social worker's concern.

"Not exactly a note, but the message was pretty clear. A big pile of shit—human shit, I think—on the Bonneville's front seat."

He closed his eyes and crossed his arms over his chest. Mr. Santa had seen a lot in his line of work—he had told me that many times—but the pettiness of this one seemed to bring him up short.

"I spent the whole night cleaning it up," I said. "You can imagine the bottles of water I went through, the hours with windows open on a cold night and day, and the 'fun' I had getting rid of the bulk of the message."

Mr. Santa smiled at that, but I saw his hands clench to his side again when he leaned in the car door to look and inhale. "You got some air freshener, I gather. Good, but when you close the windows, leave it outside. It smells fresh, but it's still a chemical. You don't want to breathe it all night long."

I nodded. "Well, I'm worried about what else they'll be doing."

"Yup. I can understand that. I'll tell Craig Span to get the boys off your case. They'll listen to him—I think."

I shrugged. I wasn't sure they would listen, and I wasn't even sure it was team members who had left the message. I wasn't the most popular girl at school; I'd fought my way through bunches of snotty fakes in hallways, stairwells, and girls' bathrooms—mainly because I didn't like gangs or cliques, or whatever name they give for a group of teenage bullies nowadays. I'd gone home with a bloody nose quite a few times, even when I lived with Mom and Dad. I'd also got bruised on my back and arms, and once I went back to the car with a black eye and a bleeding lip. Yet we lived in what people called a "good school district." Kids graduated and attended good universities, at least two or three Ivy League schools among them, every year. Most other kids, like me and most cross-country guys, would eventually go to public colleges to find and then, maybe, make a career.

"Well," Mr. Santa said, after I shook my head and we went through a few seconds of silence. "Why don't you stay with us tonight? My roommate, Jake, always likes to have people over for dinner, and you can just sleep on the living room couch for the night." He smiled. "You can stay as long as you like."

96

I think it was his smile that got to me. It was so warm and comfortable, with a genuine friendliness that made me want to cry. But at the same time, something inside my gut rebelled, and I have no idea why. At that moment I thought it was because I wouldn't be able to leave the car, but later I wondered if I just felt I wasn't worth saving. To be honest, I'm still not sure, but I know that I just stood next to the Bonneville with tears running down my face and told him I just couldn't leave my home. His eyes widened.

"Jamie, don't kid yourself. This is *not* a house, and it's certainly not a home. This is a banged up, useless pile of rust that would have been hauled away months ago if I didn't convince the mayor and the police that you needed it as a place to live."

I turned away from him to hide my face. I swear I don't know why. Sometimes real kindness makes me weepy instead of grateful, and I suppose that's what happened there.

"I don't want you to get hurt, Jamie. Not because of some stupid, fucking tennis buddy of mine, or anyone else. And I think you should be getting back to your classes. If you don't, the bullies will think they won. In fact the bullies will indeed have won, and you can't let that happen."

I nodded, still with my face turned from him, and I suppose that shows how much of a fighter I was to Mr. Santa. I wiped my shirt sleeve across my eyes and turned around. Half-resolved.

"I'll be there tomorrow," I said, "or maybe the next day."

"No, no, no. Tomorrow for sure. I'll come and meet you at the police station and drive you into school. If you want, I'll stay with you all day long, from class to class. This stuff has got to stop—literally."

That was what I wanted to hear, I guess, because I smiled and nodded. Although, I have to say, I still felt uncertain. "Meet me at the police station?"

He nodded. "At seven-fifteen then. I'll be there."

He put out his hand. I slapped it, and without another word he walked back out of the woods the way he came.

***

Next morning I stood in front of a red-brick building with a clock tower and waited among the black and white patrol cruisers for Mr. Santa's gray Honda Civic to pull up. A couple of older kids drove by in their cars, fists and middle fingers extended out their windows as they hooted and laughed uproariously, either at me or the police station. I didn't respond, but as you can imagine my mood didn't improve on seeing them. A group of four or five girls strolled past, talking loud and giggling until they saw me, and then everything went silent. At least half a block away, they all stopped and turned together to stare at me as if they had just realized who I was. They said nothing, just dawdled for a minute or so and turned back toward school.

The cross-country team was at practice, I figured, so I didn't expect anything from them. But I did wonder if any of the girlfriends, especially Michele, would go to school this way. No one did, at least not before Mr. Santa arrived, pulling his car to the curb and flashing a big smile in greeting. He reached across the front seat and pushed the passenger-side door wide open, just about yelling his good-morning. "Great to see you," he said. "I thought sure I'd have to dig you out of the rust heap just to get you to school this morning."

"I said I'd be here," I said. "I like to keep my word."

"Good. I like that. Hey, look in the backseat and meet my friend Jake."

"Hi." I looked in and saw a young, brown-haired boy with glasses, five or six years old, scrunched low in the corner behind the passenger seat. He gave me a little window-wiping wave and smiled as I got in.

"Hi," I said. "I'm Jamie."

I couldn't hold back a laugh at how cute he was, and I reached over the seat to shake his hand. Instead of shaking, he slapped me a high-five and laughed himself. "Wow," I said. "A son. I didn't know you had one."

Mr. Santa smiled. "A foster child, really. But we've really taken to each other, so who knows? Right, Jake? We're moving forward."

"Right, Dad. I love you, for sure."

I looked at Mr. Santa and saw his dark face turn into a reddish blush as he grinned. I knew he was single, and I always assumed he was gay, but this was a side of him I never suspected. "How long has he been with you?" I asked.

"A couple months. You came to live with me right around Christmas—right, Jake?"

"December 23rd, Dad. Just in time for the presents."

"Oh boy, yes. Games and drums. I still haven't regained my normal hearing."

I laughed again. "Jake was the real present, I'll bet. You're very lucky. Both of you."

Mr. Santa turned to me as he pulled into the street. He had a deep look of appreciation on his face, as if he saw something about me as well as himself. "*Very* lucky, I assure you. And it's nice that you realize that. Some of these kids . . ." He waved his hand as a car swept by us on the left and sped down the street.

He took the direct route across town, but before we reached the high school, he turned off the road and went down a few blocks to one of our elementary schools. He pulled into the school lot, got out and walked hand-in-hand with Jake to the front of the school. A woman stood at the front door, gave a big smile to Jake, took his hand and, after a few words with Mr. Santa, walked the boy into the building. Mr. Santa waved, then came back and started toward the high school.

"Jamie," he said, "just a little heads-up before we get there. I spoke to the principal and then to Craig. They were both apologetic about what happened to you and swear they will do everything in their power to prevent a repeat." He laughed at that, a little sneer coming to his face. "I told Craig that all he would have to do is control his own mouth which, I must say, he was quick to admit. Both he and the principal are worried about the kids— some of the boys on the team, and a couple of the girls you've had run-ins with."

"They hate me," I said. "They don't like it that I compete with the boys in practice."

"And win." Mr. Santa nodded. "They're jealous. In any case they're worried about what they'll do, and so they have a couple of suggestions you might like to follow."

I laughed. "What? Don't come to school? You're the one who told me I have to go back. If they—"

"Hold on, Jamie. I assure you they want you in school. But rumors are going around, some nasty ones, and you're going to have to deal with them—without getting into fights."

"Fuck," I said. "If they . . ."

"Jamie, the rumors are absurd, and only stupid, vindictive kids would believe them, mainly because they need to."

I looked at him. "You better tell me what they are before we get there, or I'm not going in. Are they saying I'm fucking the whole team?"

He turned toward me, his face gray and very serious.

"Those fuckers!" I shouted, before he nodded.

"Jamie . . . No one, I mean no one, believes it, but of course that just makes it all the juicier for repetition."

My fists clenched, and I could barely hold myself back from opening the door and jumping out. He pulled over to the curb and sat there with the car engine idling. We were about a block from school now, and I saw kids gathered on its front lawn, sitting and standing around together with their phones in their hands. Mr. Santa reached across the seat and put his hand on my knee. "I will spend the whole day with you—every day—for as long as it takes," he said. "In the halls, in classes, if you

101

want. I will smash heads for you too, but I do not want you to get into fights yourself."

"If I have to have you with me to get through the day, I'm not going back. It's not worth your time or mine. I live by myself. I'm not a baby."

"Let's see how it plays out, okay? I know you can do this, but promise me, no fighting—no matter how bad it gets. I don't want you to get hurt, and I don't want you to get into trouble by hurting anyone else."

I didn't say anything. I just held my breath and stared out the window, wondering what to say next. I guess Mr. Santa took my silence as a yes, because he put the car in gear and started toward the school again. We crossed in front of it, where the kids were waiting on the lawn and steps for the starting bell. No one seemed to look at us, but I felt like every eye in the crowd centered on the Honda as we turned and drove toward the parking lot behind the building. After he parked, Mr. Santa put his hand on my shoulder and turned toward me. "I know you can do this," he said. "Just keep focused on what you're here for—education."

I laughed, but with absolutely no humor.

"I mean it, Jamie. This is not about fighting or getting even."

Taking a deep breath, I opened the car door and looked around the lot. Mr. Santa got out on his side, locked the doors with his remote key, and came around to me.

"I don't need you here," I said.

I started directly for the building, but he caught up with me and stood close as we both walked quickly, as if we were racing.

"Jamie, don't spoil this. You have a lot of people on your side. We're not going to allow anyone to hound you from the school. We're not."

I kept walking. I figured I'd go to my locker, pick up some pencils, paper, and books, and then head to my first class. Clearly, I was not going to Mr. Span's homeroom—not today or any other. I'd go to the main office if I had to go somewhere to be counted as present, but I just figured Mr. Span's room was in another world—a forbidden one. We got to the tennis courts, walked around them without either of us saying anything, and then came to the grass at the walkway to the back entrance. I was determined to go in alone, with no one babying or protecting me, so I stopped, looked at Mr. Santa long enough to make him stop, and then just sprinted into the building fast to keep him behind. When I reached the door, I turned right and took a stairway down to the bottom floor, where the gym is and where my locker was. I went right to it and spun the combination dial with the thumb of one hand, then opening the lock quickly with the fingers of my other hand. I threw my jacket into the locker, took out a notebook and a bag of pencils, then slammed the door shut, locked it, and headed down to the other end. I took the stairwell up to the next floor and barged into the hall, thinking of running down to my music class—the first of the day. I heard loud voices and heavy footsteps coming from the front of the building, and I saw that the crowd on the front lawn had started to enter. I turned immediately toward the music room, but I saw Mr. Santa standing near the door, so I started for the stairwell instead. The door banged open. I lowered my head to slink by whoever was coming through it, but a pair of hands grabbed my shoulders and held me there.

"Jamie!"

I looked up at Misha's serious, gentle face. Grateful, I shook my head. My mouth hung open, and my lips trembled, but I could hardly make myself talk.

"I have to get out of here," I muttered and tried to push his hands away. Instead, he put his arms around my back and held me close. We hadn't hugged much, except during slow dances, and I was surprised to feel his body strength—and warmth—from head to toe. I struggled against it at first, but he just pulled tighter with his hands against my back.

"Misha, this is against the rules in the hall. You know that. Now they'll all be saying I'm fucking you, too."

"Jamie . . ." He lifted his head off my neck and shoulder and looked directly at me. His hazel-blue eyes seemed impossibly deep for a moment, but then the blush of his ears and cheeks made him much more like somebody I could talk to. I became aware of his trembling thighs, and without intending to hurt his feelings, pushed him away. All around us, people made noises, talking and laughing, but it was as if I was wood—not a part of it.

"I can't do this," I whispered. "I don't belong here, and I don't want to draw you down with me."

"If you don't belong here, nobody does, Jamie."

That was Mr. Santa, walking up to us and placing his hand on my arm. When I looked at him, I saw that the principal, Mr. Gomez, and Mr. Span stood there with him, too. "Please, Jamie, come with us for a few minutes. We'll go down to Mr. Gomez's office and work this out."

I was about to twist out of Misha's arms and run for the stairwell, but he held tight, and with such a pleading, mournful expression, that I felt I would hurt one of us if I tried. At last he dropped an arm to his side, keeping the other one on my shoulders. We turned together and followed Mr. Gomez, along with Mr. Santa and Mr. Span, through the crowded hallway toward the main office. Kids yacked and called to each other over their phones. But they suddenly stopped as we passed and, like a bunch of rubbernecks on the highway, stared at the five of us—of course, mostly at me. I put my fist and finger up as we walked, but when Mr. Gomez stopped to look, I dropped my arm to my side. "Not smart," Misha said. "You're only going to make people hostile."

As you can imagine, I laughed at his comment, although I admit I kept my fist and fingers at my side as we walked into the office. "Wait here," Mr. Gomez said to me. He gave a noticeable nod to the secretary behind the desk, but said nothing as he went behind the barrier and led Mr. Span and Mr. Santa into his office. The door closed as the noise from the hall swelled and the school bell rang students into their homerooms.

Misha and I settled on the wooden bench facing the secretary's desk and leaned apart, though Misha spread his legs so his knee touched mine. "This is crazy," I said. "What are they going to do? I might as well wear a fucking target on my back."

"I'm going to walk the halls with you," he said. "I won't scare anybody, maybe, but I'll be a witness if anything happens."

I glared at him and threw him another nasty laugh. "Are you coming into the girls' room with me, too?"

He put his head down and shook it as his face went red again. I felt ashamed at first because I didn't want to make fun of Misha, but, Jesus, how far was this going to play out? Most of the time I liked being alone, and the idea of anyone, even my best friend, following me around for protection all day would drive me into a hole. I wouldn't handle it, even for an hour.

We sat for about fifteen minutes, maybe more, staring at the secretary as she sat behind her desk and, from what I saw, pretended to be working. Her phone rang a couple times, and of course she answered, but with the snotty tone Dad used to give to telemarketers. She also seemed to hang up in the middle of a sentence: "Certainly, I will give him (she'd hang up) the message." Then she looked at me and Misha and went back to her computer keyboard with a gross frown that showed her satisfaction.

After the second or third call like that, Misha sighed, took a history book from his backpack, and started to read. I just sank lower into the bench, leaned my head against the wall behind us, and closed my eyes. After a few more minutes, I heard the door open behind the secretary, and Mr. Santa called me into the principal's office. Misha got up with me, but Mr. Santa held up his hand. "Not sure this is for you," he said. "I'm sure Jamie's grateful, but . . ."

"I want him with me," I said, though I had no idea I'd say that. "He's the one friend I can count on."

Mr. Santa flashed a surprised look and gave a nod, but then he closed the door to Mr. Gomez's office. "Fuck it!" I said out loud to Misha. While the secretary turned on me with a very nasty scowl, I started out of the office.

"Jamie, don't do this," Misha said.

I waved my hand, smirked at the secretary, and kept walking. But when I reached the hallway door, I heard Mr. Santa's voice again. "It's okay. You come in, too, Misha," he called. "You're more than welcome." I stopped and stood at the door, grinning stupidly through the glass into the hall.

"Come on. This has to be settled," Misha said. I turned and walked between him and Mr. Santa into Mr. Gomez's office. Yes, I smirked at the secretary again.

"Take a seat," Mr. Gomez said. He sat on one of three leather couches and a chair surrounding a coffee table. Mr. Span sat next to him, and, I have to say, did not look the least bit happy or confident. His head hung down, and his hands dangled in a kind of mangled ball between his legs. At first, I actually thought he was handcuffed, but really, he was just folding and unfolding his fingers to get a grip.

I squatted on a couch across from them. Misha took the seat next to me, and my buddy, Mr. Santa, took the neutral chair about halfway around the circle between us. Mr. Gomez leaned forward and put his glasses on the coffee table.

"Okay. First," Mr. Span said, "I want to make it clear that I've already apologized to Jamie. I'm

107

personally embarrassed, and I admit that what I said was stupid. From now on I will watch my tongue and be more careful. I was simply trying to motivate the slackers on the cross-country team after a particularly bad practice. I know it was inappropriate to use Jamie that way, and very poor taste to speak of her as I did. She's a very nice girl."

He glanced at me for a quick second, but then he looked down at his hands. Mr. Gomez gave a quiet smile, and Mr. Santa, I saw, studied his tennis shoes as if he was trying to figure something out. I could feel Misha stiffen beside me, but then he relaxed, and all I could feel in myself was a desire to run from the office.

"Well, Jamie, what do you think?" Mr. Gomez's smile brightened—he had really white, very straight teeth—and he leaned forward in his chair to fiddle with his glasses. I shook my head but said nothing. Honestly, I didn't know what I thought, much less what to say. I just wanted to get out of there—from, or to, what, I wasn't sure at that moment. But I knew my feet wanted to hit the floor and fast. I felt Misha shift a bit beside me and thought he would say something, but it was Mr. Santa's voice that came out first.

"Well, Mr. Gomez, it's unfortunate but nothing will undo Craig's words, though I'm sure he means his apology. My primary concern now is that Jamie continue in school without any further harassment—from anyone. How can we best accomplish that?"

Mr. Gomez shrugged and looked puzzled, as if he thought the matter had been settled already. After a few seconds he said, "There's quite a bit of history here, as I'm sure you know. Jamie's made enemies at school, and we're not going to erase them overnight. We have to keep working."

"Precisely. But we don't want to add to that history, so what can we do to make things more comfortable for everybody?"

"She can come back to the team any time she wants," Mr. Span put in. "I personally guarantee there will be no more boys' locker room talk from me or anyone else. I will not allow it."

Everybody, except for Misha, turned to look at me. I felt the blood rush to my face, mainly because I still had no idea what to say—*Good, I'd love to run with the scum of the team and their sleazy coach?*—Of course not, so I just lowered my head and stared at my NBs: "I'm not ready for this, not any of it. I should probably just drop out of school."

Misha tensed up and whispered, "No!" Then, in a very quiet voice, he added, "I think Mr. Span should apologize in front of the whole team—with Jamie there."

Somebody gasped. I'm not sure who, but I know it wasn't me. I buried my head in Misha's shoulder and gave him a huge hug, muttering, "Thanks, but I'll just drop out."

Mr. Gomez frowned and nodded. "I'm afraid you can't do that," he said.

"Because we won't allow it," Mr. Santa said before I could answer. "You're a smart young woman who deserves and needs an education. What do you think, Craig? Will an apology help?"

I shook my head, barely able to stop a scream. "I don't need his apology. No one will believe it. I don't want to be made into a special case. I've taken care of myself for almost two years, and I can keep doing it, whether people like me or not. I just want to be free."

Misha put his arm around my shoulders and squeezed. It felt good, really good—and I let him keep his arm there for a couple of seconds before I shrugged it off. Mr. Santa grinned and shook his head.

"Jamie, you're making this very hard—for everyone, but especially yourself."

I looked, and when I saw the smile on his face, the kindness and genuine concern in it, for some stupid reason I thought of the boy, Jake, and tears filled and overflowed my eyes. Misha put his arm around my shoulder again, and for the life of me I could not stop myself from throwing my head on his neck and shoulder and blubbering. Two couches and a chair scraped on the floor at once; like magic two handkerchiefs and a tissue appeared against my nose. I grabbed the tissue and wiped my eyes, at the same time I started to giggle uncontrollably at how stupid everything was, especially me.

After a few seconds, Mr. Gomez spoke. "All right, here are a couple of steps to consider. Please, Jamie, give them some thought."

I sat up straight and looked at the three of them. Mr. Span, his hands more comfortable in his lap now, looked much more like the cool coach I knew out on the track. Mr. Gomez had his glasses on and was glancing at a sheet of paper in his hands. Mr. Santa smiled and leaned back in his neutral chair, though I could see his feet were twitching to rest, I imagined, on the coffee table. And Misha followed my eyes, looking at them all while he held my hand.

"I could walk with her in the hall, and—most of the time—before and after school," he said.

I shook my head. Mr. Gomez shook his too.

"You have your own life, Misha, your own schedule, and your own classes, I'm sure." Mr. Santa nodded at him. "Besides, I'm sure Jamie can take care of herself here. It's nights and weekends I'm more worried about—really bad weather and, I guess, bad people."

"My mom and dad would be willing to have her live with us for a while, if it's housing you're talking about. They told me that last night."

Okay, here's what happened. I freaked out, especially at that word, *housing*. I shrugged off his arm and slid away from him on the couch.

"What the fuck!" I said out loud, not to anyone in particular, but mostly myself. I clenched my teeth and literally bit my tongue to keep from saying it again. I could see Mr. Gomez's smile of relief turn into something darker, as if he had just found out, definitively, that God did not exist. But then Mr. Santa turned his eyes on me, and I saw something completely different.

"Well, Jamie, think about it before you react. The Altos are friendly and have a very nice home. You'd have your own room, I bet."

"Yes," Misha said. "Between mine and theirs."

I turned to look at him, and I could see that he already knew I would turn it down. He didn't look at me. He looked past me, at the office door as if he, too, wanted to run out of there fast. At the same time, he leaned away from me as much as he could, his head and shoulders suspended above the armrest at his side.

111

"I like my present situation," I said. "It's mine. I find it comfortable, and I don't owe anybody anything for it."

Mr. Santa shook his head. "Well, I'm not sure about that. It's noble, maybe, but I don't buy it. Especially the comfort part. And don't forget that the state and the town are helping some—Washington is, too."

"Whatever you think, I like where I am," I said. I could feel Misha shaking, almost rising from the chair and drifting away. I glanced over at him, and all I saw was his grim face and tense body leaning away, as if somehow I had suddenly developed a massive case of B.O. I touched his knee, but he pulled his leg farther away.

"Jesus," I said, "can't anybody see it my way? I like the way I live—prefer it to the usual stuff? I don't know why, but I feel it's me."

Mr. Span sat there, his face very long. Mr. Gomez gave another shake. And Mr. Santa, I'm afraid, looked super disappointed—in me and the whole situation. It was as if I had turned him and Jake down, rather than the Altos.

"Well, Jamie, I know we can continue this way. God knows you're not the only kid in this state living in a car, but I'm pretty sure you'd be the only one who really wants to. It's cold in the winter, and I can only imagine how scary it is at night, or in the rain."

I said nothing, just nodding. Mr. Gomez let out a big sigh—of disgust, probably—while Misha and Mr. Santa both looked puzzled, and my pal, Mr. Span, stared at the floor beneath his shoes.

"Frankly, I don't know what else we can do here, Jamie," Mr. Gomez said, putting on his glasses. "Especially if the state and town are willing to let you remain as you are—with Mr. Santa's oversight, of course. We have rules against bullying, fighting, overly aggressive negative or sexist language, and we do our best to enforce them and educate against them. But mistakes happen. If you want to live with them, and in that unsafe environment you've chosen for yourself, you're welcome to come back to school and, as Mr. Span has said already, even work out with the cross-country team. But we ask that you not provoke people with words or deeds. Try, just try, to be a little more friendly with your peers."

You can imagine what I thought about that piece of personal advice. Mr. Gomez's pearly smile looked dark by the time he finished, and all I could do was giggle when he looked at me after the "try, just try" part. Misha found it in himself to move closer on the couch, and this time I didn't shrug his arm off my shoulders. Mr. Santa put his two feet flat on the floor, and leaned on his knees with his hands. "I'm sure Jamie doesn't look for trouble. But somehow it keeps coming at her. Whatever you can do to prevent it will be helpful."

"I'll stay with her as much as she wants," Misha said.

We all looked at Mr. Span at that point, but he just settled deeper into the couch and nodded, as if he wanted to dodge something. With all that, Mr. Gomez nodded and congratulated Misha on what he called his "gallantry".

"We'll try to be more attentive in the halls," he added, "especially between classes and free periods. I'll direct your teachers to look out for you. And, Misha, if you see or hear anything, you come and tell us right away."

That seemed to settle everything—without really settling anything, I thought—and I'm sure all five of us knew it. But there was nothing more to offer, and so, after staring at each other and breathing heavily for a few seconds, Mr. Gomez rose from the couch, Mr. Santa stood at his chair, and Misha and I, along with Mr. Span, started for the door. Mr. Santa opened it, led me and Misha past the secretary, and accompanied us into the hall.

"Well, that was pretty much a waste of time," I told him.

"But they're warned," he said. "Both Craig and Mr. Gomez. They'll keep things clean—maybe permanently. You guys go about your work and learn. I'll keep in touch, Jamie. Try to make sure things don't get out of hand again."

"Right," Misha said. Mr. Santa smiled, and as Misha and I started walking toward our classes, he headed toward the outside door.

***

VII.

For a short while, things went quietly. Mr. Santa came by the car almost every night to see how things were; I went to his office every Friday after school to talk about the week; and Misha, my dear, sweet Misha, met me every morning at the police station to walk to school and every night on the front lawn to go back to the car. We'd stop for falafel occasionally at the Cedars of Lebanon or go back to his house for an afternoon of dance and music. His mom—a really nice woman, I began to see—started coming down to sit and watch us practice, her feet tapping mightily to the beat, though she insisted she hated the stuff we listened to. I had dinner with them a few times (Mr. Alto made a mean tomato sauce for pasta), and I even got used to listening to his "philosophic" memories of the kind of music and art he liked in high school (Johnny Ray, Elvis Presley, and some Italian guy named Domenico something or other— Muldoonio, I think). And he loved Marlon Brando in *On the Waterfront*, which, he said, was the best, most explosive anti-crime movie ever made. "A single, defeated, yet victorious man against the mob," is how he described it. "Elia Kazan was a genius."

To be truthful, there were times when I wished Misha and I could just stand and leave the table in the middle of one of these memories, but we both sort of felt they meant too much to him. "My dad's decent," Misha said a couple of times. "He really enjoys telling us about that stuff, so I sit through it. I hope you don't mind."

I shook my head and, probably petted his dog, Vincent, who was around my feet a lot when I visited. Misha said it was because he thought I was kind of cool.

Anyhow, it made me remember my own dad talking, like Misha's father did, about stuff back in his own day. Now I'm surprised at how clear the things he told me still are—almost as if I lived through them myself. It's funny, but I remember more about Dad's stories than I do, sometimes, about the look on his face when he talked, or the feel of his body when he sat next to me in front of the TV. I still hear his voice in my dreams, and I hear Mum's too; but I almost never have a dream of seeing or feeling them near me. I asked Mr. Santa about it once, but he confessed he had no idea what that meant. "We talk to ourselves all the time," he said, shrugging. "In our dreams, when we're alone, and sometimes in the middle of a crowd—or, maybe, in a class. It's probably to keep from being bored or scared. So sometimes, maybe, you hear the voice of others instead of yourself."

Misha has the same idea about his dad's stories, but of course, somehow, like his dad, he had to make an abstract theory out of it. "We're both internal people, I guess. We live more on the inside than the outside."

I don't know about any of that, but I sure remember Mr. Alto's reedy, high-pitched voice that made me think of one of those singers Mrs. Alto liked us to put on in the afternoon, after we finished dancing in their basement. It wasn't opera, thank god, but singers and groups from the 70s, with acoustic guitars, rocking rhythms, and a slur of nasally, high-pitched vocals saying they were young, simple, and wild which—I have to say—Mr. and Mrs. Alto definitely did not seem to be.

Mum and Dad were like that too, although I'm pretty sure it was at a lower level. They worked with their hands—carpentry, landscaping, housecleaning— and, probably, the longest things they ever wrote were Mum's last letter to me and Dad's letter to his distant cousin, asking him to take care of me when he died. Hah! So much for the importance of the written word.

Needless to say, I heard their voices often in the Pontiac, especially at night, when traffic died down on the road and the police were in the middle of evening shifts before the dawn turnover. I heard other sounds, too, peepers in the spring—especially from the pond in the lower part of the park—songbirds in the hardwoods all around me as the sun rose, an occasional owl or whippoorwill from some distant tree in the middle of the night, and once or twice, the scary grunt or growl of an animal scuffling through the woods on the watch for food, preferably alive and, I imagined, bloody.

One late spring night a black bear came up to the Pontiac, propped its paws on the hood and then moved to the side door, touching the windows (luckily, I had closed them before going to sleep), and very gently rocked the car, as if it was trying to open the door. I held back a scream, scared out of my mind. When I sat up and saw its fuzzy face and dark eyes pressing against the glass, I dropped down to the floor beneath the steering wheel, then reached up and pushed the door lock down and held it. I will always remember the breathy snort of disappointment before the bear gave the car one last shake and dropped down to waddle away on all four feet.

I cracked open the window for air and a clearer view, but then the bear turned around and ran back toward the car at a really fast trot. By the time I closed the window again, both hands clutching the door handle while I fell back into the seat, it had gone around the car to the other side and headed straight into the park—presumably toward the pond for a drink of water and, maybe, a live rainbow trout or two.

When I saw Mr. Santa next day and told him about the bear, he didn't even smile. Instead, he repeated his mantra. "You shouldn't live there—by yourself or with someone else." I told him it was scary but interesting at the same time and reminded him that very few people—especially kids—had the opportunity to live the way I did. He shook his head, with more of a smile than a frown on his face, and then invited me to dinner with him and Jake that night.

***

He came by the Pontiac around six o'clock that evening and sat with me in the front seat for about half an hour to watch the sun go down through the surrounding trees. It was a beautiful sunset, as it often is in spring, with the fading light turning the oak and maple bark on the trunks into various shades of gold and ash. Luckily the sky was clear, and so the moon shone as a sliver of light while two other planets—Venus and Jupiter, Mr. Santa said—glowed nearby as the whole sky grew dark.

"Not bad," he said. "I can see why you like it." He leaned back and took everything in, along with the chirp of the peepers and other night sounds.

"It's great," I answered. "So, now you know what it means to me."

He turned toward me, one eye closed for a long time, and shook his head. "But then it's dark in about six months—and when winter comes everything changes. Or maybe one day a bear will look for a midnight snack. That can change things, too." He got out of his side of the car and stood, looking up at the sky and surrounding woods. Then I got out, too. "You need human company, Jamie, no matter how beautiful this is. You especially need a family to grow with. Believe me, I do not see you as the hermit type, no matter how pretty and calm it gets around here."

"I like it." I shrugged, not knowing what else to say. "Besides, I can always go visit people, if I'm lonely."

Mr. Santa walked to my side of the car and stood beside me. He looked into my eyes even though I pretended to be mesmerized by the beautiful night sky. "Jamie, you need parents again—people who will support you. And, maybe, some brothers and sisters to talk to about what's on your mind. You fight these idiots who bust you at school because you don't have any support—emotional or otherwise. You swing at them because you're all alone. In the business, we call it fight or flight."

I turned away and started to walk into the park, toward the pond this time. I heard Mr. Santa's footsteps behind me, and so I picked up the pace. I have no idea why I left him, or why I headed that way. It was the only thing to do, maybe, to show I wasn't afraid. When I got through the trees and into the open grass field of the

119

park, I broke into a run. Mr. Santa wouldn't catch me if I ran, I figured. But I'll be damned if I didn't hear him pounding away behind me and, to my surprise (disappointment, really), actually staying with me and eventually catching up. So, I started sprinting—like the last quarter, or half mile, of a race.

"Jamie," he called. "This is getting you nowhere. Stop! Please!"

I figured I had him at that point; he was out of breath. So I gave it everything I had, as if I was running neck and neck with one of Mr. Span's best boys and wanted to show I could beat him. But soon I realized Mr. Santa was still catching up.

"Come on, Jamie. You're not going to outrun me. I'm pretty damn sure of it."

He wasn't even breathing heavily now, and when I glanced back over my shoulder, I saw him about four steps behind. I tried to run even harder, really opening up, I thought—but he was by my side in just about ten steps, reaching out to touch my arm above the elbow.

"You run . . . track?" I said, gasping as I slowed down to a very disappointed jog.

He shook his head, smiling. "Just occasional road races now. I ran track in high school and college though, and I'm pretty sure I could keep up with you for quite a distance."

I slowed down even more and, in a few steps, started walking. He kept pace by my side, and as we headed toward the lower end of the park, he repeated that I needed people and a place to live. I shook my head again, but by the time we reached the row of willows near the pond, I pretty much gave up insisting. We pushed through the dangling branches of the willows and stopped a few feet from the pond, deafened now by the bass croak of frogs and the high-pitched chirping of the peepers in the surrounding trees. The moon glowed in the water, with one of the two planets and a couple stars accompanying it now, an occasional ripple from the breeze warping the reflected sky. We saw no bears or other animals, and we certainly could never have heard anything coming at us, not with all those wild songs of animal passion from land and water. Mr. Santa put his hands in his pockets and seemed to whistle as he listened and looked at it all, a huge case of wonder lighting his face.

"It's lovely, Jamie. It makes you feel small and isolated, which may be a privileged feeling nowadays. We need people. *You* need people. You need to learn how to appreciate them and their complexities—no matter how small they are."

"Well, that's a new one," I said. "You mean the people who dumped their shit in my car are complex? And I should appreciate them? They seem like simple, nasty morons to me."

Mr. Santa laughed and turned to the image of the sky in the pond again. Right where the sickle-face of the moon smiled at us, a ripple started and something small and dark suddenly surfaced, leaping and plopping back in the pond—the moon, stars, and planet scrambled, broke up, and shimmered, smoothing out like a pane of glass again as we watched. Mr. Santa chuckled in satisfaction, and after a moment we started back through the willows toward the park and the Pontiac. "Jake's waiting at a sitter's," he said. "Let's go get him and have some dinner."

We didn't stop at the Pontiac. We walked to the street, where he had parked his car, and then drove a little north of town to the sitter's house, then to his place. The house was small, but warm and comfortable, a white stucco that Mr. Santa called a Cape Cod. He had no garage, so he parked the car in a driveway next to the house, and then walked with me and Jake onto the porch in back, where he unlocked the door. "Not much," he said, "but we have a great kitchen."

He let me enter first, and I must say his kitchen was pretty cool. He had white stone countertops, blonde cabinets ("Maple," Mr. Santa said), a huge metallic silver refrigerator, and a very nice glass-topped stove. I looked at it all as Jake ran into a side room that must have been his bedroom. Fanning my palm and fingers over the countertop and the stove, I looked at Mr. Santa and asked if he had always lived alone.

"Not anymore," he said, smiling. "I have Jake, and I'm incredibly lucky to have him."

I took the hint and, nodding, smiled back. "You do the cooking, too, I guess."

"Absolutely. It's one of my most loved duties— after Jake and tennis."

I nodded again, grinning this time, as Mr. Santa went to the refrigerator and started pulling out food. "I suppose you're vegetarian, like most of the kids your age." I mumbled a reluctant yes, and he pulled out cans from a cabinet—beans, tomato sauce, and, finally, a box of taco shells. "I happen to make a mean guacamole," he said, "and Jake loves tacos. Would some kind of Tex-Mex be okay with you?"

"Fine."

"Haven't bought meat in almost a year—since I brought Jake home with me it's tofu, tofu, tofu. He keeps seeing Bambi, and maybe Elsie the cow, whenever anyone mentions meat—I mean the word, not the kind."

"He sounds like a good kid," I said, nodding. "I can see you appreciate him."

"Hey." He looked at me very seriously, his hand and arm stretched into the refrigerator for something, maybe peppers and a tomato, I thought. "My love of that young boy, or my appreciation of what he's brought into my life, is beyond question. I probably need him more than he needs me. At least it seems that way much of the time. As I said before, you need people, Jamie. I know that from my own sorry experience."

He brought out a head of lettuce and started to "assemble," as he called it, our taco dinner. Every once in a while, I heard snatches of music from the room Jake had entered, and when I passed the door on the way to the dining room to set the table, I saw him staring at a tablet while his fingers worked a keyboard, playing some game or watching a film. When I came back into the kitchen for glasses and a pitcher of water, I heard him laugh and saw him watching me walk by. "Hey, that's usually my job," he said.

I giggled. "Take the night off, dude. Your dad thinks I should practice domestic stuff."

"And this is just the beginning," Mr. Santa said. "Tell her about doing the wash and cleaning the dishes, Jake."

"And straightening your room, I'll bet."

Jake grinned, pushed a button on his tablet, and came out into the kitchen. He was a small kid, up to my waist, if I remember correctly, and he had a splash of dark brown hair flat on his head, down to his eyes and below his ears. I couldn't resist running my fingers through it and then patting him right at the top. He had changed into shorts and a t-shirt and wore a pair of ratty fur-lined slippers now that he scuffed around the kitchen floor, as if he were mopping it. He opened the refrigerator and pulled out a pitcher of colored water that I assumed was Kool Aid. After he poured a glassful, he asked if I wanted some too. I said I preferred plain water, so he shrugged and put the pitcher back in the refrigerator. Mr. Santa left the assembled taco plates and went to the refrigerator to pull out a Brita full of water.

"This'll do it for the adults," he said.

Jake looked from me to his father and back to me again. He shrugged and carried his glass of Kool Aid into the dining room. I took the Brita from Mr. Santa and followed behind him and the tacos to the dining room table. It was a nice room, small, with a sliding glass door that looked out on some trees and a small pond in the distance. When Mr. Santa opened the door for air, I heard the familiar chirp of peepers, just like at the car.

We had a nice, slow dinner, with Mr. Santa giving a brief outline of his young life as a foster child. Jake talked too, asking me about school, the Pontiac, my dancing, and even cross-country. When I told him I heard peepers like he and his dad did, he nodded and smiled, as if that was kind of interesting. But when he asked about other animals, and I stupidly mentioned the

124

bear, in addition to the deer and turkey I saw there almost every day, he told me I was crazy to stay there, especially alone.

"I've seen a bear or two in our backyard, Jakey," Mr. Santa said. "You just have to be careful not to surprise them—particularly with baby bears around."

"What did that bear want from you?" Jake asked, suddenly appearing anxious. I shook my head and shrugged.

"Food, I guess."

"Did you surprise it?"

I shook my head again. "No, but he sure surprised me. I just looked up, and there was this big, fat, hairy monster face looking in the car window."

Jake's eyes widened. "Ohhh! . . . Did you run?"

"I was in the car, Jake. Windows closed. I just held on to the door handle and prayed it wouldn't open."

"Wow. I'll bet you screamed."

"Hmm . . . actually, I was frozen. I felt like I couldn't talk."

"Hey, that would never happen to you, Jake." Mr. Santa winked. "You'd probably talk to the bear, maybe invite him in for a glass of Kool Aid."

Jake looked at his father and, for that moment, seemed like an annoyed but tolerating adult. "Dad, if I saw a monster bear's face in the window, I'd be screaming—for you."

Mr. Santa laughed. "Smart boy, though you'd be better off sitting tight in the car. With all the doors locked."

"It worked in my case," I said. "Lucky the windows were closed, too."

125

Jake looked up at me, with new light—a kind of childish awareness—in his eyes. I don't know what he was thinking, because he didn't say or do anything different. He just stared at my face, and I could sense the little motor of attitude and memory warming up and beginning to grind. Mr. Santa saw it too, I think, but chose to ignore it, leaving the table for a moment to bring more water and Kool Aid for us. Jake wiped his mouth on a napkin and went back to the taco and beans in his plate. He took a generous scoop of guacamole from the bowl in the middle of the table.

"Hey, guys," Mr. Santa said. "How about some *helado de limón* with a couple *galletas*?"

"Dessert!" Jake said. "Finally something good."

"Hey, that wasn't so bad. At least the guacamole was pretty good, no?"

The boy grinned, his mouth wide and full of confidence. "Only kidding, Dad. Everything was really good."

"Delicious," I added. "Thanks for inviting me and making dinner. It beats cafeteria food any day."

"Hah, another reason to find a family for you," Mr. Santa said.

I said nothing, just picked up plates from the table and carried them into the kitchen where I saw a box of vanilla cookies and a pot of coffee gradually dripping full in a Cuisinart maker. "I know you like it strong," Mr. Santa said, coming behind me into the kitchen. He carried serving platters and glasses in his hand and brought them to the sink near the dishwasher. After putting stuff into the washer, he arranged cookies on another plate and started filling three small bowls with lemon ice cream. "You like a lot?" he asked.

"Whatever you and Jake are having. It's nice to have a home-cooked meal, with dessert."

Mr. Santa gave me a very cagey look. "You're digging the hole pretty deep now, Jamie."

I shrugged, but didn't say anything. Hey, enjoying a meal isn't like needing or wanting it every night. But I didn't feel like insulting Mr. Santa with that kind of stupid remark. He had lived in almost a dozen foster homes while growing up, and he said he still bore the scars of the experience: From a foster "brother" being adopted by the family while he was cast into the homeless world again; to being beaten and deprived of food and water for almost a week because he had broken a garage door window with a poorly shot basketball; to waking up abandoned in the middle of the night while adults in charge left the state to run away from bill collectors. He had been made to feel unwanted, inadequate, and "very, very alone," he said.

"Well, let's get these dirty dishes in there so we can finish the magnificent repast I've prepared. I still have to get you back to the Pontiac. Unless you'd like to stay here."

I shook my head. He continued to load the dishwasher while I retrieved a few more bowls and glasses from the dining room. He poured two steaming cups of coffee, and we brought the ice cream, cookies, and drinks into the dining room. We walked onto the deck and sat on some wicker chairs around a glass table to eat. By this point peepers and frogs had basically taken over the night, sounding (to me) like a crashing waterfall all around us. We could barely hear each other, and after a few mumbling sentences, we just sat there quietly and stared up at the stars while we ate dessert and drank the coffee before Mr. Santa drove me home.

***

VIII.

I had lived in the Bonneville close to two years at the time, spring, summer, and fall—bookended by two cold and lonely winters. When the second one gave over to my second spring, I began to believe in the situation again—that is believe I could live in the car indefinitely until . . . I guess until something better came along. My English teacher gave me a used paperback copy of *Walden*, by Thoreau, and I started reading a bit of it every afternoon before dark. I turned the dog-eared, yellow pages of the book as if it were some precious religious text I read to make some sense out of my life. I loved the part about Thoreau cutting wood and warming himself twice, although I couldn't follow his example for the simple reason that I had no ax or fireplace. I did build a couple of campfires late that April, although I have to say I gathered sticks and branches of wood instead of cutting it and managed to warm myself only once—maybe half that, really, because only the side of my body facing the fire really got warm. I also liked his chapter about planting beans, and later that season I started a vegetable garden from a couple packets of seeds and a few tomato plants that Misha brought me one weekend afternoon. I found an old blunted spade in a pile of junk someone had left in the field one day, and I brought it back to the car, thinking I might need it someday. When I saw the packets of seeds and the three or four Styrofoam cups with tomato plants in them sitting near the rear wheels of the car, I decided to start digging the garden right away.

About half way between the Bonneville and the pond there was a space warmed by the sun from about ten o'clock in the morning through most of the afternoon because of an opening in the surrounding trees. I used the spade to outline a small rectangle of about five feet by ten feet in the middle of that space, turned the outline into a six-inch trench for water, and then stepped inside it to turn over the earth. It was tough at first. The roots of the grass—and rocks beneath them—blocked the shovel almost every time I pushed it into the ground, even when I stood on it with both feet and jounced up and down as if it was a pogo stick. I ended up pulling out about a hundred rocks by hand and throwing them to the side, making a mound that was higher than my shoulders. The soil that was left seemed moist and rich, so I planted the three tomato plants in the sunniest part of the rectangle and then placed the lettuce seeds, the French beans, and the fava beans in the rest of the space around them. I had done stuff like this with Mum and Dad from the time I was two or three, when I started digging with them, so none of it seemed hard or mysterious. I figured I'd find or buy a bucket somewhere and use it to walk down to the pond for daily watering and washing.

It all worked out pretty much as planned, I have to say. The sun shined a lot that May and June, and since I watered every day it didn't rain, I had a romaine lettuce crop before summer came in. Meanwhile, I watched the French and Fava beans gradually take over the rest of the plot. The tomatoes took a little longer, but the plants grew pretty well in their special spot, and so I felt confident about them until one day I came back from a run through town and found beans and tomatoes pulled up and left lying on the ground. I didn't make much of it at first, but then I realized that no animal had done it, because none of the plants were eaten and no claw or paw prints showed in the soil. Clearly, someone was messing with me, and I decided I couldn't let them stop me. I bought more seeds and tomato plants, replanting a couple of the beans and one of the tomatoes too, because they didn't look too damaged. But I must say I felt less comfortable leaving the Bonneville from that day on.

Nothing happened afterward—at least for a while. Occasionally kids ran by, chasing a baseball or just walking a dog—and every once in a while I'd see an old guy in plaid knickerbockers (that's what he called them, anyway) and long white socks walking past the car with a golf club in his hand. We started talking one day when a ball he had hit from the grass field flew through the trees, bounced off my rock pile, and landed in the middle of my fava vines and beans. "Fun-looking place," he said to me, when I handed him the ball from the short end of the vegetable patch. "Are you the one who lives in that car?"

I said no, of course, but I could tell right away he knew better. He said it must be interesting living here, but he couldn't imagine how hard it must be during terrible winter weather—especially the nights. I nodded, too quick probably, because he looked very closely at me and shook his head. "Well, I used to have a car like that when I was young, but whoever lives here now has a lot more guts and moxie than I ever had." He winked and started toward the grass field again, saying he had to work on his nine-iron shot for a foursome he was playing in next day. "Name's Will," he said as he started toward the trees. "You'll probably see me pretty often when the weather's nice. I like to work on my irons around here."

I nodded and did see him a fair amount that spring and summer. His iron shots never came under full control, as far as I could see, and so he regularly followed two or three balls at a time into the garden or in the weeds near the Bonneville whenever he came to practice. He didn't say much at first, but soon he brought sandwiches and snacks ("To pay for the garden damage," he said. "Those tomatoes will never come back."). And as the weather cooled toward the end of September, he even carried thermos bottles full of hot soup and coffee that he insisted on leaving with me until the next time he drove a ball through the trees. "Dinner," he said, walking around the car to the driver's side where I had been reading. "Whoever lives in this dump certainly needs to have some hot food."

He spoke to me while smiling through the closed window, and I realized he had me. There was no way I could deny that I lived there—or at least spent a load of personal alone time in that front seat. I smiled back at him and opened the door. When he handed the thermos to me and then reached into a little backpack for another, I could only look down at my feet and mutter in embarrassment, "Thank you so much."

"Hey, I owe you something," he said. "I lost count of the balls you found and saved for me this summer. Consider this payback, okay?"

I grinned and nodded. When I crawled under the front end to retrieve the ball he had just sent in to me, he handed me a card and told me to call him if I ever needed anything. "I've been where you are," he said. "I know it isn't easy, especially when you're so young. But if you keep working at learning and changing things, something good will happen, I'm sure."

He left with the ball in his hand and the golf club on his shoulder, and I regret to say I never saw him again. I tried calling him once or twice that winter, but there was never any answer. Assuming I would see him in the warmer weather that April, I bought some soup and coffee from the Panera in town and put them in the thermoses to give back to him. He never came back. One day Mr. Santa told me he had passed away.

That second spring other stuff happened—none of it any good. I'd come home from school and find the Pontiac painted up occasionally—white-washed windows, scrawled messages in black on doors—and junk people purposely left behind as garbage: old batteries, torn-up couches, a doll's house with broken furniture, refrigerators with doors taken off, and loads of Nintendo games that probably still worked though nobody played them anymore. Instead of the old man in Knickerbockers, gray-haired dirt bikers drove through almost daily, swerving in and out of trees. One even rode over the rock pile near my garden, into its mud, then roared across the grass field toward the distant trees and pond, where the sound of his pipes gradually, and mercifully, diminished and disappeared.

About two weeks after that, from an afternoon dancing with Misha in his basement, I returned to the car and found a note taped on the windshield. It was from Michele, the girl who had warned me to watch my back after the incident in the boys' locker room. Her note gave me a number to call right away "because it is important," and a place to meet—a corner behind the park—the next afternoon, if for some reason I couldn't call. Having no phone, landline or cell, equals no call in my book, so I rolled up her note and threw it into the basket of paper and other recyclables in the trunk of the Pontiac. And then I debated with myself for the rest of the night whether I should go to the police station and ask to use the phone there or walk back into town where one single phone booth stood near the town library. I did neither, though I wondered all through the night what Michele could have to tell me that was so "important." My first thought was more shit coming my way, and I don't mean that symbolically at all. I just figured that whoever left the last load probably wasn't finished—might in fact have developed a case of awful diarrhea by now—and my car was about to be the recipient of his body's generosity. But the joke, even for crude people like the shitter had to be, must eventually get old, and so I began to wonder what else he/she/they might be tempted to do.

So, I decided to meet Michele in person next afternoon. She suggested she would be at the corner behind the park around 3:30, so I went there right after school finished for the day. Misha wanted to come with me, but I wanted to keep him away from my problems—if for no other reason than it kept him clean (the way I wanted him to be), and then I could cry on his shoulder without feeling he was already part of the ugly mess my life had become.

It was a clear day, plenty of sunshine and a nice breeze, and I found myself thinking how stupid this whole mystery was. Yet I stood on the corner anyway, checking cars rolling by, the occasional kid on a bike, and the dozen or so people walking, probably to get to the bus stop two blocks down the street. It was 3:45 the first time I checked my watch, 4:00 by the time I looked at it every minute, and 4:15 when I decided to leave. For good measure, I waited another five minutes before walking away. When I reached the police station again, I saw Misha sitting on the front steps, but I passed him by, turning directly into the park.

"Jamie, wait!" I waved my hand, telling him to stay where he was or go back home—in any case, not to follow me. But he persisted, and while I knew I could easily outrun him, I also knew he'd get to the Pontiac within a minute after I did, so there really was no point.

"Misha, I really don't feel like talking to anyone right now. Let me be, please?"

"You don't want to go back there now," he said. "Not alone."

I stopped and turned around, looking closely at him as he approached. His face had the serious Misha look, as if something very important was about to shake out. "I've seen shit before," I said, "so I think I can handle it again, no matter how much there is. Or where it is."

He shook his head but said nothing. I turned to continue toward the Pontiac, but he ran and caught up with me right away. "It's worse," he said. "You're not going to be able to clean it up."

I stopped again and looked directly into his emerald eyes, as if I could read a message in them. I couldn't. "Misha, what's going on?"

He shook his head again. "It's not just shit. It's everything."

"What? They trashed the place? I can still clean it up."

"You'll have very little left. You're not going to be able to live there anymore."

"It's gone?"

He shook his head. At first, I couldn't understand his meaning, but slowly I began to fear I did. As we crossed the open field before the trees, I saw what looked like tire tracks through the grass and pieces of paper, metal, and plastic here and there. Now I broke into a run and kept running toward the oak and the large rock. When I passed them, I looked toward the Pontiac and blinked. For a second, I saw nothing—just a clean white wooden chair sitting absurdly in the middle of the brush, as if it was an empty throne. "What—?" I blinked again. The car hadn't disappeared, as I had feared, but everything was trashed or smashed—my clothes, my store of canned food, my books and papers, my photos of Mum and Dad, and, of course, my bed and home. The headlights and windows were gone; the rocks and shale I had dug up from my vegetable patch filled the front seat. The wind whipped papers and leaves all around, into and out of the rear and side windows, as if it had lifted the Bonneville and dumped it there in a hurricane.

"Jesus," Misha said, as he came up beside me. "I couldn't believe it when I saw it. Somebody had a tow truck, but decided to trash it instead."

"Those bastards! Michele set me up for this. And Jody . . ."

I stopped, because the rage was turning to sickness. I felt liquefied inside, as if there was not an organ in my gut that wasn't drowning. I stared at the white chair and, without thinking, sank to my knees. "My home," I muttered. "They've actually destroyed my home."

Misha kneeled beside me and put his arm around my shoulders. Without a word we stared at the chair, as if it had some important meaning, or explanation that we couldn't figure out. What the fuck was it doing there in the first place? I stood up, studying the wood and paint more closely. I saw nothing, learned nothing, just that the brush and trees surrounding it revealed a lot of movement and sound: birds, bugs, butterflies, leaves. But the Pontiac, at least in my memory, had more life in it than they did.

"Misha, what am I going to do? This was my life, all of it."

He said nothing, but I knew what he was thinking. Don't ask me why, but I knew I'd say no even then. I'd prefer sitting in that flimsy painted wooden chair all night—with cold, rain, or even snow—instead of giving in. For the life of me, I could not tell you the reason.

"Jamie . . . "

"Misha, I have to work this out by myself. You know what that means?"

"Yes, I know. But come live with us until you find something else you like."

"I can't," I said.

"You can't live here either. That chair is nothing. And someday soon . . . "

"I'll figure it out. I'll go to Mr. Santa. He'll tell me what to do."

His eyes closed, then brightened. "You'll go now? Good idea. I brought my car, and it's parked down the block. I'll give you a ride."

I shook my head. "Misha, I love you for that. But I need to walk. I need to relax—to be by myself for a while."

He shrugged and shook his head. But he gave in, mainly because I lied and said I'd go see Mr. Santa that night. Not nice, I know; it was like guys saying they were going to practice and hanging out at the Sugar Bowl instead. So I walked with him back to the police station and past it, rubbing his back most of the way. I watched him get into his car and start the engine, then drive toward the center of town and, eventually, I expected, home.

My first impulse was to go back to the Bonneville, now just a white wooden chair with a pile of metal and glass, and—I know this sounds crazy—search the woods for clues. But really, anybody with a tow truck—or at least riding in one—could have done it, so what would I find? I'm not a CSI agent. I could follow the tracks through the grass and figure out their direction here and back. But that wasn't enough. Not nearly. The tire tracks crossed the field, followed along the stand of hardwood separating the park from the street outside, and then came to a driveway out to the street. From there, they disappeared: No mud or tire track anywhere.

I looked on the other side of the drive and at both ends—street side, park side—and saw nothing. So, I went back to the chair and brooded for a while until the sun went completely down and I was surrounded by the quiet madness of the nighttime sounds. I jogged toward the willows in the distance because I wanted to stare at the pond and lie on the bank to sleep for a while. The sound of the peepers and frogs was raw and magnificent. I thought it might help me sleep at first—it was the sound of home, after all—but I had too much nervous energy. I pushed through the veil of willow branches, stood under them as if in a dry waterfall for a brief couple of seconds, then slipped through them again to the banks of the pond.

I gasped—not in fear or surprise—but because the pond looked too perfect, clear, with moon and stars like lanterns glowing beneath its surface. The moon shone a bright, gorgeous light, so I went very close to the water, stepping carefully on and over rocks lining it. Something splashed to my right, and when I looked over I saw widening circles on the water's surface. I moved closer, hoping to catch a glimpse of some amphibious being, whatever it might have been, but as I stared down into the water, I spotted something else just beneath its mirror cover—not an animal—my two boxes of running shoes, two or three of my personal notebooks, and above them, the plastic cover of the book on dance I had borrowed from the library. Everything glimmered in the moonlight. I spun around, left the water, and ran back to the white chair as if someone was chasing me.

Normally, I would have taken a flashlight from the car to check out the pond a little more, but of course the flashlight was now a part of the metal pile. I stood near the chair for about a minute, wondering what to do, and then bolted toward the street without a plan. I

wandered about for a while, first running toward the
school as if I was late for the morning bell, then turned
back toward the park before heading left and up one of
the main avenues toward Mum and Dad's old house—
maybe I should say *my* old house. I hadn't been there in
months, but I knew I needed some comforting vibe to
calm me for the night.

Our street wasn't fancy. It had small houses, as
ours had been, on small lots and not a lot of professional
landscaping. Two or three places had vegetable gardens
in back, one used up most of its front lawn as one,
because of sunshine patterns, but the rest were made up
of wire fences, kids' play toys, several basketball hoops,
and an occasional lonely tree or shrub, usually maple and
rhododendron, along with a mix of rose bushes and irises
for added color. I stopped outside our old house, about
halfway down the block, and noticed immediately that
all windows were dark and, more importantly, a tree that
Dad planted the day they brought me home to live with
them, had just been cut down. Trunk and branches lay on
the ground beside the house, cut down to foot and a half
lengths and piled to dry out for burning in a wooden
stove, whose new metal chimney pipe came out the side
wall, near where my bed used to be, and extended up the
shingle siding in an ugly gray bulge that rose above the
old slate roof.

I shivered as I looked at the changes. For a few
seconds I started to feel sick to my stomach again. But I
stared at the house, remembering my sweet life there
and, to my relief, the nausea started to pass. I sucked in
my skinny gut, breathing calmly for a few minutes, and
ran down the block again the way I came—first a jog,

then a trot, and finally a full-fledged distance run, as if I was on the track. Where do you think I was heading?— Wrong, if you said Misha's; right, if you said Mr. Santa's.

He lived about five or six miles away from Mum and Dad's, and I went straight for his place at an easy cross-country runner's pace, arriving in a little more than half an hour. Not bad, considering the hills, the traffic at a couple corners, a railway yard just beyond a pocket mall, and the highway I had to cross while waiting for two or three semis to pass. After I got to his street and arrived at his front door, I paused at the top step and held back from reaching for the knocker. I knew what he was going to say. I also realized I had trapped myself in coming here because I wouldn't be able to say no.

"Bastards," I said, cursing whoever had put me in this situation. I headed back down the steps, again not thinking with a plan. I just felt I had to do something else or I might lose everything—life, sanity, self. But when my NBs touched the sidewalk, they stopped. I couldn't go further. I turned, faced the door with the Santa name and an ugly-faced knocker whose tongue stuck out at me. "You've already lost it all already," it seemed to say. "You haven't got anything else—just torn jeans, a sweaty shirt, and those very cool shoes."

I turned to leave again, bird flipping in the air, but as the toe of my right shoe left the ground the front door opened behind me. Instead of the knocker's sardonic eyes and tongue, I saw Mr. Santa in cut-off jeans, a pea-green t-shirt, and leather sandals staring out.

"How nice of you to come," he said. "I was about to have dinner with Jake. Come in and join us."

For a night that began so awfully, I can only say it was more than strange—weird, maybe—that it ended so "normally" (yes, Dad's semaphores again). I had a hot chicken dinner, helped Jake and Mr. Santa wrap and put away leftovers, then sat down with them and watched a Disney movie. I said nothing about the Bonneville, just went along with their talk about school, work and plans for the weekend, as if I were part of the family. When the Disney movie ended, around ten, Mr. Santa went to the bedroom and bath with Jake to get him ready for the night, and then they both came back into the living room and paused for a moment, staring at me on the couch. Mr. Santa smiled and pushed Jake gently on the back of the shoulder. Little Jake ran across the room, flashing a giant gap-toothed smile as he leaped onto my lap.

"I love you, Jamie," he whispered.

I felt his arms slide around my neck and shivered. Without any reserve or bashfulness, he gave me a huge, wet smacking kiss on my cheek. "Can you stay with us tonight?" he said.

Except for Misha, I had not been close enough to anybody for a hug or a kiss in a very long time; it seemed like forever. So Jake's leap shocked me. My whole body seemed to blush, and all I could answer was "Oh, my gosh!"

"We'd love to have you, Jamie. You could probably use a real bed and warm house for a change."

I stared at Mr. Santa, ready to run, but deep inside my gut I suddenly felt incredibly tired—of my attitude, of my insistence on going it alone despite my fears, and even running. I nodded at Jake, returning his hug with a sloppy kiss on the cheek to show my appreciation. The warmth of his bare hands against my cheeks and neck went right through me, and before I could say anything more clearly, I felt tears running down my face onto his PJs.

"I'm getting you wet," I said, laughing and sniffling at the same time. I took out a handkerchief, wiped my face, and then dried his head and a spot or two on his pajama arm.

Mr. Santa took Jake's hand and, after another goodnight hug, led him off to bed. I sat on the couch, actually thinking I could walk out while they read and said goodnight to each other in the bedroom. But a more powerful thought fought me in my gut. The night was turning cool, and even I had to admit that I had no place to run now that the Pontiac sat crushed and open to everything—animals as well as weather—in the woods.

When Mr. Santa came back into the living room, I didn't give him a chance to ask me again to stay. I just stared at him and let my fear and anger come out in a wet flow of sobs and tears. "They trashed my Pontiac," I blubbered. "Crushed it. I haven't got any place to go home to. Ever."

"It was trashed?"

"Crushed," I said. "That gang of bastards and bitches is partying somewhere, laughing at me right now."

He sat next to me on the couch and put his arm around my shoulders. With a loud moan and a quiet whoop, I buried my face in his neck and let more of that shit pour out of me. "I've got nothing," I heard myself say over and over again. "Nothing. All my clothes—gone. Pictures of Mum and Dad—dumped in the pond.

Along with notebooks, books, and my diary! How could anybody human do that to someone? They're lousy, fucking shits!"

"That's *terrible*, Jamie."

Mr. Santa kept patting the back of my head and mumbling in my ear—to calm me, I guess, but the longer he did it, the more unraveled I became. Finally, he walked me into the dining room, then onto the back porch where the sound of peepers and frogs filled the night, helping to quiet me after a while. I pulled away from his neck at last and stood against the wooden railing. I looked up at the sky, toward the air above the town, and gradually, without another word from either of us, allowed myself to feel like I could live, at least until tomorrow.

"Of course, you'll stay," Mr. Santa said. "There's no question of you leaving. We'll figure something out during the day or tomorrow night. If nothing else, you can stay here until you've decided you want to live somewhere else."

I shook my head at first. But then I realized what my real choices were and nodded, following him back into the house with a half-hearted "Thank you."

***

So, once again I began to learn about living with other people, particularly a family. Mr. Santa, whom I could never relax enough with to call Dom or Nick, let alone "Dad", treated me like a combination niece or daughter and friend, which didn't surprise me but somehow embarrassed me at the same time. I felt like I didn't deserve what he gave me, that because of my stubbornness I was taking him away from important stuff at the job and, more importantly, stuff with his newly-adopted son. But Jake was surprisingly independent, more independent than I was in certain ways. He just enjoyed having people around, and Mr. Santa enjoyed obliging him. "It's for the good of all of us," he said. "I'm too much the lonely brooder myself. Sometimes I think I prefer it that way."

What could I say? I'm that way too, mostly, and so I felt uncomfortable although they both made it clear I was welcome to stay as long as I liked. One night I tried to give money to Mr. Santa to pay for food and the couch I slept on, but of course he refused. He would not even consider it; in fact he went out the next afternoon and insisted on buying clothes for me: jeans, underwear, two pairs of NBs, and two or three cool shirts and sweaters. He also bought me a jacket for cold weather and some gym stuff in case I wanted to run or work out somewhere. I offered money again, saying I would withdraw it from my bank's ATM next day, and he just waved the idea away, looking at me as if I was out of my mind.

"Jamie, I'd be insulted if I didn't know you so well. You've been my responsibility in the Pontiac and my office for over a year. That doesn't stop—not now. I'm taking care of you, period."

I didn't know what to say, to be honest. I welcomed it and hated it at the same time. I hung my head and thought for a moment about how I might pay him back, month by month. I couldn't think of anything else, at least at that moment. I'd never been a babysitter, but I figured I could stay with Jake and play games with

145

him whenever Mr. Santa needed it. And I would clean the house regularly because that was one thing Mum made me do with her on Saturday mornings. But Mr. Santa wouldn't hear of either idea. He didn't go out much at night, he said, and when he did he always took Jake. As far as cleaning, he had a former client and her daughter do it because they needed the work and did a very good job. Well, I couldn't disagree; they did excellent work, and they were quick. Mum and I couldn't have done as well, no matter how hard we tried.

So I stayed put—for several weeks, at least— although I never really settled in and felt comfortable. For the first few days I felt pissed at whoever trashed my car, but very soon I realized I was acting that way to Mr. Santa, and even Jake, rather than the assholes who did it. I remained silent during meals, hardly giving more than one-word answers to Jake's questions, and sometimes not saying anything to Mr. Santa at all, no matter how good the food he cooked was. Then, about three weeks after that first night with them, Mr. Santa sat next to me on the couch after putting Jake to bed, picked up the remote, and shut off the movie I was watching on TV.

"This is not good, Jamie," he said. "You're punishing the wrong people."

As you can imagine, it was not a comment I wanted to hear. I sat still, frowning at the blank screen for a few long seconds, and wondered how soon I should leave, if not immediately.

"I'm not forcing you to stay," Mr. Santa said. "You're independent as far as I'm concerned, but you obviously need a bed and a roof, and for now, I can't think of a better situation for you. If you have a better place, you're free to go. I'll drive you whenever you want."

I smirked a bit. As my case worker, he had to approve of my living conditions, no matter what they were, and for any length of time. But I also knew he supported me in almost every way, and so I owed him a lot more than this recent snot-nosed lack of respect. I lowered my head to hide the ugly look on my face and muttered some thanks for all that he had done, along with an apology for my behavior since I moved in. It was enough, I guess. He put his hand on my shoulder and drew me close, actually hugging me, side to side. I stiffened at first, pulling my head and body away, because I didn't expect the hug, but also because no one except Misha had hugged me like that—I mean with affection and no sleazy expectations—since Dad passed away. Mr. Santa just held me still for a few seconds, letting me lower my face out of kissing range onto his neck, and allowing me to feel the support of his arms against my shoulders. When I looked up at him and smiled, he immediately dropped his hands to his side.

"I'm sorry," I said. "For my behavior—and the attitude. I appreciate everything you've done for me. Really. I know I owe you—too much."

He smiled and waved his hand, leaning against the broad, round arm of the couch. "We'll work things out," he said. "Don't worry. Meanwhile, we'll see if we can find more comfortable arrangements for you. I still think the Altos would be a good alternative. They're very concerned about your welfare, especially Mrs. Alto. And then you and Misha seem to get along very well. What could go wrong?"

"Stepbrother porn," I said—stupidly, I admit.

He looked at me, not puzzled but wondering, and I shook my head immediately. Then I shrugged to show him a feeling of indifference. Mr. Santa stared at me, taking in my expression very carefully. Finally, he added nothing, just picked up the remote and, with another wave of his hand, turned on the movie again. He settled his head into the couch back while the TV screen flashed and filled with color. I have very little recollection of the film we watched after that, one about Queen Elizabeth II, maybe, but I do remember very vividly the way the room and Mr. Santa's body next to me suddenly came together as a comfortable place to be. I fell asleep in minutes, my mind absolutely blanking out on the world and whatever it was about it the film had to show. When he woke me later and I listened to the theme music while watching the scroll of credits on the screen, Mr. Santa's hand felt so gentle on my shoulder that I put my own hand over it and thanked him again, adding a second apology for having doubted him in the first place.

So, that's how it settled. We threw a sheet and blanket over the couch, as we had every night since I arrived. Mr. Santa retrieved an extra pillow from the front hall closet, and, after brushing and other bathroom stuff, I slipped under the blanket, took off my jeans and socks, and tried to sleep. I heard Mr. Santa check on Jake in his room and then go into his own room and close the door. The house went quiet and stayed that way as I lay on my back in the dark. I watched the ceiling and occasional traffic from outside casting light and shadows like some dystopian science-fiction film. Once again I wondered where all of this was leading me. I did the same in the Pontiac, of course, although the light and shadows there were less interesting and more than swallowed up by nighttime sounds outside, but I never came to any conclusion about my future. Didn't at Mr. Santa's house either, although I also felt less pressure about it. "I'm safe," I whispered—several times to Mum and Dad because I sensed them near me in the dark. "I feel comfortable. I can eat three meals and then sleep on this couch tomorrow. Whatever happens—with Misha or anybody else—I think I can be happy."

I must have fallen asleep soon after that, because the next thing I remember is Jake running into the room from the kitchen and jumping on top of me on the couch. "Time to get up, Jamie. It's a school day," he shouted. My eyes popped open to his an inch or less from my nose and his knees kneading my stomach. I laughed as Mr. Santa came into the room with a glass of orange juice and put it on the coffee table beside the sofa. Light streamed in from under the shades and curtains, and I heard talk from a radio somewhere in the kitchen.

"Okay, Jakey. Let's leave Jamie to herself so she can get ready on her own. You and I have some breakfast to eat in the kitchen." He took Jake's hand and led him from the room, telling me just as they walked out the door that coffee and muffins were waiting on the counter. I pulled on my jeans, checked through the shopping bag full of underwear Mr. Santa had bought me a week or so before, grabbed underpants and a bra, and headed out to the bathroom in the hall. I heard music playing, something classical, I think, though it could have been just old-fashioned movie stuff. As I closed the bathroom door, an announcer began to tell us about the weather and news. "Same old, same old," I whispered, as Dad used to when we drove to school with the radio on.

I brushed my teeth, combed out my hair (which didn't take long since I wore it short at the time), changed underwear, and put on a clean sweatshirt over my jeans. I stopped for juice and a bran muffin in the kitchen and then took a fresh cup of coffee into the living room for putting on socks and my new NBs. By the time I was done, Mr. Santa came down from his room, looking fresh and handsome, I thought, in a crisp blue shirt and yellow tie, worn with khaki chinos and brown moccasins on his bare feet.

"Okay, troops, off we go." I followed them out the door, feeling slightly compromised, because I had just spent another night with a handsome grownup and his son, and now the world of high school teenagers would know it.

He dropped Jake off at his school and then drove down Main Street toward the high school, pulling into the parking lot in back when we arrived. I asked him to let me walk in alone, which he agreed to, but before I got out he reminded me that I could stay with him and Jake as long as I liked, though I should think about the Altos because it might be nice to have an older woman to talk with once in a while. I thanked him, smiling, almost leaning over to give him a wifely kiss on the cheek because I felt so grateful. But he had the car in drive already, and with curious kids walking by us toward the school entrance, I just opened the door and slid out, waving as he drove away.

***

IX.

I went downstairs to my locker first thing and took out books and stuff after hanging up my jacket. When I turned to go to my first class, I saw Michele and her boyfriend, Jody, staring at me from across the hall. I resisted the urge to say something, as I usually did, by just walking past them toward the stairwell as if I didn't see them. Jody reached out to touch my arm when I pushed open the door, but I pretended not to notice that either and started up the stairs. Michele called my name, but I kept walking anyway and, finally, I heard footsteps bouncing up the stairs to catch me. It was Jody, grabbing my elbow. I spun around and shook his hand off.

I knew him, of course. I had run with him pretty often in cross-country practices, and always thought he was one of the sweeter guys on the team. Tall, he wore dark hair down to his shoulders—sometimes in a braid, sometimes flat out in a young Jesus mode. His shoulders were really broad. He swam with our high school team, in addition to running cross-country, and you could see the obvious results in his body: long, muscular thighs and calves, big shoulders with very thick arms. Because of him, Michele, pretty and athletic herself, was the envy of most of the other girls in school.

"Please don't touch me," I said, trying for ice rather than bitchiness. "You might get some of my shit on your skin."

He pulled his hand away, as if he might. I laughed.

"Look, Jamie, I'm trying to help. So is Michele." Still grinning, I looked past him down to the bottom of

151

the stairwell, where Michele stood gaping up at us. She had a very serious pleading expression on her face, and I could have sworn that I saw a single blue tear streaming down her left cheek. It was a new tattoo.

"Please, Jamie. We have something to tell you," she said. "Really."

I forced another laugh, but with nothing to say, except maybe another stupid comment, I just kept quiet. "We know what happened," Jody said. "And we also know it wasn't one of the guys on the team."

"Right," I said, and turned to start up the stairs again.

"Jamie, somebody told us it was some people—you know, community people—who wanted to clean up the park, get rid of all the junk in it. And . . . "

"And then dump it in the pond to keep everything tidy? That's bullshit," I said.

Jody grabbed my arm again, with a strong grip that I couldn't shake off. "Somebody else did that. They piled your stuff on that chair and left it while they went for the tow truck. They figured you'd want it, but somebody got to the stuff on the chair before you."

I looked from him to her, two high school kids like me, but a lot luckier. "Fortunate," Mr. Santa would call them. And of course he worked to even out the odds for unlucky suckers like me—skinny, maybe not so healthy, and without the lives they took for granted. Something in both their faces told me they were sincere that morning, but at the same time I couldn't imagine Mr. Santa knowing about the cleanup and the mess they made of my car. He would have told me.

"How do you know all this shit?" I said. "You have special contacts?"

Jody looked at me, ready, I could see, to drop the whole thing and walk away.

"Mr. Gomez and Mr. Span know. My uncle— who's chief of police, by the way— thinks Mr. Gomez had something to do with moving the car. I bet your social worker friend knows about it, too."

I didn't say anything, just turned away and continued up the stairs to the main floor, fuming. I went to all my morning classes, ate a quiet lunch with Misha—who didn't know anything about the car or the cleanup, he told me—and then walked with him to his house to listen to music and, because I needed to get the anger out, dance. Mrs. Alto was in the kitchen when we walked in and immediately offered snacks and something to drink. I took a small half-sandwich of prosciutto and provolone, and the three of us sat at a long marble counter to eat. Mrs. Alto asked about my car, how I was doing at Mr. Santa's house, and that kind of stuff. All I could tell her was that I missed my own place. Of course, she looked sympathetic, but at the same time something about the look told me she wondered if I had shit for brains.

"You miss it?" she said. "A rusty old car in the back of the woods? I would think you'd prefer a warm house and running water. Mr. Santa is friendly, I assume."

I nodded, making sure she had no doubts about that. "I know it was chancy and pretty rough, but I actually liked my Pontiac because of that. My dad always told me we lose something if we don't take risks, so . . ."

"So, you took one heck of a major risk," Misha interrupted. "The whole town . . . well, maybe just some of it, worries every day you're out there—especially in winter."

Mrs. Alto laughed—though I couldn't see the humor—and patted Misha on the back. "Oh, Misha, it would be nice if you were right, but I have to say I doubt that very much."

Misha blushed, but I could see how upset he was. He bit hard into his sandwich and swallowed some iced tea while chewing it, but he didn't say anything to his mother. I felt bad for him, but I also knew she was probably right. "People have a lot on their minds. They don't get much outside their own families—or themselves," I said.

His chin sank deeper into his chest, and I wondered how much he believed his own story. I knew he really cared about me, but he didn't want to say how much. I could also tell he wanted to bring me deeper into his life, but he wasn't sure about the best way to do it. The Pontiac gave him an excuse, and now he was looking for other ways. As for me, I can honestly say I don't know what I wanted. Listening to music and dancing with him a few times a week was great, but I wasn't sure what I wanted beyond that even though we had kissed a bunch of times and rubbed a couple of places on each other we weren't supposed to—especially if we were family.

"Well, whatever," I said. "Call me crazy, but I miss my rusty old car more than just about anything else."

Mrs. Alto smiled, as if she thought that was actually cool, but went on to other things, Mr. Span and cross-country mainly. I could tell she wanted to know more about what he said and what he might have done before I spoke up. But I told her nothing, mainly because I'm not proud of any of it; and also because Mr. Span had been nice to me once—just letting me run with the team, even though I wasn't supposed to. "I don't want to talk about it," I said. "There's been enough trouble already."

Again, my first impulse was to run away, out the door, across town to Jake and Mr. Santa. But I looked at Misha, and of course I couldn't do it. Then his eyes lit up, and he grinned at me. "What do you think? Should we dance?" he asked. "We could dig up some really cool music and work on a routine. There's a contest at the county art space next month. We could enter."

I nodded, reluctantly, thinking about all that might happen if we went for it—how much we would need to see each other, how much time he would have in my life, how often I might stay with the Altos if we had to practice late. Looking back, it doesn't seem so bad—actually it was a really good idea given the funk I was in—but there was something, maybe something destructive, in me that wanted to fight it off. Misha was sweet, his mother struck me as really nice the few times we talked, and his father, an aloof nerd at times, seemed like a nice guy, too. So I nodded again and, as Misha's face went bright and happy with relief, I told him that it might be fun.

"Then let's get started. We have to pick the music and begin working on a number."

"But I'm not break-dancing," I said. "No way."

"No pressure there. The contest is for couples, and one partner's feet must remain on the floor."

"Guess who that's going to be," I said.

We went into the basement laughing and began rummaging through his father's vinyl and CD collection. Jesus, it was huge. Misha said at one point they had over a thousand recordings down there—classical, instrumental, opera, jazz, lots of American, French, and Italian folk, and plenty of Broadway musicals and popular singers from the thirties through the sixties. So, where were we going to begin?

"Bolero?" he asked. "Or maybe something cool by a modern singer—Adele?"

Misha looked at me, his eyes fixed, as if he had said something crazy. I just shook my head, and the two of us began looking through the CDs nearer the speakers. "I don't know. I just want to find something that feels right," he said. "Maybe something really new?"

"Modern," I said. "I like things spare and bouncy to dance to."

"But not too many steps." He grinned. "I think the routine has to last around ten minutes. I don't want to lose my breath or balance."

I poked him in the side and patted his stomach. "We're going to have to work you into shape." Then I squeezed the muscles on his arm, which were pretty firm, but nothing like Jody's or some of the other guys

156

on cross-country. "Start doing push-ups," I told him. "Daily."

He laughed, dropped to the floor, and started doing them while I counted. Not bad—the first ten went quickly, but by fifteen Misha was clearly struggling. He barely made it to twenty, and then he just collapsed to the floor, laughing and wheezing at the same time, though I think the wheezing was exaggerated. The legs are more important than the arms, I knew, so I told him we had to run together every day to build up his breath.

"You're trying to turn me into a jock, I think."

"It was your idea," I said. "Besides, dancers are great athletes, better than most of the guys in major sports. They have more stamina and strength."

Misha groaned. He pushed himself to his knees then stood. We continued looking through the CDs and vinyl, and finally decided on something Misha called wild and primitive by a guy he said his family once knew when he was just a kid. His name was Zach—Zach Douglaston—and he had played with some very important bands, one being Coltrane (cool name, but I never heard of him), another Phil Woods (not a bad name, but I never heard of him either), and a third being Miles Davis (nice name, and I had heard of him since Dad liked one of his records, "My Funny Valentine," which he always played for Mum on her birthday). Frankly, they meant nothing to me; except for "My Funny Valentine," Dad and Mum never played their music and certainly never danced to them either. But Misha liked them all, said they were really hot in the jazz world, and that this guy Zach was so famous in France that almost all of Paris had come out for his funeral.

157

He put on a CD of Zach's music, and we just sat on the couch facing the speakers to listen. He played jazzed up versions of French classical music—Poulenc and Satie were two of the composers Misha mentioned— and did some great upbeat American stuff where he and the drummer went boom-pitty-boom-pitty while the sax player, Coltrane, nearly broke our eardrums with the screech of his horn. But my favorite was a solo bass version of something my dad used to sing to me and Mum almost every fall: "September Song." He sang it along with a Tony Bennett album we had, and I still remember the chills I felt when he whisper-sang the end: *These precious days . . . I'll spend with you.*

But Zach Douglaston did something strange with it, and at first I didn't like it. He began it as a solo, not another instrument coming in until the very end when a piano and drum joined his bass. And he used a bow instead of his fingers, making the music start with an incredibly slow and mournful drone. It seemed fitting, given the subject, I guess. But he gradually sped it up and augmented the volume, the way I've always heard "Bolero" done, until in the very last few seconds, with piano tinkling and drum booming, this sad, slow September afternoon just bursts into a happy Indian summer night filled with woods sounds, human song, and lots of dancing animal footsteps. I told Misha that it reminded me of that poem by Keats that we read in our English class: "Pipes and timbrels, whatever they sound like," I told him. "I hear them in his playing, even before the piano and drum come in. It's a soulful moan that turns into a ringing, dancing hymn."

Misha nodded. "My dad says no one else could do that—not when we knew him. Probably still can't today."

"He was a friend?" I said.

"Of the family. More of my father than my mother and me."

I was impressed, and I'm sure I showed it.

"We spent a few weeks near him in southern France when I was a kid. I used to dance with his French girlfriend, who I think was my father's girlfriend when they were very young." He laughed. "It's complicated. Maybe my dad isn't as stuffy as he seems."

I nodded, but couldn't bring myself to laugh. This stuff with Zach and his French girlfriend was not anything I could identify with, at least in relation to Mum and Dad. As far as I knew, they fell in love very young, in their teens, I think, got married when Dad found a regular job, and just stayed together—spending their lives trying to have babies, adding to and working on the house they bought, and finally, taking care of me when they brought me into the house—or "family," as Dad insisted. Actually, it took five years before I could really be called one of the family because my birth parents had to be found, then somehow convinced to give up their rights to me—though they never exercised any rights or responsibilities as far as I ever heard. They had to be paid off, I know—which is why it took so long. Mum and Dad had to save up and pay them bit by bit until my bio-shits (as I still call them) were satisfied enough to let me go. "Cheap," Dad said, though that's a lie. I'm sure they wanted lots of money.

***

After a couple days, Misha and I finally decided that Zach Douglaston's "September Song" should be the principal music we danced to in this competition. His mother looked a little noncommittal when we told her what we chose, but Mr. Alto absolutely lit up and smiled as if he had won some major prize. "Terrific," he said, grinning. "It's unique and original, yet based on a universal theme."

Misha looked at me, and I could almost hear the groan he kept buried in his chest. Mrs. Alto looked at both of us and smiled, though I could see it was a lame dad joke that she and Misha shared. "Never stops being a professor," Misha said. "Or a critic."

I knew what he meant because at dinners we shared, his father almost never stopped lecturing the classroom, especially about things relating to art or music. But I could see he was a good dad too, because he appreciated his son and especially his son picking a former friend to honor with a dance. The music grew on me, I have to say, and though it began with little more than a crawl and a howl, by the last three minutes— especially when the drums joined the piano and bass—it just seemed to lift you, feet and all, and float you above the ground. All with the moan and whoosh of a bow across some very thick bass strings.

We sat and listened to it over and over for a while, sometimes with Mr. and Mrs. A, sometimes with just one of them, trying to feel the music in our muscles—especially our feet and thighs. Strangely enough, I felt it move my gut more than my legs; as if the skin of a drumhead stretched across my belly and each beat of the song, soft at first but gradually building minute by minute, shook and vibrated the stuff inside me until I stood up and moved my feet.

"That's going to be tough at the end. I don't know how we're going to keep up with the music and make any sense."

"It's about getting old," Misha said, "and holding on as long as you can. I think we have to show that we're trying hard because we love it and don't want to lose."

I looked at him and grinned. He was adopted—from Russia, as I've mentioned before—when he was six months old, but if anybody sounded just like his father's son it had to be Misha at that moment. He even looked like his dad, the same lanky body with dramatic hands, the same polite excitement in his eyes, the same happy certainty that he saw something other people probably didn't notice. "Well, that's something I can understand. But sometimes people take it away from you, whatever 'it' you want."

We started trying different movements, positions, ways of using our feet and hands as the music played around and through us. My gut always vibrated, even while we moved, but it seemed to paralyze me somehow, more than make me want to dance. Finally, Misha had us start on the floor, crawling on our bellies as if through some deep mud with bullets flying over our heads while that slow bass beginning hummed and boomed.

"It feels right, I guess. But how is slogging through the mud for all that time going to get people's attention—especially for a dance competition? We have to move our feet."

161

"They'll hear the music. They'll know what's going on. Besides, if we end up doing something wild and inventive in the last few minutes of the dance, they'll admire the evolution. It's like life."

I nodded at that, and I confess I smiled. Because he was right, but at the same time I wondered if people judging the steps and bounce of a dance would actually wait for an "evolution." The name of the game, as far as I saw it, was jumping in and making sure you shake your booty for as long as the music lasts.

"It will have to be a thoughtful crowd," I said. "Not many like that around here."

"Well, the music will help. It's a famous tune, and people will see the way it changes—and see us change with it."

I shrugged, deciding to go along, mainly because I liked practicing with Misha, and partly because his mom, Lee, as I was starting to call her, agreed with him. She believed that art had to educate more than anything else, so she liked the idea of leading the audience as we performed our dance. "Try to make them feel it," she said. "They'll understand it. It's not just doing entertaining steps."

What could I say, without turning all three of them against me? So we crawled for about the first ninety seconds or more, kind of snaking in and over each other as if we were on one of those Mobius strips we looked at in geometry. We gradually rose to a squat, smacked each other's butt (lightly), and then hopped to our feet to do the rest of the dance, a waltz transformed into a ballet that became more and more modern until we were basically doing jazzy gymnastics for most of the last three minutes—a kind of breakdance when the piano and drum lifted the whole piece into a summer celebration.

We worked on it in the Altos' basement for about a month—sometimes alone, sometimes in front of Misha's mom or dad—until Mr. Alto brought us to a dance studio that a friend of his managed, or owned, somewhere in New York. This guy had chops; that's for sure. He had studied in London and Paris, performed with some famous dancers and dance masters, and spent a year or more with the American Ballet Theatre. I was impressed, and not just by his résumé. The muscles in his arms and legs were huge, yet he could move them with more grace and fluidity than I could even imagine, at least for myself, let alone Misha.

He seemed to admire what we were doing, liked the way we reacted to each other while we moved, and particularly mentioned me as having a "wonderful" line and control of my body for the latter parts of the dance. What could I say? No one had ever told me anything like that before, and I have to admit it filled me up—with what, I'm not quite sure. I knew I was fast, with a body that most people, including Mum and Dad, called "wiry" and "supple" (to me it was flat-chested and ugly). But this guy (Gil was his name) made me feel like I was floating whenever Misha lifted me. My arms, hands, and legs seemed to rise separately, yet in a unified, harmonic way whenever he told me to be expressive. He actually made me feel beautiful—more than beautiful, *lovely* I would say. And he seemed to make Misha more confident, too.

We did the routine all through one time. Gil suggested a few changes that seemed minor to me, and then we worked for about an hour on the different parts of it to see how the changes felt. They felt great, I thought, and I told Gil that. But I think Misha was less excited about them. Mr. Alto went along with Gil, and so, the outvoted Misha went along with the rest of us, though it was clear he didn't like seeing his ideas fixed or fiddled with. Back at his house, we showed Mrs. A the new routine, and she agreed too, which won Misha over completely. So from there on we practiced with the new ideas permanently in place and got to feel completely confident with them.

"You guys are good together," Mrs. A said. "I don't know if you're going to win this competition, but you're going to make people sit up and pay attention. I bet they'll even learn."

We really started busting after that. Mrs. A's words motivated Misha more than his father's, and he committed completely to the changes Gil had made. Mr. Alto drove us into New York a couple of Saturday mornings that month, and Gil worked to improve things a little more each time. He flattered Misha about his choreographic ideas, even while he changed them, and he made me feel lighter and more beautiful than I had ever felt in my life. Of course he loved Zach's double bass solo too, and said that after we competed in our state contest he was going to use it and some of our choreography in a dance performance he was working on for a summer tour with his company. "With your permission, of course," he said to Misha.

Admittedly, just the thought of a professional using our dance ideas blew me away. Misha and I rode home in the backseat of the Alto family car as if we were floating on something strong and illegal. Mr. Alto looked as if he had inhaled something life-changing too, and he kept rattling on about how talented and fortunate we were—especially having caught Gil's attention. He was proud of himself too, for making the connection with Gil and even raised the possibility of us becoming part of the traveling troop, if we wanted to. "They tour out west to northern California, Portland, and Seattle. We could easily follow you, if you wanted, Misha. It might be fun."

Well, that tuned me out right away, and when I looked at Misha I saw him frowning. Neither of us said anything to his father, but the silence was loud and clear. *Ugh.*

We were just getting to the Jersey side of the GW Bridge at that time, and Mr. A was busy looking at road signs, lanes, and the trajectory of other cars as he maneuvered onto I-80 West to take us home. When he finally did get into the express lanes through Patterson, he looked in the rearview mirror. "You know, most successful people get their success because of intense family support. Mom and I never received it, Misha, so forgive me for trying."

"Dad, you brought us to Gil. That's plenty for now. Let's not start making plans."

"I could ask . . ."

Both of us shook our heads, and he immediately brought his attention back to the road.

In a certain way, that became a special secret for all of us. Though Misha and I never mentioned it out loud, I could tell that it was always there between us. Could we really, possibly, become professional dancers? Were we actually good enough? Did we really want it? We thought about it a lot as we practiced the routine each afternoon—sometimes in his basement, sometimes in the woods near the old Pontiac (parts of it still there, but people had come in and added to the mess with sledge hammers, dog shit, and piles of junk). "You guys are good," Mrs. A told us whenever she watched. "I'm really impressed."

So, we were happy as well as hopeful. Misha and I busted our butts to clarify our intentions as we practiced (which Gil had advised us to do), and we kept looking for suggestions from people we trusted. Except for the Altos, Mr. Santa was clearly the most happy and enthusiastic of anyone we knew. He and Jake literally cheered for us, stamping their feet and shouting "Way to go!" when we performed for them.

"No question you have something valuable here," Mr. Santa said when we finished one of our performances in his living room. "Whether you win or lose, you've done something really good—and important."

Misha smiled, satisfied in a way I had never seen before. He told me he respected Mr. Santa a lot, and in a certain way I think he thought more of Mr. Santa's opinion than his dad's. I felt bad about that. Mr. Alto was really smart—especially about artsy things—and I had no doubt he loved Misha more than anyone else, except for Mrs. Alto. You could tell he wanted Misha to

166

feel the same about him, though Misha didn't—not in any relaxed, natural way. I think he respected his dad, the way I did mine, but you could tell they had never had many "BFF" bonding moments. When I asked Misha about it once, he just shrugged.

My own dad was the best buddy ever for me. He shared my interest in just about everything from music to food to sports, and especially Mum. He started my interest in running by taking me down to the park and timing my sprints across the open grass field near the pond. He got me to love music enough to want to move my body to it, no matter what the movement was. And he always had me thinking about enjoying life in special ways: food because it was beautiful and healthful, for instance, rather than sweet and gloppy. He had grown up on vegetables, fruit, and pasta, he said, and as far back as I can remember—maybe when I was three or four—he and Mum fed me those things together. My skinny frame and runner's legs come out of what they taught me, either by example or just hanging out as a family all those years. My uninflated boobs? Well, that's another story. "DNA," Mum always said.

Misha never had times like that with his parents, he told me, and when I spent time at his house I could almost understand why. They were just three positive, but independent people with a lot on their minds, and so you got very little sense of touch and feel and shared emotions between them. They talked, they enjoyed their time together, especially while traveling, I think, but they never danced or played a sport together. They always seemed to talk about their own things—painting, writing, funky music—things they did on their own. As you can imagine, Misha saw this dance routine with me as the beginning of something very unique. Also (maybe) very big.

***

X.

Two years older than me, but in certain ways, I guess I mean boy-girl ways, you could say Misha was a year or two behind me at that time. Maybe more. He was handsome; I think any girl would agree with that. His gorgeous eyes could do embarrassing things to your legs and face, unless you were very careful. But he didn't have any kind of swagger, probably because his mind was too complex—*Sensitive*, his father might say. He didn't play any sport particularly well, and, worse, he didn't hang around with anyone who did. He liked to read, listen to jazz and folk music (though occasionally he'd venture into hip-hop), and watch lots of classic foreign films, or old black and white American ones. So, though he was nearly seventeen years old, I thought of him in the same way I thought about some nerdy little kid with glasses or worse, a thirty- or forty-year-old man like Mr. Santa. Not bad to look at, you'd say, but way, *way* out in a different league.

At the same time he basically begged me to love him. Whenever we met, he looked at me with those milky blue-greens, and though my legs shivered and the blood rushed to both sets of my cheeks, something inside me—the runner, I guess—kept yelling to move forward and maintain a safe distance ahead. At times like that I missed Mum more than Dad, because I used to be able to talk to her about boys in all kinds of situations. We'd lie on a couch, or her and Dad's bed, and I'd tell about guys talking to me at school, or in the park, or on the track that I ran around for fun. I'd also mention guys who made me feel funny in good or bad ways, and no matter

169

what I told her, she'd admit to similar experiences, some funny or embarrassing, but also very romantic—even with guys who weren't Dad. She always told me my responses to boys were absolutely normal, "natural," as she called them, and so I didn't need to feel weird or— *God forbid*, she'd say—immoral. "Being human is sometimes very different from being moral," she used to tell me. "Growing up is learning to bring the two together in a very nice, harmonious way, though it's not always easy, or even possible."

Mum was gone more than three years at this time, and though I was going on fifteen when I met Misha, I was still not sure what "moral" or even "human" meant. But I never passed a day without thinking about her words, specifically in relation to people—especially boys and other girls I knew.

So with all the things spinning around Misha and me—his "love," his mom and dad as the parents Mr. Santa wanted for me, and, of course, the "September Song" routine we developed together—I was never able to figure out what to do with this warm swelling in my heart and throat (and the antsy legs) whenever we got together. He didn't seem to have that problem, at the dance or the following afternoons and evenings. He didn't try to force anything, but he didn't hide anything either—it always seemed to me that I'd have to make up my mind sooner or later about what I wanted. Even without other girls running to knock me over and get in front of him.

Well, he waited pretty long. But one of the nice things about Misha is his patience, which I suppose again is what makes him seem to lack confidence. He got it from his dad, I think, but his dad told me once it came from something deeper; "the thousands of years of frustration in his bloodline, the peasants and serfs who suffered in Russia," he said.

Lack of boobs and plentiful patience—good old DNA again, making us who we are, even when we don't want it.

Well, peasant or not, Misha was wonderful for me. As we developed our routine, the shaky stuff between us became a lot easier. Not clearer, but definitely manageable because we felt more comfortable with each other, happier, more natural, though we had no idea where we were headed. Sometimes we were like brother and sister—laughing and joking, with no sense of sex and romance—sometimes like an old married couple—fond, but years past the excited, heavy-breathing stage. And then sometimes our bodies seemed to blossom like a pair of summer roses, and the simplest touch or look could prick like a thorn or evoke the gentle smoothness of petals. I had no complaints, really, but I remembered Mum and Dad together, even in their older age, smiling, kissing, even fondling each other in warm embraces several times a day and night. I wondered why it didn't happen with Misha and me.

Clearly, Mum and Dad felt something special for each other, and I suppose that's what I looked and hoped for with Misha, although we never seemed especially close. Was a spark missing? Was I not capable of striking one in him? Would I not welcome a blaze of heat between us? I still don't know the answers to those questions, but I do know that if he walked away from me at that time, I would not have known what to do with myself. I spent ten or fifteen minutes waiting for him in front of the Sugar Bowl once, and when I saw him walking toward me from the high school with a beautiful red-haired girl who looked like she belonged in a bathing suit commercial, I took off at a run and didn't stop till I got to the park and the spot where the Pontiac used to be, just then remembering that I no longer lived, or hibernated, there. By the time Misha arrived, huffing and puffing through the trees, but with no redhead beside or behind him, I was down by the pond staring at the water to see if anything from my car or its contents was still under it (nothing was).

"Jesus, why did you take off like that, Jamie? I wanted to introduce you to Kelly. She's interested in dancing, too, and wanted to talk about the competition."

"I'll bet she did," I said.

"I thought you'd like to know her. She's a very interesting girl."

I stared in his eyes, imagining I was in some kind of police procedure movie and knew this guy was lying through his teeth. "You think you could lift her?" I asked. "She doesn't look like wire or a piece of thread."

He laughed, flexing his biceps for me. "A feather," he said, "floating on the wind. No problem."

"More like a fart smelling up a room, I'd say."

Misha's smile disappeared, and he came up beside me to look into the pond. Despite myself, I felt tears burning in my eyes.

"Look, Kelly's a nice girl. I've known her since kindergarten, but she went to a private school for a while, and we just ran across each other in the hall."

"So?"

172

"So, I thought she could use some friends. She doesn't know anybody here anymore."

'Well, she isn't going to want to know me. She'll be lonelier than before."

Misha's shoulders and face drooped into a full curved body-frown. He stared into the pond as if he wanted to dive through its surface and find something better on the other side. Meanwhile, tears rolled down my cheeks now, gathering into a large, obscene water spot on my shirt. "Jesus, we are a pair of really heavy dumbbells," I said. I put my hand on his shoulder, and then, on tiptoe, reached up with my lips and kissed him on the neck. It was a cool kiss, nothing sexy about it— actually, just a cozy begging for forgiveness and warmth. He turned and pulled me in his arms. We stood that way for a long time, arms around each other, and finally, for one of the first times ever, pressed our lips to each other's without any silly nervousness or obvious preparations. Naturally.

"That's really nice," he said, catching his breath. "You just made my run down here worthwhile."

I punched his arm and laughed, and things turned light and comfortable between us again. We stared at the pond and the gathering purple darkness in it as the sun sank behind us. We held hands, hugged, and kissed often, so that afternoon ended happily enough; and then we walked back to the Sugar Bowl for coffee and a snack before working out at the school gym to practice some of the harder steps without music. By now I knew something about myself that I never thought possible: Not only could I be jealous, but I very obviously liked— no, *loved*—Misha more than I ever cared to admit. Was that the spark I thought missing, or something else? At least my legs weren't shaking. "It's a kind of spark," Mum might have said. "But then you have to wait for the lovely warm afterglow."

To be truthful, our afterglow wasn't so warm. We didn't leap into each other's arms very much (except when we danced), and so nothing much happened—with lips and hot fingers, anyway. We worked on the routine, showing off to the school during one of the weekly assemblies we had. Mr. Santa and Jake attended—along with Mr. and Mrs. Alto—and after Mr. Gomez introduced us and the curtain rose on the two of us crawling downstage to the opening growl of Zach Douglaston's bow and strings, I spotted them sitting together in the first row, all smiling as if it was a proud moment. But then the whole auditorium erupted at the same time—catcalls, howls of laughter and general disgust, some shrieking "*ewws*" and "*yucks*" from girls who couldn't understand ordinary school clothes used to dry mop a stage. My first impulse was to run, of course; my second was to yell "Fuck you!" Then I looked at Misha, grinning in the spotlight as if this was the greatest response he could imagine, and I kind of hunkered down with more insistence, smiling myself now, keeping time to the music as we leaped to our feet, hustling through our routine as Zach's counter bass gradually built up to its final, life-accepting celebration.

Finally, when the music faded to a stop and we stood side-by-side holding hands and bowing, I didn't hear any boos or catcalls at all. But I didn't hear cheers either. I just concentrated on Jake's happy face, Mr. Santa's huge smile that reminded me of my Dad's, and the Altos' nodding, bobbing heads as they clapped and shouted. Mr. Alto actually cried out "Bravo!" bringing the whole auditorium—kids and teachers—along with him onto their feet. After about a minute, maybe more, Mr. Gomez walked out on stage, waved the curtain down, and took both our hands in his before we left. He smiled, pushing us through the center opening, and we stood alone before everybody as they continued to applaud. "Thunderous," Misha said, when we heard kids whistling and cheering while some of them stomped their feet. I felt naked for the first couple seconds, actually folding my arms before my flat chest, but after about a minute, I also began to feel proud and confident, as though I was just reborn and had everything good to look forward to. Misha nodded, leaning over to take my free hand. He stepped forward and drew me beside him. "Let's milk it," he said, grinning. "Remember, these are the kids who think we're weird." He bowed, pulling my hand down with him as the whole audience, kids and adults, clapped and shook the floor with their feet.

That night the Altos took us, Mr. Santa, and Jake out to dinner. We went to a new French restaurant in town with a chef who, Mr. Alto had heard, was trained in Provence and Paris. He loved French cooking and insisted that we try some of the Provençal dishes, although Mr. Santa and I reminded him that Jake would prefer pizza, and I liked safe stuff now that I wasn't eating out of cans and boxes—give me roasted chicken, broiled burgers, lots of green salad, and a plate of spaghetti smothered in hot red sauce. That night I had my first *pâté*, some meat stew called a *daube*, a delicious squash and eggplant dish with a name I couldn't pronounce, let alone spell, and some incredibly smelly cheese from a town called Brest that we ate with apples. I have to say it was very good, although I can't imagine anyone eating that stuff a lot without turning into a blob of butter and fat. Luckily, they had a small individual pizza that Jake could eat, and he and I shared a couple pieces of it along with the apples.

Afterward, we went to the Altos' house for dessert, and somehow it worked out that I stayed for the night instead of going back to Mr. Santa's. I had slept in their guestroom once or twice before, and since it was a Friday night, Misha and I decided to work on the dance and then watch a movie before going to bed. Mr. Santa told me to keep in touch over the weekend and let him know when I was coming home. I hugged Jake goodnight and walked them to the front door while Misha and his parents cleared up dishes and cups. At the door Mr. Santa took both my hands in his and looked at me with a very serious face. Uh-oh, I thought, this is going to be about condoms and STDs. But no, he fooled me again.

"You did really well today," he said. "You both should be very, very proud. You made the whole school go from mocking to stomping their feet in support. Even Mr. Gomez was happy for you."

I laughed. "How about your buddy, Mr. Span? Was he stamping his feet?"

He laughed and shrugged at the same time. "I don't know, but maybe I'll hear tomorrow, at the courts. We have a tennis date in the morning."

"Do you need somebody to watch Jake? I can get over there early, if you need me."

He shook his head. "Jake's our regular ball boy, so we're okay. It's nice of you to offer. Anyhow, I just want to remind you that this might be a good place for you. I mean a home. The Altos like you a lot. It's clear Misha adores you, which might be a temporary problem. But he's a reasonable kid, and so I think that can be worked out in the long run."

"We get along," I said, staring at my feet. He didn't say anything to that, which surprised me because I thought he'd be the first to see through my run away habits. Instead, he held on to my hands and looked at me, as if he had more important stuff to say.

"You're always welcome to stay with me and Jake," he told me, "but it's probably better for you to have a family—especially a mother. To me that's key at your age, and I get the feeling that Mrs. Alto . . ."

I just looked down at the floor and shook my head. I guess it's clear I had no idea what I wanted at that time, much less what I needed for my future. I knew I was a lost cause, for reasons that I did not understand and could not change. But I also saw no clear way to improve things, or at least make them comfortable, without somehow changing who I was inside and who I wanted to become. I thought of Dad's wildness after Mum died, and something of that lost, brave soul that he tried to show me every morning seemed like the only possible person for me to be. "Permanent sadness," he used to call it. "You stiffen your back, close your eyes and mouth, and just trudge along—taking care of business without any complaints."

I pretty much attempted that, I think, at least most of the time. When Misha came around along with his parents, and showed me I could have some easy happiness too (and a pretty clear picture of at least a pleasant, normal future), I couldn't believe it. So, I prepared to run, and every once in a while I really did, especially from Misha—which made staying with the Altos on any but an overnight guest basis just about impossible. Yet I was beginning to think about them a lot, and I especially looked forward to seeing Misha after school when we talked and touched each other so easily, without the sense that people were watching and having expectations. Mrs. Alto usually left us alone after the first half hour or so of watching us rehearse. She said positive things and occasionally made some very perceptive recommendations. For instance, she thought the opening few minutes of groveling on the floor should be scrapped in favor of lying still during Zach's opening solo and then vaulting to our feet in a kind of reverse squat-thrust when he picked up the tempo after the first few bars. We tried that a couple of times and liked it; then we moved through a brief balletic two-step, with both of us on our toes while Misha led us around the room at a flowing, easy pace that gradually built in speed until we broke into our final celebratory jig—dancing separately, raising and swinging our arms in joy and happiness, but in opposite directions—until the music faded and diminished, suddenly stopping with us in mid-stride, me on my right foot with the left leg extended in back, and Misha squatting and preparing to lift me, flying like that, into the clouds.

Most of the time Mrs. Alto would leave after that, although we welcomed her suggestions. She said that we needed time to ourselves to work everything out.

"Details," she said. "Make sure you nail down the details." Then she left.

I was sure Misha had confided in her, sure he had let her know what and how much he felt for me. So I guessed she left to help him slow my running feet. Details certainly kept me there longer on those afternoons—and maybe, she might have hoped, still longer in their lives.

***

Fred Misurella

PART THREE:

THE COMPLICATED PART

XI.

So here's the complicated part, the problem. I had to face it back then, and I have to face it again right now because I have been holding something important back from everyone, including Misha and Mr. Santa; and it seems to me, I have to come out with it now. It's about Coach, Mr. Span, and me—and before you go running off into fantasies about him and his crude words with the cross-country team, let me just admit that I was at fault too—and not just a little. A lot.

Sure, I was only fourteen, but despite Mum and Dad's best efforts at protecting me, I knew how things work, especially between a man and a woman—or, slightly differently, a man and a girl—even more differently, a married man with children and an underage, skinny-chested girl with a lot of animal energy. Not a pretty topic, I'll admit, but pitch it to Google sometime, and you'll find out that in many "civilized" countries around the world, fourteen is not too young for a girl to say yes, and in some places the age is even younger—it's ten in one or two, although even I see that's a setup for harem building, which disgusts me.

In any case, having just crossed a line, leaving Mum and Dad's house to live alone in my Pontiac (missing my Dad and Mum so bad I thought of walking with heavy weights into that pond of mud and rusty water in the park) and feeling, or developing, what—a crush? A lustful longing? Maybe we should call it an awakening of love and loins—for Mr. Santa's tennis buddy and our high school running coach, Craig Span.

He was incredibly nice to me back then: friendly, generous, careful and caring about the way he talked to me—or about me—when I first started running (and carrying equipment) with the team. He'd take me along with the guys to team parties and meetings; he let me travel in the van with them to nearby meets, seating me beside him as he drove us to other schools and towns. Once or twice he put me up in a room of my own when we had to stay overnight because of weather or distance from home. It was all innocent and proper, but he must have felt something in the air because the tension I felt inside filled the cab we were riding in, whether the whole team went with us or we drove alone. And you could tell he had a special response for me, innocent at first, in his own fatherly sort of way, but that changed fairly quickly as we worked through practices and meets that first fall season. He got distant for a while early that November, and I thought about quitting the team to do something else with my time, but he invited me and Mr. Santa to his house for a family Thanksgiving dinner (this was before Mr. Santa adopted Jake) and was very warm and friendly again, even giving me a goodbye hug and kiss on the cheek when he drove me back to the park since Mr. Santa had to leave early and canceled eating dinner at the last minute.

It was a wonderful day—the best for me after Mum and Dad died—and it renewed my interest in the team (and Mr. Span), maxing as we moved toward Christmas when he and the team pooled enough money to give me a beautiful cozy, and light, down sleeping bag that kept me warm and alive in the back seat of the Pontiac through that horrible, snowy winter. I suppose you could say that the sleeping bag was the arms and legs of Mr. Span making love to me, because from Christmas Eve onward he held me every night—in dreams, thoughts, and fantasy adventures—until I saw him again two or three mornings after New Year's day, when school started and the team began its spring practices.

It continued innocently enough, at least on the outside, when he began driving me home from practice at night, dropping me off in front of the police station so I could run across the street through the trees and open field to the car. Once or twice I carried a backpack, heavy with books from school and some gym clothes, and of course one night he had to offer help. One thing led to another, I guess you could say, but it wasn't that sudden or accidental. We were feeling each other out. Occasionally, we'd sit in his car and talk—sometimes about the team or school, sometimes about his family, life, love, men and women in sports, and, you know, men and women, period. I'll say this for him—I led him as much as he led me, especially to the emotional, racy stuff.

Was I lonely? Of course. It was terrible and cold in the car. I was a loner, but sometimes I wished I had someone to share it with. It was freezing that first winter month when I ran home in the dark and had to stumble through drifts of snow across the field behind the trees. One morning I crawled out a window because the snow had drifted up to the car's midsection, and I couldn't push the door open. Boy, I thought, it would be cozy with another body to share this stuff with me.

That kind of thinking, cheesy as it may sound, carried me through the awkward moments with Mr. Span when I was deciding whether I should lean over and kiss him—on the cheek, or even the lips—or just walk up and give him a full body hug. I have no real idea what he was thinking—or feeling—but I could tell he was wobbling. Mr. Span or Craig—coach and homeroom teacher, older married friend (with kids), or my lover? Even when he smiled and laughed, I could see something grabbing him near his belt. I remember once looking at my naked body in the mirror of the girls' locker room and imagined him walking in on me. I asked myself, in all seriousness, how would *he* respond? How could he want such a skinny, flat-chested girl like the one staring at me now, no matter how fast she ran? I was three or four years older than his son, maybe six older than his daughter—but to my needful, undemanding eyes, I saw all the signs in him of someone who wanted to get skin to skin and bone to bone with me—illegally, immorally, and pretty damn soon.

No, I wasn't a complete virgin. Tomboy that I am, I had roughhoused with boys in a couple sports. I had wrestled with a few for fun, and I knew a woodie when I felt one, especially on my legs or ass, and once or twice against my face and neck. Strange . . . and nice. Powerful. Mum and Dad would have disapproved, of course, but I'd seen enough hugs and deep kisses between them that I put the pieces together in my mind and felt the need for physical friction in my soul. In all the forties and fifties love songs Dad used to play for me,

I always felt the music as romantic sex, and in the old films he watched with me—black and white, with Fred Astaire and especially Humphrey Bogart—it was always there as deep yearning, which you could see in the men's faces while the women smiled and looked away as if they had something else in mind. A pie to bake? Really?

Well, I didn't, and I wouldn't pretend that I did. When Mr. Span (I could never call him Craig, or anything more informal than Coach) smiled at me in the morning as I ran by him on the track, I could feel the blood surge through my face and body. I knew it wasn't from the running. So, I'd smile back—prettily, I hoped—and whisper a promise to myself to kiss that smile and the rest of him neck to toe before the school year ended. Then, I'd dally in front of him, showing off my smoother form as I pumped my arms and legs— white socks with no ankles, and tighter Spandex fit on the shorts. I guess you could say it worked, but only much later. I don't know if it was self-doubt, or him being cool because he knew I was gaping at him, but he never showed a reaction. No mention of the socks, my running form, or the shorts—the stuff I usually heard from the guys. He'd just turn away, look at the clipboard he always carried, and then lean against the fence to watch the rest of the team as they ran along the track.

One afternoon in late winter, he passed by me as I was jogging home. He didn't stop, just drove on for a block or two, and then pulled over to the curb between a couple cars. It was near a supermarket, and I assumed he was going in to get some food for his family. He stayed in the car instead. I noticed the passenger window slide open as I approached, and by the time I reached the car his head was leaning through it. "Jamie! Need a ride? You ran enough in practice today." I waved my hand to say no. But then I saw his face with that quiet, hungry look I had seen and felt in those old black and white movies, and without even thinking about it, my feet skidded to a sudden stop, as if a ten-ton school bus was rolling across my path.

"Jesus," I said, "I didn't know it was you, Mr. Span. I thought it was some creep."

"Not a creep. Just a coach, which may be the same thing," he said.

I laughed, though he didn't even smile. "Some of the guys might think that, but not all of us," I said.

And that was how it started.

***

XII.

Mum and Dad were two people you could always count on whether you wanted to or not. They'd be *there*, as people say now, and as they both told me at least a hundred times, they especially loved being there for *me*. Mum's death was a terrible shock, a heart attack, while I was away at school, trying to follow classes. Dad rushed her to the hospital, and the staff carried her in on a gurney, keeping her alive in the emergency room just long enough, Dad said, for her to scribble me a note. She gave the note to Dad, murmured what would be her last goodbye to him, and died on the way to the operating room before I had a chance to read a word. When Dad picked me up at school later that afternoon, I saw tears in his eyes and, of course, I knew something awful had happened to all of us.

"Mum," I said. "What is it?"

My heart still does flip-flops when I remember that moment, my stomach tightening into a vicious knot, as if it wanted to trap something poisonous inside.

"Passed," is all he said. "No one, including the fucking doctors, saw it coming." He shook his head and handed me her note.

"Mom . . . ? How . . . ?"

"There're no explanations, Jamie. Goddamn it. It just happened." He shrugged his shoulders and pointed to the small envelope in my hand. My stomach felt empty just seeing her scribbled handwriting on it, and then my flip-flopping heart tried to emerge from my mouth. I bit it back and opened the envelope. When I began to read the note inside, he started the car.

"She wanted you to have that," Dad said. "Maybe she knew what nobody else did." He looked pissed, and at first I thought he was pissed at me. But then he added in a kind of loud and booming shout, "I sure as hell didn't," and stepped on the gas.

For a few minutes—for the whole ride home, as a matter of fact—I held that small white envelope and the folded paper in my hands. I didn't want to look at them, and I didn't want to read her words because they wouldn't mean anything without her there; they wouldn't hold anything I could respond to. What could I say? I enjoyed knowing you? Have a nice trip? Give me a call when you arrive, so I know you're safe? Anything I could do or say would be crazy, inappropriate, and I couldn't see myself just calmly reading her goodbye, filing it, and asking about that night's dinner.

Dad said nothing. I could see his mind was confused—an angry (*really* angry) riot. His face had stiffened into a pale white mask, his eyes glowered at the other cars on the road as if he wanted to ram them, his mouth and chin tightened as if he had swallowed something impossible to chew. I let the envelope and note lie in my lap and reached across to touch his wrist. He gave a quick look at my hand and then turned back to the road, as if I hadn't touched him. That's when I began to get scared. Was he blaming me somehow? Was he getting ready to leave, wander somewhere stupid, and, maybe, off himself? Did he in fact not want me with him without my mum? I couldn't believe any of it, but at the same time I kept thinking about how hard it would be, and how grief can change people—make sensible men do crazy, even awful things.

"Dad," I said. "Please, remember I loved Mum, too. *Love* her . . . very much."

He looked at me, pulled the car to the curb. We just sat for a couple minutes without moving. I could see his face had changed, because the hard look of his jaw and eyes softened. His lips trembled a bit, and that scared me almost as much as the anger. "I hate this," he said, his head down, almost touching his hands on the steering wheel. "I hate this so much it hurts. She was too good to go this early. She wanted to see you graduate college, help you pick a wedding gown, maybe even mind your kids. What the hell is this all for if she's gone before anything's finished? Shit! Shit! Goddamn shit!"

He pounded the wheel, threw his head back, and just bellowed at the automobile ceiling.

Jesus, it scared me. For a few seconds I slid away from him and leaned against the door, ready to open it. I was close to running away as fast as I could, but I couldn't make myself leave him that way. One side of me thought I would die without him, another side thought he would die with or without me, so why stick around for the ugliness? Stupid. As I said, grief makes men (and girls, I guess) do crazy things.

Finally, he just took a deep breath, smiled at me faintly, and then reached across the seat to pull me close. It was a weird couple of moments, because my gut told me I shouldn't be doing this, especially without Mum in the car. I didn't want to replace her or, God forbid, even think of cheating on her with him—but at the same time I was just past twelve years old, and all I saw was years of days and nights living in the same house with him, cooking, cleaning up the dinner dishes, and watching hundreds, maybe thousands, of hours of crap TV while he slept in the chair next to me. And snored. What kind of fun was that? How romantic was it? I hated my thoughts; I knew that Dad and Mum had saved me as a baby, so how could I abandon them now just because he was alone?

"Honey," he said. "I'll take care of you. It won't be the same—not nearly as wonderful—as with Mum, but I'll do my best. You have to concentrate on being a girl and enjoying a young girl's life. Mum would want that."

I nodded. Just hearing him say her name made me feel more confident that we could work it out. I smiled at him, for the moment comfortable despite Mum's absence, not happy but at least no longer weepy and overwhelmed. I didn't know what was coming, had no idea that the thousands of hours and nights would boil down to nothing in less than two years, and so for a short while I felt almost happy—a contentment that I look on now with quite a bit of naïve guilt because I wonder if I should have been sadder at Mum's passing.

"You have a life, and you must go on living it," Dad told me several times that night, and more than once afterward, especially when friends upset me by leaving me out of things or laughing at something I had said. He always tried to make me see that what others thought should never be as important as what I thought myself, and in the end (I never really understood—still don't—what end he meant) I could only be accountable to myself.

"Dad, how do I know I'm not crazy, or sick, or just some selfish, self-centered bitch? Sometimes I get weird ideas."

He laughed. "You're not crazy; you're not sick. As for selfish, I'm not so sure." He grinned and laughed louder at that, his big face and eyes lighting up at the joke and showing me a glow I hadn't seen for a long time. It made me feel he really liked me, was actually proud of me and happy to have me in his life—even without Mum.

"Well, I don't get it from you," I said. "At least not the sanity." And together the two of us just stood there and giggled like a pair of kids. It was the one time in the weeks, months maybe, since Mum passed away that we were able to laugh and enjoy our lives, though she had already reached the end of her own special journey.

You could say that after those moments our lives settled down into a normal, quiet pattern that made us— not happy, but at least satisfied. Dad would wake me in the morning with a sharp rap on my bedroom door, open it a couple inches, and peek in. "Up and at 'em, Jamie. Get those running shoes moving."

"Be there in a second," I'd say. "I'll just close my eyes for a bit."

"Jamie . . . Let's go. Your public is waiting."

At which point I'd throw off my covers, leap from the bed, and rush the door to push it shut. He'd smile at me with his foot stuck between the door and the doorjamb, and then he'd whisper in the softest, kindest voice I think I'd ever heard, "Sorry, honey, the clock moves forward whether we want it to or not. Oatmeal is waiting on the stove. I'll be down there, with my coffee, waiting for you."

That was us, day after day, for more than a year. He'd make my breakfast, watch me eat it while he drank dark coffee, then walk me to the door and wave after I slipped on my backpack and began to run—literally—toward school, nearly three miles across town. Normally, girls didn't run much in our school district, but as I said, I'm good at it and, later, when Mr. Span saw how much I loved the running, he listened to Mr. Santa and let me run with the boys. I'd stretch and do timed workouts alone from about 7:00 in the morning until about 8:30 (indoors on snow days in the winter)—and then go right to my first class, which was music, because Mr. Span was allowed to keep me on his homeroom roster since I began every day at the gym. After music came history, then English (my favorite class, except for gym), and then lunch followed by an afternoon of algebra, science, and Home Ec. I'd run home after school, unless I went to the weight room to lift for a couple of hours, which I did at least two times a week. By the time Dad arrived to pick me up near the locker room entrance on those evenings, my mind and body would be pretty much finished for the day. He'd take me for a snack at a local diner, and then he'd drive me home to nap before dinner.

After a while, it became a comfortable life, one I look back to with a warm feeling, as if nothing essential was missing, though of course it was. Like Dad reminiscing about his childhood, I knew the days were very hard, often a little depressing, but still important and very special. Oh, I thought about Mum a lot, especially in bed at night when I looked at the stars in a dark sky out the window and imagined that she was still with us, a scattering of brightness lighting the night. Then I knew I wasn't alone. I'd hear Dad puttering in the kitchen or the TV room. I'd hear his hum, or the sad mumble of a sports announcer building to excitement, and for some dumb reason, I'd know that, yes, Mum might be gone, but she was still with us—and the world was absolutely full of her love.

"Hah!" as Dad would often say about that kind of idea. "Fat chance, Jamie. The world operates in different, very dangerous ways."

Then, too suddenly, he was gone as well.

***

"I have no excuse, except the obvious one that no one will accept," Mr. Span told me one afternoon. "I'm in love with you."

So . . . there it was. How do you think a fourteen-year-old would feel hearing stuff like that—especially a girl living without parents? Especially if it came from an older, hot-looking man—a man she saw just about every weekday morning, and who went out of his way to do nice things for her once her parents had died? Mr. Span bought me coffee and doughnuts, or bagels; he massaged the backs of Principal Gonzales and a strict, by-the-rules school superintendent to let me work out with the boys' cross-country team, and then he made up a volunteer student job that would let me travel with the team (and him) to meets all around our state. "You're good for us, Jamie," he told me. "You're the force, the driving spirit, behind all our efforts to be respectable. Seriously, when we win a meet, we owe a lot of the victory to you. Just being there."

"In other words, I'm the mascot," I said, only partly as a joke.

He laughed (I did too), but we both knew there was truth to it, and I was secretly pleased to be that important—both to Coach Span and the entire team. Finally, I belonged. And what was he to me? Maybe a mentor? No fucking way after I held him in the car one afternoon. Lover? Well, Hollywood would call him that, but I was never really sure—three times my age, already married with two kids, and, as he told me more than once, a "ton of mortgage payments and college loans."

He was something I could not really figure out because, really, what could I give him other than the energy he said he loved? But it was just so cool. Even I understood (though I lied to myself every time I saw him) that real love—physical, emotional commitment—had little to do with what went on in that car. We were charged, no doubt, but I'm not sure what kind of current passed between us. He wasn't Dad, or even some kind older man who took care of me, like Mr. Santa. All of which made "us," whatever that simple connection meant—in the Pontiac or some hotel on the road somewhere. So, he was weird, hard to define, and, yes, unbelievably wonderful to me at the same time. I knew we were outside all the normal stuff everyone wrote songs about—except when we were alone. Then only the stars existed, and maybe the moon. Coach Span felt it too, in his own terms, of course, although he struggled to keep everything between us in the Pontiac.

"I should know better," he'd often say, solemnly, during those afternoons and evenings we spent together in my car. But the look on his face offered something more. Oh sure, there was something not quite right between us, but a fresh, relaxed smile on his face more than hinted at some inner happiness. And for me the idea that we shared something very, very special made my heart swell because our differences truly didn't matter. He was hooked—I was too—and we couldn't possibly stop because my boobless body gave him something he very much required. This way, I would never be alone.

To be honest, he gave me something special too, and so I couldn't stop myself either—wouldn't even think of trying. An impossible weight—some incredibly large, invisible structure, as I imagined it—had collapsed and pinned us under its walls and roof. I felt powerful, yet helpless beneath it. Stupid too, because I had done nothing but let everyday human events sweep me up as if a sudden wind lifted me from the vulcanized rubber track I ran on and carried me away. I had no idea where it would set me down. I was beautiful when it held me. In the back of the Pontiac or some figment of my memory or me imagining about it, I felt free of everything—stronger and more independent than ever. Yet at times I felt lonely, too, like the day Dad handed me that last pain-filled note from Mum.

It was a big, puzzling secret, holding me close to Mr. Span and, I believed, binding him to me—at least for the present day, but maybe forever. He had more to lose than I did—his wife, children, career, and (I only see this now) professional and personal self-respect. People thought of him as a great coach and very caring teacher, but it would have meant nothing in light of fucking one of his youngest students in a wrecked Pontiac after nightly cross-country practice. Mr. Santa would have deplored it, smashed his tennis buddy's head with a graphite and fiberglass racquet without any qualms, I'm sure. His wife would have dumped him; and I think the whole town would have run him out on a rail—tarred and feathered, too, I'll bet—or whatever else people do nowadays when they decide somebody is a piece of shit. So, compared to myself, I thought of Coach as brave. For me it was a sexy, romantic challenge, not necessarily painless, but an adventure. I had nothing to lose except my "emotional virginity" (as I heard one girl describe it in the halls one day) and a lot of useless, cheesy innocence. But the *ooh*'s and *ah*'s in the Pontiac's back seat made the happiness pretty complete. It was just great fun, like nothing I had ever done before, so of course that meant it had to be just as great for him.

"Creep has something nice to give today," I said during one of those secret afternoons, running my hand down his abdomen to his groin. He'd flash a nervous smile that couldn't hide a flicker of panic coming to his eyes. To me it was golden. *He's a shy one*, I thought. *But he's going to enjoy this, no matter what it takes.*

So, I kissed him, unzipped what my palm had come to rest on, and then laughed with a kind of gasp as that hidden lump came tumbling sweetly onto my fingers. Then his hands slid from my shoulders to my back, and he embraced me, thumb and palms near my neck. In seconds I lay on top of him in back of the Bonneville, pressing his shoulders down and smothering his lips with mine. He was usually docile; to my pleasant surprise, I felt I could ride the swiftest stallion in the world, the wildest and most muscular—yet Coach just lay there, smiling, head against the arm rest, passive. Nothing hurt, nothing felt sick or wrong, nothing struck me as sad or dangerous. But—looking back now—that's not exactly what his expression told me. "I'm digging the shit out of this," I whispered. He said nothing, just let his hands rest lightly on my waist and hips—allowing a wild, incredible ride, with his beautifully tender, softly massaging touch—urging me on while he stared deeply into my eyes, letting his own face cloud up in a mix of puzzled affection and fear. "What have I done to you?" he asked one day when we were resting. "What have I done to us?"

"'Done?' I'm fine. Wonderful. I wanted this, wanted it as much, or more, than you. Believe me."

I felt beautiful at that moment, inside and out, but he shook his head, steadying me as I lurched toward him, trying for a kiss. He stared at my face for signs of something—maybe pain or fear.

"I haven't felt this good in months—longer," I told him, raising my arms and hands to the car ceiling. "How could it be bad?"

I felt strong enough to take on anything, any challenge, on those afternoons, maybe ride him forever. But that strength began to ebb and then rapidly flow away, as I felt his hips' restless wiggle, his hands dropping from my face to my thighs, and his eyes showing more panic and fear than satisfaction. Pissed, I swung my leg over his head and dropped it beside the other on the Pontiac floor. I squatted on my heels, elbows on my knees, and propped my chin on my fists.

He sat up on the covered seat beside me, shoveling what was left of his muddled feelings back into his goddamn khaki chinos.

"Fuck. Well, it was quick, at least."

He looked at me, saying nothing.

"And Coach, don't forget your goddamn stopwatch." It was hanging from his belt, on the floor between my feet. I picked it up and handed it to him. "Good time today, but we should do better tomorrow."

"Jamie . . ."

He looked at me, more injured and shaken than I could have imagined.

My stomach turned—the look on his face, the surrender and regret in his eyes. I knew immediately what was coming next.

"You're only fourteen," he said.

"And living—happily—on my own. I don't want anything—especially pity—from anyone, including you."

"I'm forty-one," he said, as if that had something to do with pity.

"We've gone through this already. In my car age doesn't exist."

He laughed, genuinely, and that made me smile again, even though I hadn't really said it to be funny. I slid beside him, nuzzled my head and neck onto his shoulder, and reached around him to rest my arm on his waist and hip. "This is very good for me, Coach. I've needed somebody to hang on to. I've been with a boy a few times, but no one who could make me feel so strong. And happy."

"Safe, you mean."

199

He smiled, but other than resting his hand on my naked thigh, he gave no other sign that the conversation was okay. Thinking about those afternoons now, I can only imagine the regret he must have felt in his heart. He had a son a couple years younger than me, a daughter who was even younger, and I guess he thought of them in similar situations—an older man (or woman) taking advantage of their adolescent needs. Of course, that afternoon, I could only think of a soulmate—with engorged dick, to be sure—someone I wanted to clutch and never let go.

We sat for several minutes that way, breathing quietly together but not saying a word. Then he sighed, lifted his hand from my thigh, and let the cool afternoon air separate and chill us for one long moment. I kissed his neck, put my hand to his face, and stroked his cheek. He pushed open the Pontiac door and slid outside while I began pulling on underpants and jeans and straightening my hair. "I hope this isn't over," I said, as I had a few times already. "To me it just began."

He stood beside the car, zipping his pants, closing his belt, making sure of the stopwatch in his pocket. He stared at my legs as I came out of the car. "It probably shouldn't have begun," he said. "It's no good for either of us, especially you."

"Don't say that! Don't fucking say any of it!" I screamed. "I'm human. I have nothing else."

He put his arms around me, squeezing me in a bear hug from head to toe. My own arms went around his back, and again I nuzzled that tender place between his shoulder and neck and stared into the surrounding trees. I could have stood like that all night, maybe forever. This isn't Dad, I kept thinking, but he can take care of me, he can protect me until I'm ready to do it all alone. Just have to let him keep his family—especially his children—he has responsibilities to them, too.

Remembering all that as I tell it, I can see the silliness or, really, the impossibility, and the absolutely false sense of my own righteousness. That afternoon it seemed like the easiest thing in the world to have him in my life. I wouldn't push him or bother him. I wouldn't demand more of his energy and time than he could give, or drain the emotions that belonged within the walls surrounding him and his family. We would have a very special, secret relationship because we were both very special people. Understanding. ("Hah! Understanding what?" Dad would have hollered. "What kind of scotch are you drinking, Jamie?")

He left soon after that, hunching and turning away, walking behind the rock and through the hardwoods as if I was a minor teenage problem he would have to discuss with the freshman guidance counselor. At first I regretted his leaving, but I made a show of accepting it because I saw that we had wandered into a very unusual web of circumstances that threatened to strangle us both. For a short time I wondered what Mum and Dad would think, which immediately made me grateful that they would never know. But of course that thankfulness went on to make me sick. I felt this sudden, overwhelming knowledge of just how selfish I could be and how my thoughts revolved around myself, excluding everyone else. Awful.

"No one gives a shit about anyone, Jamie! That doesn't mean you have to be the same!"

I don't know how many times I repeated that dirty ditty to myself that day and for weeks afterwards, but it never did more than make me hunker down and insist that I get my way. I began to talk back, badmouth my teachers again, didn't take shit from anyone—especially the girls (and some of the guys) who in my eyes seemed to think God created the world for their benefit. Fights became a normal part of my school week, and since I was quick (with fists as well as feet) and didn't give a shit, I'd get my shoves and punches in while other kids were wondering if it was really worth it. Detentions followed, along with two or three short suspensions for second and third rounds of action, but the school psychiatrist thought I was sick and Mr. Santa came to my defense, pointing out that I was smart, traumatized at an early age, and in need of some formal security that only high school could provide: "Warmth, days with purpose, opportunities for friendships, and expanding knowledge of the world in its complexity."

To which I replied much more than once to this wonderful, amazingly caring man, "Mr. Santa, you must be fucking dreaming—or on some kind of illegal doctor's pill."

He smiled despite that jack-of-all, smart-assed comments, and went on to talk Mr. Gonzales and the rest into letting me stay in school.

The secret . . . ?

Everyone knew I had nowhere else to go.

***

So, it was established that school was good for me—surprise, surprise! As a result, Coach and I walked around each other at the track or in the gym bright and early every weekday morning, with occasional weekends together when the team had away meets. But nothing happened, really. Like two embarrassed lovers, we avoided staring at each other or being obviously chummy during practices and competitions. And to my surprise Coach played this game much better than me because, despite everything, I always looked for some special secret recognition or meaning—a smile, a certain hint of regret in his eyes, or just a softer, more personal tone in his voice as he spoke my name during roll calls. But nothing like that happened. If anything, he was more deadpan than usual when he talked to me, especially when he mentioned me to someone else. As one bright bonehead put it one day, after I passed him on the track and came around to lap him just after we reached the second mile, "You ain't on the team, Jamesee boy. Run all you want, as fast as you fucking want, but you haven't got real balls!"—which made the whole bunch of slackers jogging with him give out a huge guffaw and flip me the bird when I looked back.

It went on like that for more than a month. Neither of us broke down. We didn't "see" each other anymore because neither of us made a move to change things, as if we were both happy to let a couple of strange afternoons slip into some buried romantic past that no longer existed except as a secret, maybe useless, memory. But one weekend, after the team had traveled three boring hours to another part of the state on a Friday night and still woke up to win a meet next morning (me cheering those bastards the whole time, even carrying bags of equipment from the bus), the guys decided to party after we got home, making a loud point of inviting Coach but not even mentioning it to me.

I heard them, but said nothing, though my face burned in anger and even a little shame—because I did things for the team and still got no respect. So after carrying equipment from the bottom of the bus back into the gym, I just threw stuff on the hall floor and left without saying goodnight or giving a high five to anyone, not even Coach. I jogged to the Pontiac—ran really, as fast as I could—choking on every breath, with tears streaming down my face and an acid cloud gathering like rain around my heart. I threw my clothes and bag onto the front seat and immediately climbed in back, grabbing a handful of tissues from a box on the floor, blowing my nose a couple of times, and covering my face with what was left. I'm not exactly sure how to explain it, but I bawled and howled to myself for over an hour—louder than when Mum and Dad died and I knew I was all alone forever. Sometimes I think I just realized that night how broken my life had become and, worse, how helpless I was to change it now that they were gone. I turned to my side, buried my nose and face in the opening between the seat and seat back, and breathed all the mold and shit fouling the air inside it. It was an awful smell—choking, sweet and bitter at the same time—but I found it satisfying for some sick-ass reason, as if I was punishing myself for thinking I would be alright, things would eventually work out happily, my life would come together if I just kept plugging away. Now all I heard was Dad's voice in my ear. *Fat chance, Jamie! Life doesn't happen with silver linings.*

As I lay there, I heard Dad's voice say that more than a dozen times, loud but somehow very distant at the same time, and always with a murmur of hope and cheer from Mum just beneath it, as if she was saying not to worry, he was just being Dad. I get chills remembering that, and I still feel weird writing about it now. I know I'm kidding myself, but sometimes I think that opening in the back seat gave me a personal entrance into another, deeper world of experience. I'm not sure if it was the afterlife or just my messed up fourteen-year-old imagination. I didn't see much, but I certainly heard plenty, as if I had tuned into some other shape of human existence, like a Snapchat session maybe, based on sound where anybody can talk, no matter what the language or country.

I drifted off to sleep with those parental voices and others behind them filling the car's cabin, even with—if you want to hear more weirdness—a chorus of singers above them that seemed to come from celestial spheres in the sky beyond the stars. And then, as I was about to scream because I felt so strange, somebody knocked on the side window above my head and a familiar, quieter voice called my name. It was Coach Span. I looked up and saw his face through the glass, though at the moment I was sure it was just another goddamn sick dream.

"I'm sorry I bothered you," he said when I opened the door and shook my head. "I wasn't happy with the way you left."

"Happy?!" I shook my head again (to tell the truth, I *was* happy now that he was there, but I wasn't going to let him know it.) "Well, I sure as fuck wasn't ecstatic. What did you expect?"

He said nothing. He just shrugged his shoulders and looked above my head to the trees on the opposite side of the car.

"This is hard on both of us, Jamie. I regret we ever started it."

"Well, it's fucking finished now, isn't it? So don't worry about consequences. Besides, as I said, I wanted it as much as you." I looked up at him. "Probably more."

He stepped closer, nodded, and without a word put his arms around my shoulders, giving me a full, meaningful body hug. I'd like to say I pushed the bastard away or, maybe, spat in his face and called him a terrible name. But god, I missed feeling him close to me—his hands, his legs, and especially his face looming so near I barely had to pucker my lips to kiss him. Which, of course, I did. Then we both did. He held me tight, not enough to hurt, but enough to show he meant it and would be willing to die to keep us that way. I curled one leg around his, and without another breath or wasted movement, we fell into the back seat of the Pontiac and started pulling off each other's clothes. At that point the sounds and smells—and whatever else came from the back seat's smelly other world—seemed fresher, more human, with a sweetness and bitterness that pushed all that other existence back into its scary cave.

I would like to draw a curtain around the Bonneville windows now, although I can't tell you the number of times I looked out that night and was happy to see things beside or above me, as if a bird or a deer could somehow make up for the emptiness in my life. But at that moment I felt full and, aside from shame or possible trouble if a policeman or Mr. Santa came by to check on me, I just wanted to enjoy the moment, memorize it, and keep it all to myself. Because it dawned on me that this handsome hunk of a man, with a wife and family but also plenty of beautiful muscle on his arms and legs, really cared for me and wasn't just after easy teenage pussy. His breathless moans sounded too real; the nervous, but surrendering want in his eyes reflected the same kind of stuff I felt, and the automatic, spontaneous moves to make our bodies connect and begin a chain of shudders and screams wiped away any doubts I should have had. "I'm in love!" I shouted at one point. And although he didn't respond with words, his embrace grew warmer, his movements about me became more tender, and his hands and arms touched and caressed me with a sweetness I could only remember from Mum and Dad.

Afterward, we lay next to each other for at least an hour. The air was cool, but we didn't feel it. I just looked through the back window and saw a white sliver of the moon looking down on us as if to make sure we were okay. I felt his breath in my ear and, warmed by it, reached down to feel his soft penis swell again in my hand. "I have to go," he said, with a look of regret in his eyes again. "There's school tomorrow, and—"

"And you have to say goodnight to the boy and girl. And wife." I put my hands against his chest and slid back on the floor, covering myself with jeans and shirt and throwing his stuff in his face. I watched him struggle into them awkwardly, and then climb barefoot out of the car. When he sat to put on his socks and shoes, I pulled on my underpants and jeans and threw my shirt at him. I put on a denim jacket and slipped out of the car. He stood next to me, handed the shirt back and, without a word or any loving gesture, began to walk away.

"You wanted it," I called. "I didn't ask you to come by tonight, so don't blame me."

He didn't even look back, just stepped behind the large rock and disappeared.

***

PART FOUR:

MR. SANTA

XIII.

"It's a sick world sometimes," Mr. Santa told me once, "but there's always reason to hope."

And because of that he's spent most of his life—his adult life, anyway—trying to erase that sickness, or at least weaken it, but without much success. He was in his office every day—still is—with almost no help but a huge heart full of hope, which never seemed to outweigh the paperwork or the county's need for more of it.

"So why do it?" I asked him. "You'd have more time and a lot more money with another job. I'll bet people would appreciate you more, too."

He looked at me, that smooth, expressionless face I knew so well just telling me nothing, but, maybe, monitoring. After a long minute, probably more, he nodded his head and sighed. "What else do we have, Jamie?" he said, softly. "Somehow, God made a mess—I think we have to admit that to ourselves. I'm just trying to clean things up so they don't get worse."

The surprising thing was that he didn't even smile or wink, so I knew what he said came from the heart. He was raised to be Catholic, but I knew he didn't attend church or read the Bible anymore, and as long as I've known him he's never expressed belief in anything except science. He did go to Christmas Eve masses with foster children, but he came out of them "feeling empty," he told me, as if the time spent had disappeared in a blast of nasty wind. "I felt nothing, saw nothing, and heard nothing, Jamie. I don't even remember the priest talking, or the choir singing. Apparently, I wasn't consciously there, except for the hand I held of the lovely child in white standing next to me."

I was that child one Christmas Eve, though I'm not sure about the "lovely" part. I remember the mass we went to vividly because it came the Christmas season after Dad died, and I was praying as hard as I could that he would be on his way to heaven, and Mum would be already there, waiting to welcome him. And yes, I prayed for my own happiness, too—here on earth, not up in heaven. I know I was completely bewildered at that time. I couldn't believe God (or life, or fate—whatever you want to call it) wanted me to live the rest of my life without a family. I was a difficult, though decent kid (I think); I had done no major damage to anyone or anything. But here I was, thirteen and a half, my dad's distant cousin forcing me on Mr. Santa so he could go off to his family in Ohio to enjoy the holidays. No question of me going with him, he said with an awful shit-eating smile. "You wouldn't fit in," he added as he walked out of Mr. Santa's office. "You're better off here where you know people."

I remember looking at Mr. Santa at that moment and seeing the most primitive expression of anger, shock, and disbelief I had ever seen. He dropped his feet from the desk to the floor and leaped from his chair to slam the office door shut before this cousin of mine could touch the handle. "Just wait a minute!" Mr. Santa shouted, as if the man was already on his way. "I don't run an animal shelter. You can't just drop her off and leave."

This cousin, who had none of Dad's smile or soul or sweetness and called himself Charlie but could've been "Shit" as far as I was concerned, gave a quick annoyed glance at his watch and nodded his head. "I got to get on the road," he said. "It's a long ride to the airport, and it might snow."

Mr. Santa's eyes went wide. If he had a hammer, I'm pretty sure it would have been planted in Charlie's skull right then. "This girl has needs," he said. "You're family. You can't just leave her with no responsibility."

Charlie-boy smiled and shrugged, looking at his watch again, without so much as a flicker of concern or apology. "My lawyer says I have no obligations toward her. Whatsoever. I'm here for the house, land, and contents—nothing more."

In college, one of Mr. Santa's professors used to urge students to keep things clear, uncomplicated, telling them to look for specific primary causes behind (or rather, inside) the terrible disturbances in people's lives—especially in the lives of kids. "We have to find a virus, something that attacks and sickens, and suggest a way to kill it, or render it powerless. If money or the lack of it is cause, find a way to redistribute; if it's abusive power, name and shame the abuser—and work to remove him (or her); if it's ignorance, provide the care and education people need to grow into full, independent citizens. 'Society' doesn't need to change, it's the individuals in it, and for each one there's a single, tender crisis point. Find it, name it—eradicate it."

"Your relative," Mr. Santa said to me that night, "is another strain of virus, completely unique: he simply doesn't care." So he took Charlie's name, address, and phone number at the door, put them in his register, and waved him out of the office, saying—with disgust—he would hear from our state offices "before too long."

"Send it to my lawyer," Charlie responded. He handed Mr. Santa a business card—his lawyer's—and grinning like a murderous little puppet, left.

***

That Christmas Eve night and mass was Mr. Santa's attempt at virus killing for me. He had tried to place me in a foster home, but I hated the two places where he found beds, mainly because the family rules were grating. To be fair, I can't say they wanted anything awful—no kitchen-maid Cinderella duties, I assure you—but I couldn't face the fact that these strangers thought sharing in on washing and drying dishes, helping to set the table at dinner time, or doing my own wash were ways to welcome me into their homes. I felt sorry for myself, I admit. I wanted to be a guest, a very special one with a deep crack in my heart that needed to be mended with tender, loving care. Instead, both families welcomed me as if nothing awful had happened, and I just needed to familiarize myself with a new set of happy circumstances: family, home, routine. "I hate it," I screamed at Mr. Santa, when he came to check on me in the first new place. "They aren't my people; they haven't a clue about what I need, or how much love I lost. Get me the fuck out of here before I blow a hole in the ceiling!"

He tried with another family, and after I came back with the same complaint less than a week later, he just shook his head and said he couldn't find another place right then. He might do better after the holidays, he told me. "People are genuinely trying to help you, Jamie, give you a home. Are you sure you're not being too fussy?" Of course I said no, and after he left the house, I walked up to the room I shared with two other foster girls, packed my stuff in my backpack, and, without a word—not even a thank you, I must admit—jogged back home—Charlie's house now, no longer Mum and Dad's. I stayed a couple of nights, with no electricity, heat, or light, until Mr. Santa's gray Honda rolled into the driveway one cold morning and he knocked on the front door.

"This is not working, Jamie," is all he said when I answered. He asked me to pack my stuff and took me home—to his house this time—and I guess you could say I finally accepted that my life had turned upside down. There wasn't a fucking thing I could do about it.

Jake didn't live with Mr. Santa then, so he put me on a couch off the kitchen in what would become Jake's room eventually and fed me warmed leftovers— meatloaf, mashed potatoes, and green beans—from the night before. I hadn't eaten much for several days because I had nothing to cook with at the house, and so you can imagine how hungry I felt. Mr. Santa sat with me at the table and grinned while I shoveled food into my mouth and gulped down a couple glasses of milk. He brought in more meat and potatoes when I finished the first helping, and beamed when I went at it like I hadn't already eaten a huge plateful.

"Skinny girl, big stomach," he said. He brought out another plate for himself and a platter with more meat and beans for both of us. He took just a little for himself and let me have most of what was left. "Now I know where your energy comes from," he told me, laughing. "You take as much as you like, I don't need anything. I had a pretty big lunch."

I nodded but wouldn't take any more, partly because I felt stuffed, mainly because I felt embarrassed. He offered a bowl of fruit for dessert, and I took an apple from it but nothing more. While I ate, the two of us sat across the table from each other without saying a lot. He mentioned that he was stretching social workers' rules by letting me stay with him, but he thought the trouble I was having adjusting to the foster families justified it. "This is temporary, Jamie," he said, "until we find accommodations that you're comfortable with."

Comfortable? I never did find anything I liked, although he tried me with at least two other homes. I have no excuse; I just didn't like them, mainly because I kept looking for someone to be like Dad and have fun with me, or for someone to act like Mum and love me completely. It didn't happen. And although I felt a real closeness with Mr. Santa, I could not get over the embarrassment of living with a man so much younger than Dad. I imagined some pretty raunchy things, I must admit, especially at bedtime—and while he kept his distance, except in the kitchen when he was cooking for us, I always felt a shiver of something extra right down my legs, as if I could just reach out, touch his hand, and the rest would be this amazing romantic flame. But then he'd say something about washing dishes, taking out the garbage, or dusting furniture, and the hot fire in my imagination would turn cold as ashes. I wasn't disappointed, but the whole thing felt very, very strange. And when Christmas Eve arrived and he offered to take

215

me to midnight mass if I wanted to go, I sort of grabbed at it to make things feel normal between us—like family.

I had a white, gauzy dress that Mum had bought for me the Christmas before, and though it looked a little too short for me now, I liked the way my legs showed beneath the frilly hem, and I decided to wear it again with my new white NBs matching it on my feet. Mr. Santa gave me a red and white corsage of roses, lilies, and holly berries, and before we went to mass he made me open a second present: a beautiful red down coat that went to my ankles and kept me really warm whether I zipped it up or not. I hugged him and kissed him—on the cheek, mind you—without thinking of anything but thankfulness. And then, a little bit ashamed, I gave him a red baseball cap with an "R" and "F" painted on it in white and green.

"Oh, wow, Roger Federer!" he said, his face blushing like a little kid's. He tried it on, giving himself a jaunty, teenage air. "Thank you, Jamie. A lot. I can't think of a better hat."

"I couldn't either," I said. "At least for you. I hope you don't mind the painted letters."

He shook his head. "They're perfect. Thanks."

And then, believe it or not, he hugged me and kissed me on both my cheeks.

***

So, he and I were like a family from that night on. I'm not sure why, but it just helped me relax with him; mostly because I didn't have any more of those creepy sexy feelings that had us rolling on floors or couches with no other goal than reaching some loud, dramatic gasp. He was calm and easy with himself, and I found myself becoming that way, too. In a certain sense, I think, the corsage and down coat made me feel like a daughter again—a young child who didn't have to do anything but show appreciation and respect. A kiss on the cheek with a genuine "thank you" did all of that, and of course the Federer cap showed some forethought about making him happy too. In a certain way, it was just like giving gifts to Mum or Dad—nothing too expensive, just thoughtful enough to show you cared, which I guess we both did that Christmas Eve.

The church was crowded, as it usually was for Christmas mass. Decked out with white lilies and other flowers, red and green streamers, flags with silk-screen pictures of scenes from the nativity all around: shepherds and the three dark-skinned kings, Mary on the donkey with Joseph walking beside. I never thought much of that stuff before, mainly because Dad laughed at it. He called it gaudy and rich when the family in the story was poor—a carpenter and his pregnant wife living with animals in a barn because they had no place else to stay. I took Dad's thinking to heart, usually, and hoped for something a little less grand in the decorations. But that night, standing beside Mr. Santa, I saw the whole scene as a lovely welcoming gesture, as if it was all for me in my own time of homelessness. Selfish, I know, and mostly a result of finding a friend in this man looking to place me with a new family; but holding his hand, feeling his shoulder and arm very near, I just felt like I naturally belonged.

We went through the motions of the mass together, a beat behind the people in front and alongside of us, smiling a little because we felt like strangers in the midst of all the automatic native movement. But when the officiating priest stepped into the pulpit and began to talk about Jesus as a migrant child with parents who never left him alone, I felt the shock of emptiness in my stomach, as if I had stepped into a hole and fallen down a shaft. Mr. Santa saw it, I'm sure. He put his arm around my shoulders and held me close, whispering that I should think more about the meaning of the child's story than its physical details. "It's about saving the world, Jamie," he said, "no matter how desperate your circumstances. We're in there, too—both alone, but somebody has our backs."

"You mean God?"

He looked at me, smiled for a moment, and shrugged.

I had never thought of anything like that, certainly not about Christmas. To me holy days were about God showing his power—all the amazing stuff he could do, even as a baby in a manger, or a corpse lying in a tomb at Easter. It's the way my dad saw it, and maybe Mum too, although she never really talked much about her beliefs. She just loved the church music— Bach especially, who she said she descended from through some very distant, third or fourth (maybe fifth) cousin several times removed. She played his music constantly during holidays and especially loved "Ave Maria" and "Jesu Joy of Man's Desiring" performed on an organ. From Thanksgiving to Christmas she hummed those tunes morning into night, especially when she cooked my breakfast and our dinner. And I remember the thrill her voice brought to my heart around those times when she pronounced the words. She sang very well, her voice clear and sweet so that you felt she lifted you among the floating clouds. It's what Dad and I missed so much when she died, I think. The silence of the house covered us both in gloom that first Christmas, and it felt no better when Dad put on one of her favorite LP's before we sat down to dinner. The darkness of December seemed worse than ever, as if no light would ever pierce it. And, of course, when Dad passed the following year—just before Thanksgiving—the gloom was overlaid with murky dark shadows that never lifted, even on sunny December days.

Of course, Dad's cousin Charlie made the darkness worse for me. He arrived at the door one Saturday afternoon with a key in his hand and an unfriendly smile on his face. Within half an hour he told me I could stay in the house, but only for a short while, and that I should begin to look for another place right away. "The house is mine," he said, "in case you're wondering, but I'm not going to live here at all. First, I'll auction things off, and then I'll sell the house itself as soon as I can. There won't be much room—or time—for you."

He smiled and said he'd call the county children's agency to see if they could help, and, after a couple days, they sent somebody over—which, of course, is how I met Mr. Santa.

I didn't really like him when we first talked; I'm not sure why. He was friendly enough, but to me he thought more of Cousin Charlie than me, talking about his burdens, the difficulty in settling a distant family estate. Later he told me that wasn't his intention. He was simply trying to assess my situation—whether Charlie and I could get along, whether I'd be able to live with him and his family in Ohio, and whether there was anyone else I could live with if Charlie and his family didn't work out. He caught on pretty fast that it wouldn't work out, I guess, because in a couple days I was sharing a room with another foster girl, Camilla, who was my age but did nothing more than lie in her bed and stare at her phone all day and night. She was waiting for calls, she told me, from a boy she knew when she lived at home. "A boyfriend?" I asked. She nodded, said he was the quarterback on her school football team, and they planned to marry as soon as she turned sixteen. Well, I don't know if that ever happened, though she would be well over sixteen by now, but I do know that during the week and a half that we shared a room, he never called once, just texted her two or three times to say he was busy with the team.

"Hmm . . . the team," I said to her one day, trying not to look too much like a know-it-all. "I'll bet."

As you may guess, Camilla and I didn't get along very well, and although the family switched my room with one of the other girls', Mr. Santa had me out of the house at the end of the second week. "It's a less crowded place," he told me as we drove up to the second house, just out of town on a very rural street. Trees—"Hardwoods," Mr. Santa said—surrounded every home, and there were no sidewalks—just a road, a berm, and then lines of bushes and trees leading up to very well-trimmed lawns. Something about it grabbed me—as if the street was shelter for whoever lived there, especially kids. "Nice," I told him. "But how about the people you're putting me with? Are they going to be nice, too?"

"Should be," he said. "They're an older couple. They've been taking one or two kids in steadily for over fifteen years. They miss their own children."

"Miss them—are they dead?"

He shook his head. "Scattered," is all he said. "In different parts of the country. They like to have youthful energy around the house, and I told them you have plenty of that."

They may have liked it, but they sure as fuck didn't know what to do with it, I'd say, or how to allow it into their lives. Oh, they were nice enough, I'll tell you that. They bought me things, took me places, even went for hikes on mountain trails and around lakes. I loved the hikes, admittedly, but the things they bought me, the places we went to tended to leave me cold. I'm not big on museums, plays, or even malls, to tell the truth, and as far as things are concerned, I like practical stuff I can use—jeans, NBs, and maybe, one or two pretty dresses for special occasions like Christmas mass. No phones, no iPads; just a few books and a backpack to carry them in. Whatever might fit on my back, or in a car, will suit me, you know? I don't need a lot of stuff.

They appreciated that at first, but they were stymied because they couldn't entertain me or make me happy, though they sure as hell gave it their best. Mr. Santa explained the obvious to them—the swift loss of Mum and Dad had stricken a very deep, painful chord in me, and it would take a while to bring me back. But that twisted them even more, I think, because we spent nights sitting in front of the TV, and though they didn't fall asleep like Mum and Dad, they just stared gloomily—sometimes at the tube, sometimes at me, not seeming to understand either. I confess I didn't understand much more. In their house a fog seemed to swallow us all and carry us into a huge dark cave, as if it intended to trap us there, or bury us alive and go back to a happier, safer place. Jesus, I found it scary—and then there were nights when I couldn't stand being near them, let alone being in the same room. I told Mr. Santa that when he returned to check on me—and so he decided to take me back to his house until he found something else.

"Those people are too nice for me!" I told him. He just looked at me and nodded his head. I guess he agreed.

For some reason, probably because of the holiday season, there was not a single other foster bed available in the county. "Christmas," Mr. Santa told me with a little shrug. "People want to open their homes, but then the holiday strain on dysfunctional families makes bunches of kids suddenly available. It's like a perfect storm."

He said I could stay with him until something better became available, and so, from Thanksgiving to just after the New Year celebrations, we were each other's Christmas family, for better or worse. I had a pretty good time—much better than I would have guessed. We went to Coach Span's house for Thanksgiving (which is how I met the dickhead), then to another social worker's house for Christmas dinner, and nowhere but home on New Year's Eve, which Mr. Santa said always depressed him because of the false cheer and heavy drinking. We watched a pretty stupid movie on

TV (a cheesy one about meeting at the top of the Empire State Building), then looked at the Times Square celebration on a couple of channels, and shortly after the ball fell, Mr. Santa said goodnight and went to bed. I washed up and went to my room.

Next morning, I asked him if I could go out on my own, "for some fresh air," I told him, and—mainly—a little exercise for my legs. No problem with that, he assured me, so I pulled on a pair of spandex leggings, a sweatshirt, and running shorts, tied up my NBs, and left—running into the cold, clear air of the New Year's first day. I felt happy, for some reason, at least happier than I had since Dad died, and so I took off at a good, excited pace to try to work up a sweat and bring on some of the good feelings that flow through me on long runs. I headed out to Main Street, turned toward the high school, and just enjoyed seeing the town so quiet and clean on this particular sleepy morning. All the stores were closed, but I knew that a couple restaurants would open later—for lunch or dinner—and things would gradually get back to normal.

At the school, I ran past the gym and out onto the track, where I saw one person jogging at a very slow, almost walking pace. So, I got onto the track myself and followed at an easy trot. It was Mr. Span ahead of me, so I picked up a little speed and caught up to him in about the length of a 110, nodding and passing him as I continued at a faster gait. I lapped him before he came around in a second quarter, and I slowed and nodded once before taking off again.

"Hey, Jamie," he called. "Slow it down a bit." He caught up, a little breathless, I was happy to hear, and settled back to my pace as I basically slowed down to a walk. "Good stride," he told me. "Too bad we don't have a girls' team. Do you run much by yourself?"

I nodded. "As much as I can. At least three miles every day, and if there's time and weather, I can do at least another three—sometimes five."

He nodded. "Pretty good. You must like it."

"My Dad used to say, 'Better than a shrink, Jamie. And cheaper.'" Coach laughed, but believe it or not, the sound of the word "cheaper" brought the sound of Dad's voice to my ears, and in less than about fifteen steps I pulled over to the side of the track with a handkerchief in my hand and tears streaming down my cheek.

"You alright, Jamie?" Coach stopped and came over to where I squatted in the grass. I felt stupid at first, especially since I wanted to show him how well I could run for distances.

"Fine," I said. "Just a little runny nose from my allergies this time of the year."

"Good." He handed me another handkerchief and squatted beside me. I felt embarrassed, of course, but at the same time I felt good—kind of comfortable—having him beside me. I had seen him in gym classes occasionally, and once or twice I ran a quarter or two in the grass while the cross-country guys sprinted on the track. I knew his name; he, of course, remembered mine from Thanksgiving, and that was that. The warmth of his sweaty body crossed the very little space between us and got to me, even as I was crying.

"You sure you're alright? You want to go sit in my car?"

"I'm fine," I said and, without another word, jumped to my feet and started down the track at my fastest pace. He didn't try to catch me, but just stayed where I had been and waited. I fooled him, though, because when I got to the gate in the fence at the far side of the track, I went out and ran to the street instead of coming back to him.

That's not quite the "meet cute," they show us in romantic movies, but it sure started something powerful boiling in my belly. I began leaving for school very early in the mornings just to watch Coach run the cross-country guys through their practices. I'd run the track daily before they came out, and then sometimes I'd run beside them to see if I could keep up—and to get Coach to say something nice again about my running. We both passed the test, I guess; I easily kept up with the front-running guys, and he, almost daily, complimented my running form as we crossed the finish line. That made me feel great, of course, and when I told Mr. Santa about it, he spoke to Mr. Span and they went to the high school principal. In about two days I was made part of the cross-country squad and allowed to work out with them every day, though because of division rules I could not compete in a meet.

It was a bummer about the meets, but it let me run in the morning and see Coach Span every day, which was what I wanted the most—along with the return of Mum and Dad—during that particularly bitter winter season. Mr. Santa did everything he could to cheer me up, but he could not find me another home in the county. And despite his sweet and generous soul, he could not make me feel fully comfortable in his little house. I didn't need his TV, his bathroom, or even his running water. I wanted my own place, the cruder the better, I thought; and while I tried crashing in one or two abandoned houses in the poorer section of town, I never felt right, never felt at home—whatever "home" might mean to someone who had lost it the way I did. Once or twice, I decided to give everything up and just wait for Mr. Santa to find something, but then the itch to be alone would return and off I'd go in search of empty buildings. One day I overheard a couple kids at school talk about an empty boathouse on the river behind the park, and when I learned it had been unused for many years, I hiked out there one March day after school.

There it stood, red brick with three or four barred, but unbroken windows, and when I looked inside I saw a huge empty floor with a bunch of loose bags, plaster, and papers scattered about. I tried the door, but found it locked, and when I tested the windows, found they were sealed up too. I left, thinking to come back with a crowbar or something to pry open the door. I took a shorter path back through the park, and at the street turned toward Mr. Santa's house to see if he could tell me more about the boathouse.

"Five years. That's the last time anybody used it," he told me. "They built another one up the river and just left this one to rot."

I nodded, not saying anything more than I had found it accidentally as I hiked along the river. But by this time I knew Mr. Santa almost as much as he knew me. He figured I had an idea of making it a home, and he immediately warned me that the police checked it regularly because, for insurance reasons, the county could not let anybody—especially nesters—live there. "There are problems with mold," he said, "and even some structural damage in the roof. It could fall in at any time."

I figured that was all scare talk to keep me away, but when I went by the next day after school, I looked through the windows at the ceiling and saw huge patches of cracked and hanging yellow plaster. I spotted brown water stains too, and when I looked at the walls above the windows, I saw more of the same. Part of me said "Fuck it, I'll stay here anyhow." But another part remembered how awful I felt in the run-down houses I had tested, so I ended up just walking away.

I started back toward the park, thinking of a pleasant, though miserable, walk through the trees before reaching Main Street where I intended to jog down to the public library for some books before heading back to Mr. Santa's. I stopped at the brook that fed into the town's main stream, and after walking along the bank for a bit I headed through the trees again. When I got to the open field I crossed in front of a large rock I had never noticed before. It was surrounded by oak and maple trees, and as I walked among them, I pulled up suddenly, thinking a car was heading toward me. It was a car alright, but of course it wasn't heading anywhere, except into the next couple years of my life. The Pontiac, a Bonneville, stood before me. In some sudden surge of electricity and urgent vibration, it seemed to call out to me, as if it had a spirit. Aqua blue and metallic gray where the paint had peeled off, with a banged-up right front fender, a crumpled grill, and a pair of smashed headlights, it

227

seemed like a wounded animal stumbling through some epic battlefield in a war that had no meaning or end.

I walked toward it and slowly circled it, picking up a torn cushion and a hubcap that lay alongside. The back trunk had been left open, so I tossed hubcap and cushion in there and pulled out a muddy army blanket that someone had left. It was made of thick brown wool, and I immediately saw it would keep me warm through some pretty cold winter nights and days. One of the doors was open a crack, and I yanked it open all the way—it made a loud screech that set the starlings in the trees out over the field and back again. I don't believe in spooks, but I have to say that in the sound of all those wings overhead I heard a whispering voice make a single protracted moan: "Home . . . " is what it said to me.

Home. I looked up and turned around, seeing and hearing nothing but the birds and their excited chatter as they darted from branch to branch. Don't know why, but I felt a chill run down my spine. In less than a second I recognized it as a happy chill—not a sign of fear. I stepped inside the car, sliding behind the wheel, and sat for several minutes with my hands on the dashboard and my eyes on the bushes and trees that surrounded me. Comfortable, I decided, well-protected from prying eyes and hostile winds. And of course I realized that Main Street and the town police were just the other side of the open field and trees—a quick run of less than a minute for me, I guessed. I did not think of the winter dark; I did not think of the impossible cold of January and February nights. I did not think of the lack of the Internet. I thought only of the quiet, the view of the stars from the open field, and the opportunity to discover, maybe, the secret bravery of the loners I knew who found in solitude a happier way of life than a crowd of people.

I looked around more carefully inside the car, checking on things I could throw out and making a list of stuff I should bring back with me next day. There was no key, of course, so doors would always be open when I was away, but I noted that I could lock the doors from the inside and at least protect myself from a surprise attack. I also saw plenty of small, secret places I could hide important stuff like letters and books, and I assumed no one would be interested in a pile of blankets for warmth and another pile of jeans, underwear, and sweaters that I could stack in a newly cleaned out trunk and interior. Obviously, I was running away with my dreams, not thinking very carefully, but really daring myself into bravery—no matter how impossible everything seemed. And of course I didn't give a thought to legal issues, like whether the town and county would let me live by myself in a wrecked car, and if I had thought of that, I'm sure I would have assured myself that Mr. Santa could work some kind of deal to make everybody happy—including me.

***

"Whoa, Jamie, slow down!" is what, in fact, he said later that night. "You can't do this kind of stuff. No one in their right mind will allow it."

"I keep reading about homeless kids," I said. "Millions of them. You mean it's better to live on the streets than in an out-of-action car that will keep them dry? That makes no sense."

"Street kids have slipped through the net, I grant you that—but I won't let that happen to you. Not while I'm here."

"Even if I want it—desperately?"

"You can't," he said. "For your own good."

That pissed me off. "You don't know what's good for me!" I shouted. "No one knows better than me—because I know myself, and you don't!"

I saw that hit him somewhere—deep inside that secret Catholic conscience he kept buried, I'll bet. He leaned back, folded his hands high up on his chest, and stared at me with his deep set, soulful eyes. After a long couple of minutes, he shook his head and told me he thought the idea was foolish—"Foolish and dangerous, actually," he said. And of course I heard an unspoken "but maybe" in there, though next morning over breakfast, he insisted again that the idea was not going to fly—with him or anyone else in county social services.

"Jamie, I don't care how fast you run, or how close you are to the police station—it's just not reasonable. You're too young to live alone, even in a reasonable situation, let alone an abandoned car! Let the idea go. Please!"

"I can't. I truly love it. I want to know what it feels like to be alone—fully alone—with the stars instead of the fucking internet to tell me how my life is going!"

He shook his head and leaned back in his chair. Once again, those eyes, dark brown Italian olives, as I saw them, seemed to look through me to another room, maybe even another house.

"Mr. Santa, I love *Walden,* not *Little Women.* I've often thought that it's the perfect model for the kind of life I want to live. With the Pontiac I can test that theory and learn if I'm just full of shit."

He laughed, shaking his head again. "Even if you could get badly hurt, or worse? We can't risk that."

I must say I hated him at that moment—the grin of condescension on his face, the absolute certainty that I was a nutcase, the sense that somehow I had lived for nearly fourteen years and still had my head up my ass as far as the real world was concerned. I was about to leap to the toes of my NBs, run out the front door, and find my way back to the Pontiac to spend my first night alone under the stars. But then I realized he probably could keep up with me if I ran, and with the police near the park he could have me out of the car and back in his custody in less than the time it would take me to open a door, jump inside, and lock it.

"I want to try it," I said. And without the slightest effort, I suddenly found myself with my face in my hands and choking sobs swelling in my throat. "I have to," I blubbered, with snot now bursting from my nose. "Please, Mr. Santa, I just . . ."

Damn . . . I knew that reached him—touching and massaging that soft spot I knew he harbored inside the science. But at the same time I hated myself for letting it happen. No, *making* it happen. I didn't want sympathy from anyone—especially not from a man I really admired and whose respect I absolutely craved.

Without a word, he stood and put his arm around my shoulders, then squatted next to my chair. Still sobbing, I pushed my face into his armpit and sniffed and snuggled there. I felt all the angst and awfulness of my past two years fill me in an overflow of whimpers. I became a fountain of misery. In certain ways I think that moment was when I first felt how really bad my luck had been, the awful cards God had shuffled into my hands, and the near impossibility, except by a magnificent bluff, of winning anything good with them.

Mr. Santa squatted that way for a good fifteen minutes maybe half an hour—I don't know. He just let me moan against his chest and kept smoothing my hair back from my forehead and ear so that I could breathe and blubber a lot more easily. What can I say? He felt like Dad for those few moments, this strange older man who just wanted to give me warmth and strength—not grab my pussy. He didn't try groping, no gradual slide of fingers or hands to parts unknown. I imagine his knees must have hurt quite a bit after a while—him on his haunches next to the chair like that. But he didn't show any discomfort at all, just steady warmth and patience. I have to say I dug it immediately because it made me realize that Dad wasn't the only man I could count on for such demand-free affection, or even love.

"Look, Jamie," he said, when I finally started breathing like a human being again. "Let me talk to a few people this week; we'll see what we can do. I just don't want you to get scared out there, or hurt."

"I don't either," I said, sniffling. "If I can't use the boat cabin, the Pontiac will do the job. I want quiet—and gobs of solitude."

"You're a unique young girl." He squeezed my shoulders before rising to his feet. "But you have to find some way of connecting to people your own age. A Pontiac in the woods is not the way to do it."

"I'm not much interested in people my own age. I want some action, not just smart phones and hanging out."

He nodded slowly, and without another word went to the stove and ladled out some hot cereal for me. Then he poured a cup of black coffee for himself before sitting at the kitchen table. It was kind of a cozy moment, and of course I felt better about everything from that moment on. No thoughts of sub-zero, heatless nights, no fears about crazies invading my little campground and taking things away, no worries about anybody—crazy or cruel—wanting to do me any harm.

Looking back on all that now, I can't really say what was driving me. There were times when I thought of myself as an ostrich, a Caucasian-colored big bird with clothes and sneakers who, because of her fear of life's awful possibilities, wanted to bury her head in the sand to hide. I knew it left my ass vulnerable to attack, but I didn't want to know about it or see it. I just wanted to feel alone and safe whatever was really going on around me.

That week at school went terribly—slow, sorrowful, completely shallow as far as classes went—and I found myself arguing with other students, especially girls, just about every day. Again, I'm not sure why. I just felt that somehow everyone I met was phony and not to be trusted. What I wanted to trust them with—when all we were doing was sitting at the same lunch table, or in the same classroom, discussing the day's math homework—I can't tell you. But somehow I felt

233

myself hating them—again especially the girls—and to my surprise, wanting to hurt them, maybe because I thought they were leading such happy, perfect lives, while mine had just been torn apart. I held terrible cards; why shouldn't they?

The boys, especially the ones on the cross-country team, struck me in a slightly different way. I knew they were phony too, but I thought they felt much less proud of themselves because of their family lives. They seemed to realize there was some mistake—that, really, we all should be equal—at least if you were a boy. Was I wrong, or did they really see themselves as lucky rather than deserving, that the world was a mess, but they had somehow skipped the shit that splattered other people? It didn't matter, I guess, because I didn't get along very well with them either. Some cross-country guys were jealous when I outran them or even made them struggle, and guys who were not on the team thought I was butch—at best, not a very attractive girl. Basically, I didn't care what they thought of me—boys or girls—and so maybe Mr. Santa was right that night when he said it was just another set of walls I put around myself.

Walls . . .

Mr. Santa tried to knock them down while I stayed with him and, later, Misha tried to climb over them in his own nerdy Misha way. I never knew I had put up walls, but when I think about it now, I can't think of any other way to explain my thoughts or the way I behaved. In less than fourteen years I had experienced the loss of four parents, the cold-shoulder abandonment of Dad's fucked-up distant cousin, Charlie, and the good-natured, but self-centered interest of three sets of foster parents. And now Mr. Santa's genuine but awkward bachelor's care had to make up for everything—including my natural tendency to put on my shoes and run away.

I enjoyed his cooked cereal breakfasts, his meatloaf, and his emphasis on fresh fruit and vegetables over the sweet stuff. But I never felt at home, never came back from school thinking I belonged in his little stone house. Yet when I went to the park, walked through the trees to that little clearing beyond the huge rock, I felt myself inhale without any stress or effort. And when I sat in the car, I sensed every wall or hard surface inside me collapse. Wednesday of that week, I walked through wind and heavy rain to get there, and when I slid behind the wheel and closed the Pontiac's door, I spoke to myself out loud through the tinny patter on the roof and windows. "This is truly where I belong," I said. And with a deep sense of comfort and belonging, I took out a flashlight I had stashed in my backpack and started to do my homework.

***

XIV.

That was the start of my time living in the Pontiac. I didn't go back to Mr. Santa's that late afternoon, but I saw him trudging through the field and woods about six in the evening, and when he came around the rock and entered the clearing, he waved, but with a pretty serious—maybe pained—expression on his face. Again, I thought of running, but I didn't, and not because I figured he could catch me. As I looked at him, I realized that I liked him too much to make things worse. The yellow slicker he wore, the red fisherman's hat he propped on his head as if he was balancing it, and the controlled look of earnest care on his face made me feel I didn't want to cause any trouble. So, I sat there. I even opened the door to the passenger's side of the car and waved him in from the rain. "I'm wet already," I said. "You're not going to make things any worse."

He stopped, shook his body like a spaniel to get some water off, and then just slid into the car and closed the door. "Cozy," he said, without the slightest smile on his face. "Too bad you can't drive us home."

I giggled a bit at that, uneasy, I guess, because I didn't know what else to do. Then, without thinking, I took a big gulp of air and told him I was sorry that I didn't let him know where I was. "I should have called."

He just nodded, saying it was no problem. "I figured you'd be here," he told me. "And I'm glad you told me where to find it the other night. Otherwise police would have been on the lookout, and I would have felt like a blockhead if they found you right across the street from the station."

I shook my head and laughed. "So, what do you think?" I asked him.

He snorted, but clearly he had more to say. "At least it's dry—I'm not sure for how long with all this rusted metal."

"Mr. Santa, I want to live here. And no matter what you say or do, it's going to happen."

He took off his red fisherman's hat and held back his head, looking down at me along his wise, slightly hooked dark nose. "You know you're just fourteen, Jamie. You don't have much legal standing as a minor. Someone has to take you under control—assume responsibility—for your welfare."

"My dad's cousin and his lawyers sure as fuck didn't think so—not that I'd want that prick to control me. He doesn't care."

He looked through the windshield, took a long, deep breath, and said nothing. I could almost see the disgust building in his soul, but after his silent pause all he did was turn back to me and say nothing. Which scared me a little because I had never seen him at a loss for words before.

"Well . . . ?" I said. "Can I live here?"

"Jesus, Jamie! I'm working on it, believe it or not, but you have to stay with me until I get things correctly arranged. Maybe, and I mean just that, *maybe*, you can stay here for a while under certain rules and conditions. Those are what I'm working on right now."

"Conditions . . . what kind? I don't want anybody telling me what to do."

Again, he looked at me and shook his head. "Jamie, you have no power. None. The state could take your case over and force you into foster care. We don't let teenagers run around uncared for. Well, as little as possible, anyhow," he said.

"I could check in at school; I could come to your office whenever you want. My dad left me some money in my own bank account, so I can use that for food and clothes."

"Great. But we want you to be safe, we want you to be healthy, and we want you to think about your future—while having the means to do something good in it. College and whatever else. You're a bright girl—you should be able to do fine things."

"'Fine things'. . . I have no idea what that means. Husband, kids, house with a fence right near the school bus stop? I wouldn't know what to do in that situation."

"You're getting ahead of yourself, Jamie."

"Well, you're the one who's talking about my future."

"Because I'm thinking about potentialities—now. You're not going to sit in this car for the rest of your life."

That little comment stopped me in my tracks; no running away no matter how hard I tried. I had never really thought of my future before—not in practical terms. I had assumed Mum and Dad would take care of me until I grew up—whatever that meant. And I had no idea how to define growing up, except that somehow I'd be on my own, have some money, a home, maybe even a job and a family. Somehow I'd be equal to Mum and Dad and even get to the point of helping them out as they got older. But now? How could I even measure that while they were in the ground and some glacier-hearted cousin couldn't wait to get his nasty fingers on whatever Dad had left him? The Pontiac certainly wouldn't help, but neither would a mansion. It almost made me collapse into tears again when I thought about it, and so, once more, when Mr. Santa reached across the seat to put his arm around my shoulders and invite me to stay with him for a few more days, "to let the emotions settle," I just let all my sorrow and fear come out at once. I howled then blubbered like an infant—a one-year-old suddenly aware that she was lost and had no Mama to call for help. I felt pretty alone. And empty.

Mr. Santa said nothing—just hugged me after the invitation to stay with him—and probably, that was for the best. I couldn't hear above my own grief, and if I did, I would have been unable to make any sense of what he said. Bitterness filled my heart and seemed to hollow out everything inside me because I had no one to hate or blame for it. Two lives of good, innocent people erased in a very short time, and for me, any hope of adult support and example rested in this dripping wet stranger with a silly red hat sitting beside me in a moldy abandoned car rusting in the woods. Some fucking prospects.

"Well," he said, "I guess I should apologize for starting this." He pulled a handkerchief from his pocket and handed it to me. As I sniffled and blew into it, he took a quick glance at his phone and dialed a number. When no one answered, he canceled and sent out a text, probably to the same person. For about ten more minutes, we sat there listening to the rain on the Pontiac's roof mix with my occasional mumbles and moaning sighs. After the rain finally slowed down, we left the car and hiked back out of the woods, around the rock, and through the open field to the street. We crossed and went into the police parking lot to get into Mr. Santa's car.

"Home with me, if that's okay with you," he said. I nodded, grateful, but still a little resentful for sure.

"A foster home is a shit alternative," I said.

"A Pontiac is no better," he answered. "And despite everything, I think you know that."

I said nothing, just scrunched up in the corner of the seat, shoulder against the door, and looked out the window as we drove down Main Street toward his house. I certainly did think the Pontiac was better, and though I didn't say it that evening, I never really changed my mind. In about two weeks, Mr. Santa drove us back to the police station, introduced me to a couple of the officers, and then opened his car's trunk and helped me carry stuff to the Pontiac. I don't know what strings he pulled, whose permission he had got, or what office had to give the final approval, but from that day I lived in the Pontiac Bonneville, though my official address was his office, and I had to check in with him regularly and report on any problems. I could not miss school without calling him first; I had to eat breakfast and lunch in the school cafeteria; and I had to attend church dinners for the poor at least once a weekend. Plus, I had to walk across the street and wave to the desk sergeant every morning.

I hated all that stuff at first, but I must say I came around to appreciate it after about a week of dark and cold nights and days. With the money Dad had put into my account, the few dollars Mr. Santa managed to coax from the state welfare office, and his constant personal supervision of my daily situation, I actually did very well. I was scared every night for the first month or so, but nothing beyond weird animal sounds happened, and seeing a policeman or policewoman pass by at least once every afternoon gave me a lot of comfort. Nothing like having Mum and Dad around, of course, but I didn't feel so abandoned or alone. To tell the truth, it became annoying after a while, so I told Mr. Santa to ask the police to stop or cut back, and after another couple months they actually did.

Gradually, the whole town got used to it, I think—especially after a reporter from the local paper came to interview me and write a story for the Sunday issue. He called me the "Bonneville Girl" and really laid it on thick about Mum and Dad and the distant shit-faced cousin. Pretty soon people started bringing me things—blankets, clothes, cans and boxes of non-perishable food that I'd find on the roof or hood of the car when I came back from school. At first it made me laugh; then it made me angry. Then it made me cry because I realized that people actually liked what I was doing and wanted to help. Kids at school were a little different—less enthusiastic, maybe even jealous of the attention I got, and of the balls I had in living the way I chose. To my real surprise, it eventually became something everyone took for granted and actually stopped talking about. Food, clothes, and blankets stopped. Police kept me on their minds, probably, but not so much in their sights, and Mr. Santa, bless him, had to pay more attention to the hundreds of other cases he had in folders in his cabinet, so that when I saw him he had to drop a bunch

241

of them on his desk, raise his eyes, and refocus for several minutes before speaking to me.

Which, of course, opened the way for Coach Span to enter my life—and my car. I don't think of him as a predator, but I do think he had his eye on me since the day I passed him running on the track. At first I thought it was because he liked athletic girls, or girls who could run, because I thought maybe he'd like to coach a girls' cross country or their track team. And maybe I was right, but I doubt that I'll ever know. I do know that he had no hesitation in cooperating with Mr. Santa about attaching me to the boys' team as a helper and letting me work out with them every day. And it was his idea to start bringing me on team trips to meets in other towns—even a couple out of state. So, he definitely had some ideas, though I'm not sure what kind. He was perfectly proper on our trips and practices, and scrupulous as a homeroom teacher taking attendance. So I could never be late or miss roll call without a written note from Mr. Santa, and in school he made a point of calling me Miss Sasso whenever we talked.

But something different (maybe *amazing* is a better word) happened to me when we were together, especially whenever we talked alone. It was a strange feeling for me, maybe what they call chemistry—or electricity—between a man and a woman. Whatever it is, I felt it, hard. No bells clanging—but muscles tensing, boobs tingling, and I can't even describe the messages coming from my legs and in between. I kept shaking my hair away from my eyes, but for no obvious reason. At first I thought I was sick or just tired, but then I realized the feeling went away immediately when we stopped talking and turned to go in different directions. "Love?" I remember whispering to myself out loud as I went down the hall one school day afternoon. "Impossible. He's three times my age. He's married—I think happily—and he has a daughter. Geez . . . she could be my sister."

Yes, but . . .

"And I've been there for Thanksgiving dinner, for god's sake. He has a real life!"

So . . .?

So, none of that made any difference because I could not get him out of my head, and I could not think of him in any way but—I'll admit it—physically. Normally I'm not that kind of girl—I don't think dreamily of boys I want to sleep with; I'm not a groupie for any of the teenage heartthrobs in movies or on TV; and I don't collect pinups of muscular guys in thongs or cute ones twerking and singing on some local bandstand. If anything, I just think of Dad gracefully dancing with Mum to some Guy Lombardo tune in our living room on New Year's Eve, or Dad's voice crooning like Sinatra or Fred Astaire while he motored me to school in the morning before driving himself to work. It's all retro stuff, I know, but I liked it because it seemed to come from a time when people treated each other nicely, especially men and women, because they were raised to be polite rather than aggressive.

But in any case, here I was, walking down the school corridor with all kinds of jingle-jangle pulsing through my body just because he had smiled at me a few moments before and said hello. I had no idea how to express it, or handle it, so without thinking—that strangely beautiful morning—I just broke into a run down the hallway outside his homeroom, and when the math teacher saw me heading toward her classroom, she held up her hand and screamed, bringing me to a sudden halt, though I still had my head in the clouds. "Jamie Sasso! What are you doing? You know there's no running in the halls. Someone could get hurt."

I took two or three deep breaths as I tried to bring myself to earth, not because I was tired or scared, but because I wanted to keep my cool in front of the crowd of students behind her at the door. "I know," I said. "I couldn't stop myself."

To which one of the jerks gathered behind her shot back, "Why? Is somebody putting a buzz-buzz into your cute little put-put?"

They all laughed hilariously at that, of course, including an approving smile and giggle from the shrieking math teacher. Not to be outdone, I flipped them all the bird, spun on my heels and, ignoring the gasping chorus behind me, ran at full speed back toward the principal's office. Nobody stopped me this time, so I sprinted past the office, into the main vestibule, and through the front door out onto the school's front lawn. From there it was out to the street and down past the gym to the track, which I circled three or four times before turning back to school and facing everyone I didn't want to see, except, of course, Coach Span.

He stood at the front door, arm extended, palm out toward me, and when I slapped his hand he held on and walked me down to his office near the locker rooms. There we had a heart-to-heart about running, the cross-country team, respect for your teachers, and personal relationships—none of which seemed to enter my brain or my heart because I could not take my eyes off his face or the peculiar, insightful way his eyes kept studying me and the movement of my lips.

"Sorry," I told him when he reminded me to report to homeroom on time, which I had failed to do that day. "My head is not where it should be lately. I'm not sure why."

He laughed, sighing as he did. "Mine isn't either, Jamie. But somehow we'll have to work ourselves through it." He laughed again. "Charging down the hallway isn't an effective way to do it."

I nodded in agreement, and as the bell rang for next class, he waved his hand and told me to enjoy my classes.

Which I did, I guess, because all of this happened on the day I saw him after practice in the afternoon, waiting in his car on Main Street near the supermarket.

***

PART FIVE:

CROSS-COUNTRY

XV.

I've told you that my "real" mom and dad—sperm and egg providers, nothing more—abandoned me when I was born and somehow, through the magic of Catholic youth services, I ended up in Mum and Dad's lovely, loving hands. The full story's a bit more sinister, perhaps, but not that much. At least I don't think so until I talk about it with all its sick particulars. I don't know much about the sperm and egg part of it, of course, though I can't imagine it as having any more romance than a mutual collapse and embrace under a cloud of meth or heroine. "Mother" was famous, I am told—a genuine party girl with a history of few inhibitions or reluctances. She performed in porn movies—social workers have told me—turned occasional tricks for a "lot" of coin, and loved to pose nude for various local artists and photographers, especially ones she was pretty sure would put her portrait in some kind of gallery or show. "Father" was nothing more than a two-bit pimp and drug pusher who hooked her on the stuff and then joined her on the miserable descent to nothingness. Dad always talked about both of them, especially her, as a bit nutty, but in an artsy-craftsy way that would sometimes make her seem sad and, maybe because she was pretty, he said, excuse her in people's eyes. I wanted to meet her when I was very young, to ask how she could abandon me after bringing me into the world, and maybe also to see something of my own future self. Both Dad and Mum always assured me I'd be disappointed. There were things about her, they said, that were highly unattractive.

"Have you met her? Have you actually talked to her?" I asked them—many times.

They'd shake their heads, saying they were going by hearsay, but I must admit I never really believed them. Sometimes Dad would readily condemn my "mother" as a slut, but always with a very quick insistence (and Mum always emphasized it) that her behavior meant nothing for my own character. "You're your own person, Jamie," they said. "Anyone can see that."

Hmm. Don't know if I ever saw that myself, or ever will, but I took them at their word because I loved them very much and desperately wanted them to be proud. "If it wasn't for Mum," I used to tell Dad, "I'd marry you. No one else."

For Mum, my feelings were incredibly special. Beautiful in her own, slightly distant, way, she was like a loving older sister, or aunt, and I felt I could talk to her about anything without fear or judgement getting in the way. Sympathy—she had tons and tons of that, as I told Mr. Santa once—could have been her middle name. My birth was nothing, the circumstances unimportant, and my birth parents—those sperm and egg spillers, as we all called them—were just a physical convenience to get me where I was meant to be. "They must have really loved you," Mum often told me, "but knew they couldn't support you. So they gave you up, luckily, just as we came out searching for some family love to fill our lonely lives."

I never believed that part of the story either, but I do know that Mum and Dad had lost two children—one to an automobile accident, the other to illness—at a very

249

early age and for years had been trying to have another child. "It tore us apart," Dad used to say. But Mum would always deny it. "In a way, loneliness brought us closer together," she said, "as if something awful and powerful hung over us, ready to fall."

Then one night Mum, who used to work in an expensive Italian restaurant called Mario's, just outside of town, walked into the alleyway behind the kitchen to get some air during a slow dinner period in February and heard a baby's distant cry. It was very dark, she told me, with no moon, and although she looked around, she saw no one—certainly not a baby or a carriage. She went inside again, but it stayed slow, so after another couple of hours she left to go home, but this time heard the unmistakable wail of a baby as soon as she stepped out the back door. "Is this God calling?" she asked herself. In case it was, she searched up and down the alley for the source of the cries. After about fifteen minutes, maybe half an hour, she realized the sound came from the covered dumpster at the far end and ran toward it as the wailing took on a desperate, almost fatal, tone. She couldn't lift the lid herself, so she called the chef and a couple busboys. By the time Dad arrived to drive her home, she stood holding the baby in her arms before the open dumpster, which, she said, "with the lid hanging open, smelled like a sewer."

Dad would smile really brightly at this part of the story. "And in your mother's arms," he said, "was the sweetest piece of sewage she or I would ever know."

Those are exact words and believe me, cheesy or not, I was happy to hear them. I was especially happy after I learned that the birther of that piece of sewage was found completely stoned a few years later and charged with child abandonment—something that even she, in her stupor, must have felt some shame for. She pointed to a pimp who, she claimed to the police, may have been my father, but in all certainty helped her lift the dumpster lid and tossed in their bundled garbage so they could get on with more important business, whatever it was.

What that experience did to me—or for me—I have no idea, of course, because I have no memory of any of it—good or bad, stink or sweet, loving, tender, motherly hands supporting my back and head—or the putrid slime and stench I'd been thrown into. Dad always told me I had tomato sauce smeared on my lips and hands and a couple leaves of lettuce and parsley and a whole pile of asparagus peels settled inside my diaper. "At least you were diapered," he said, trying to be helpful.

My first live memory has nothing to do with Mum or Dad, at least not the human sight of them. Instead, it was a kind of motion or sound—a rocking, gliding sensation mixed with gentle, windy music I recognized sometime later as humming. Eventually I realized that hands, arms, and thighs were holding me and that the rocking motion came from them. I reached for the hands and arms, went beyond them to the wickerwork edge of the chair arm alongside, and then looked up to an open, humming, human mouth—Mum's.

That wasn't my first real sight or sound, I'm sure, but certainly the first I can recall. Mum's sweet mouth "calming the sea's mad rush" as Dad might have said—so much so that the peace and balance of this particular memory has washed over my entire life, urging me to search for it even while I thrashed about at school, or in the Pontiac lying back as if on a float and checking out the stars.

Dad would rock me in that chair too, but with a jauntier, simpler tune coming from his lips. He loved Tony Bennett and Sinatra ("'Come Fly with Me'" he said. "My own father sang that for me, Jamie."). But Dad also loved the mix of other singers from the sixties— Dylan, Peter, Paul, and Mary, and some of Judy Collins because he had seen her perform once and thought she had the "sweetest voice" he ever heard.

With all that, I could say that in a two- or three-hour passage of time surrounded by the dark and vegetable musk of Mario's (and other people's) garlic and onion-infused throwaways, I soared from abandoned flotsam to spoiled, yet super-appreciated beach treasure. At least that's the way I felt from the time I can remember anything. I did my best to return as much love as I received, but I suppose those sorts of equations are impossible to resolve. I know both Mum and Dad showed delight on seeing me, and their voices absolutely warbled with pleasure whenever they spoke my name. They took me everywhere, dressed me warmly in really colorful clothes that I loved, and spoke of me to everyone as a "happy gift from God"—with Mario's Restaurant being His fragrant, friendly UPS from heaven.

My childhood was wonderful, spoiled—I willingly admit—and intense with Mum and Dad always close, ready to explain, protect, promote, and especially, reward. Problem was it made me think everyone lived that way and that my life would continue in such a manner. But then I learned about people dying and, a few years afterward, felt the loss of my mother and then my father. Tossed right back into that alley dumpster—especially with dear cousin Charlie lifting and dumping as well—sending everything, especially me, sailing into some distant, contaminated sewer wash on the way to the sea. So, I wondered, what was God and his pungent, tomato-garlic flavored square of heaven doing to me after all—teasing?

Mr. Santa never liked to hear me talk like that. I should think more positively, he said, remember that my life was saved by an accident and an act of genuine human kindness. I have "very fine mental ability," as he described it, even with my dubious biological heritage. And he said, if I put my mind to it, I could achieve some "very important, very satisfying things." To be honest, that scared me when he said it, probably because it put all the responsibility for my future on my shoulders—no Mum and Dad, or anyone else, to guide me along. Wasn't I lucky to be abandoned on a slow night at Mario's? Even more lucky that Mum walked into the alleyway *twice* while I was crying? And that she and Dad desperately wanted a child to replace the two they had already lost? Yes, I have to say, but—here's a switcheroo—why was my good fortune someone else's awful luck—like the two kids who died too young?

None of this is pretty, as anyone can see, so why call it a sign from God?

"Faith is a mystery, Jamie, but you're replacing it with something else—maybe it's not so good."

I looked at him, genuinely puzzled. I knew I was a mess, but what could he be talking about? "What do you mean?" I said. "That maybe I have shit for brains?"

Mr. Santa smiled at that. "You're a survivor, Jamie, which is good. But you don't feel worthy of your life." I shook my head, not knowing what to say. "Who is worthy of it?" I should have said.

"You have to accept that some people win and some people don't. Things change, but you can't know how or when and certainly not even why. Your responsibility is to take your good fortune right now and do your best to fulfill it—for yourself and others in the future."

So, there I was, according to him, free of the Pontiac now—and out of the garbage—doing my best to run with my good fortune. Coach had changed my life and then left it (of course, Mr. Santa wouldn't know about that); the woods and their pleasant night sounds had disappeared with the rusted car and the trash in the alley behind Mario's—and here I was living with Mr. Santa and Jake, fumbling my way into a brighter, clearer existence. Well, maybe. I certainly had fun dancing and flirting with Misha at that time, but to me it had become a teenage fling, and we both knew it. He wanted us to be much, much more, but after a little talk he said he was cool with the way things were. Friends with some, but not all, the benefits. We won most of our dance competitions, at least at the county and state levels, but then we lost everything afterward. Some judges said our chosen music was too weird, while others said the dance we performed was too abstract. We didn't care. We danced for fun from that point on, and we both liked it better, although I got the feeling Mom and Pop Alto wished for more trophies. I was flattered by their compliments and the feeling that, to them, we actually made an interesting couple. More important, that I was good for Misha—good enough to be with him in a more than friendly way. Maybe I did have something to offer, I often thought, but in certain ways I saw that Mr. and Mrs. A really wanted our dancing partnership to bring out something different from their quiet son. "Confidence, maybe even a deeper sense of fun," Mrs. Alto told me once. But honestly, I think Misha felt happy just being close to someone his own age, a BFF he could share cool music and family stories with, accompany to the movies, and—let's admit it—enjoy some friendly, not particularly committed foreplay sex.

We went to downtown New York dance clubs by ourselves a couple of times, then once or twice with his parents. It was interesting to see Mr. Alto's moves on the dance floor—never quite with the funky beat, but always heading toward it, as if it were an ever-receding lifetime goal. Misha and I also attended nearby university parties (he didn't smoke or drink; I occasionally did), and during my junior year went to every high school bash and two or three local YMCA teenagers' nights out.

We spent frequent evenings alone in the Alto basement where the foreplay sex gave some friendly playtime to his small, round butt and my hapless boobs, as well as challenging his strong arms and eager dick. We never got completely naked, just partially if at all, mainly because Misha was so timid. Though I felt sure Mom and Pop were trying to be extra tolerant—perhaps to let their sheltered boy enjoy a bit more lived experience—he worried about every sound coming from upstairs, fearing that the Altos would come down to chat or see how we were dancing, Some nights, we'd drive past the school in his car and pull into the woods across from the police station to make out for a while near my empty Bonneville space. But I became so swept up in memories (most of them good), that I'm afraid I showed little interest in him or his friendly body. We'd usually end up frustrated after half an hour, driving away with nothing more than a few semi-passionate kisses and some awkward groping that had more obligation in it than biology.

We were a known and obvious couple for a while, but nothing beyond that. Despite Mr. Santa, I couldn't see myself as his sister, as I'm sure Misha would have accepted—or as his lover, as I'm pretty sure he wanted. The only real question for me in all this concerned Mr. and Mrs. Alto. I mean I knew what they would have liked—at least I was pretty sure about it, given Mr. Santa's comments—but I had no idea how long they would tolerate someone like me. I had tons of rough edges, I admit; I didn't have one tenth of the knowledge they had passed on to Misha from his infancy, and in a certain sense I'm not sure I even wanted it. I'm a female jock, I'd tell Mr. Santa. I love movement and competition, have little taste in music— except for Dad's old-fashioned, cheesy stuff (still love it)—and adored Mum's homey affection (which I didn't feel at all when I talked to Mr. and Mrs. Alto). Sure, they told me nice, positive things; I learned a lot from their comments on our dances and the music and paintings they liked. And though Mr. Alto could be a bit of a bore sometimes, I never doubted that he meant well when he started one of his personal lectures or reminiscences.

During one night's after-dinner discussion at his house, I told Mr. Santa to cancel his Jamie Alto dreams and think of me as an abandoned girl without a family. He didn't like it, but as a social worker, he simply nodded, raised his hand as if to wave away an unpleasant or unimportant subject, and then moved on to another topic. I lived with him for most of my junior year, kept dancing with Misha and spending time down in his basement. But we necked less and less as time went by, probably out of a sense of going nowhere fast, and then one warm summer night, when we were dancing at one of our Y teenagers' nights out, I met a guy named Thomas, or Tomaso, as he liked to call himself— someone, out of nowhere, who I thought would help me change my life.

***

I don't even know how to begin describing him. Let's just say that when I looked at him and caught his eyes staring at me, there was a flash—a very strong current that went right to my belly and rapidly slid down to my hips, my thighs, and my legs. I felt like running— but toward him, not away; and I'm pretty sure I never felt that way about anyone before—or since. When I look at him now—at his picture, anyhow—I laugh because there is nothing obviously spectacular about him: a kind of droopy, oily hairline that meanders over his sleepy eyes as if it doesn't know where it's headed and, more than that, isn't quite sure if it has the energy to get there. He was thin, about the same height as Misha

257

but because he was so slim, he seemed a lot smaller, but a lot wirier, which I suppose is why I always think of him as magnetic—someone who drew me in immediately.

That night at the Y he came toward me, slipping through a crowd of dancers as if he lacked physical substance and, like the music they were playing, could be everywhere at once and at the same time move an individual—at least this one—in her very most private self. Sounds a little "woo, woo," I know, but he affected me that way. And when he stood behind Misha, tapped him on the shoulder and whispered in his ear, I stepped between them without hesitation, turning my back on my best friend as if I didn't know him. Shame on me, I thought. But Thomas flashed his toothy, everybody's welcome grin, reached his boney hands out toward mine, and then turned us completely around so I could see over his shoulder as Misha stood for a second, caught the look on my face (I think I was blushing, but I'm not sure why), and walked off the dancefloor—head down, shoulders slumped as if we would never see each other again.

Thomas took me home to Mr. Santa's late that night, after a stop at the Sugar Bowl, where we sang Lady Gaga songs with the group that filled the place, and then drove to my Bonneville's empty spot in the woods across from the police station. I did not see the stars or hear the music of the wind through the trees that night. His hands and dick were a lot more friendly and twinkling in the back seat than the actual sky above us, and my boobs did not feel the least bit pathetic when he touched them and began to remove my shirt. I held him back, of course, but with each kiss and every brush of his lips against my skin I realized how much I was faking. So, off with his shirt, down with my jeans—and in less than a minute I was on top of him and doing things that even Mr. Span didn't know that I would, or could, possibly do.

I have no idea what was so cool about this guy— Tomaso. Droopy-eyed and brown-haired with an oily sheen to his skin, he had an ordinary singing voice—a high baritone, I noticed—but nothing really special except the glow in his eyes when he looked at me and a sly, even smile, as if he knew at first glance that I would be an easy backseat bedfellow. I had never thought of myself as easy before, but Thomas certainly sliced through something vulnerable in me, especially after that quick knowing glance across the Y dancefloor. He wasn't a student in school, but a friend of several, including one or two guys on the cross-country team. He had dropped out of school in his junior year, deciding to work and make some money to have more freedom— car, cool clothes, and, as he liked to describe it, "real Pennsylvania corn", which is how he referred to the marijuana he regularly sold.

You could call Thomas a pusher—and say I was following in my dear birth mother's malignant footsteps—but he was not the really awful kind. He sold weed and nothing else—and he liked growing and harvesting the stuff himself, seeding it in colorful planter boxes hanging on the inside edge of his sunny apartment windows. He searched for exotic seeds that were "medicinal," as he put it, checking with underground marketers he knew from Philadelphia and New York. He didn't have a lot of money, but he gave a part of whatever he earned each month to politicians who supported legalization—and he went into the street and campaigned for them each time they set up for election. "Healthier than alcohol and tobacco," Tomaso always said. "Some of the strains can take away pain, maybe even cure some things—like migraines."

Most kids at the school knew him and agreed, though I never cared much about it myself, because— one, I always doubted the opinions I heard at school, especially when almost everybody said the same thing; and two, I did not want to risk my brain for a drug because my mind was my principal survival tool now that Mum and Dad were gone. Cross-country runners joked about smoking and seeing weed all the time, pretending it grew wild along the paths we followed in afternoon practices. Girls often talked about it too, and many dance teams Misha and I competed against throughout the state claimed it was part of their warmup and relaxation for a competition. We refused to use it ourselves. Misha followed his dad in thinking the mind had to be fresh and clear for any type of challenge, and I, well, as I just said, I wanted to survive the mess I was born into.

So, with all that, Tomaso was just some ordinary skinny guy who got to my groin because of something, maybe magical, I can't define. He could dance as well as Misha, at least in ordinary dances, though for sure he depended on the girl to make him look good. His movement was ordinary, not at all creative, but I'll be fucked if I didn't just love performing the most boring copy-cat stuff with him because, somehow, maybe on account of his loose, flexible limbs and always-confident smile, he seemed spectacularly smooth. When he swung you around and led you to whatever music moved him, he could make you feel, if not look, like a genuine princess. I know I made him look good too. Skinny and loose-limbed as I am, my body just naturally complemented his—and maybe that's what interested him in me as a partner. At the Sugar Bowl that first night, he told me he loved the way we sounded together—"sweet, mellow on one side, twangy and strange on the other"—and he said the dancing was really special, "like a pair of angels, on a very fluttery, cumulus cloud."

I saw him regularly after that dance, almost every night for a few weeks, even during school. Misha accepted it with his head hung down to his chest, and gentle Mr. Santa never mentioned the frequent pickups and late-night returns—though I could see he worried and wanted to. One night he was reading in the living room when I said goodnight to Thomas, and he put the book down immediately when I walked in and closed the front door. He looked at me for a long silent time as I took off my coat and hung it in the closet, nodding as I passed him and started for the bathroom to brush my teeth.

"How serious is this, Jamie?" he asked, finally.

I shrugged and said nothing. To tell the truth, I had no idea if "this" was serious at all. I had the hots, I knew, but I didn't know what for—why was I so hot for Thomas and not Misha, for example (still don't). Yet there I was every afternoon waiting for him to call, eager for him to ask to see me, then more eager to drive to the woods, climb into the backseat of his car, and start pulling off his clothes. We did not do drugs—at least I didn't—we did not even smoke weed in the beginning. Again, at least I didn't. But I sure as hell inhaled it in the air in the back of the car when we huffed and puffed against each other. And I can tell you that, even with the windows open, the stuff he smoked packed a very strong punch—much more than medicinal. It was so strong that once or twice I went blank from breathing it and remembered absolutely nothing about what we had just done in the lingering aftermath on his backseat.

I felt happy, giddy, confident that what we had just done, ordinary as it usually is, had to have been magnificent—probably more than magnificent. So when Mr. Santa asked if "this" was serious, I could only shrug and laugh—a snide teenage snort and giggle that could only offend and, maybe, embarrass a man as caring and careful as he was. He asked me to come into the living room and join him for a bit, and though I had nothing but a silly, teenage reaction to the situation, I could not say no. I went into the bathroom first, did nothing but flush the toilet and run some water, then came out and flopped onto the living room couch across from him, folding my feet under me after removing my shoes. I nodded again and settled my hands in my lap.

"What?" I said, after a pretty lengthy silence. Now it was his turn to shrug and let the heavy moment weigh on us. We stared at each other for a few minutes, him with a book in his lap (*Portrait of the Artist as a Young Man,* I noticed), me with my reddened, sweaty hands and the smell of backseat sex and weed rising all around.

"I'm not your guardian," he said. "I have no familial rights or responsibilities over you, but I have a moral one—and I have to admit that, as your friend, I'm more than a little worried about what is happening in your life. This boy Thomas is a bit strange for you, isn't he?"

"Mr. Santa, they're all strange for me. Nobody likes me, as you obviously know. Even our buddy Misha is unusual."

He looked at me, "scrutinized" me really, because he liked Misha a lot and thought (or still hoped) the Altos would be important in my future. Of course, school was important too. But that night, and during all of those bright, Tomaso-addled nights of the past couple weeks, Misha, Mr. and Mrs. Alto, and school stood far away from my mind, along with any vague, impulsive thought I hoarded about my next few years. For me everything was NOW, and then the next NOW, and then the next one after that—all of which only occurred on the dancefloor or in the back of Thomas's smoke-filled BMW.

"Are you at least keeping up with school work?" Mr. Santa asked. "As you know, that's part of the agreement for you staying here."

I shrugged and snorted yet again, but something inside told me I shouldn't hide anything from this generous man. I had gone to church too often with him, heard him defend me to school and town officials, and smiled in relief when I saw his face and head peek around the rock where the Pontiac had been, especially when he walked straight to the car after I waved.

"I'm doing my best," I lied, looking at my feet while sitting on his couch. "But I admit I've been pretty distracted lately."

"You've always been distracted—that's been your life, as I understand it—but you've always . . ."

I lifted my hand and stopped him. "I know, Mr. Santa, and I admit it's not happening right now. But this stuff is very, very strange—even to me."

His eyes narrowed, as if to squint and read my face. "I can smell that stuff, you know. Your clothes reek when you come into the house. Is that the strangeness you're talking about?"

Of course, I thought he meant the smell of sex at first, but then I realized it was something else.

"I'm not using, if that's what you mean. Tomaso, I mean Thomas, is. But it's nothing serious—only MJ."

I stopped when I saw him shake his head and look down at the floor. Except with cousin Charlie I had never seen Mr. Santa angry, never even heard him raise his voice—certainly not with me or Jake—so that little shake and the compressed lips broke through my thick post-Tomaso haze. "Not that I think it's right to do that," I said. "It's better than drinking."

He nodded, but again said nothing. We sat there brooding for a good ten minutes or more— just staring at each other while an occasional car wheeled down the street, engine racing, its lights brightening the shaded windows though they left the two of us retreating into the gloomy lamp glow behind him.

"Well," he said, closing the novel in his lap, "I think it's time I went to bed."

He placed the book on an end table and, with a nod toward me, began to leave the room. For some reason, despite his quiet, gentle tone, my heart pounded, and I leaped to my feet and beat him to the doorway, where I stood facing him with my hands in front of my chest. I couldn't imagine what to say, but at the same time I didn't want to disappoint him. He had seen me at my saddest after Dad died; he had supported me during my troubles with Mr. Span and the team at school—and, in some strange way, with the trips to mass, the visits to the Pontiac, and the simple, laidback process of allowing me to live with him and Jake and maintain my sense of freedom at the same time, he had dug into my heart and planted something fresh and rewarding there. I didn't want to kill it.

"I'm sorry," I said. "I mean it. I know this isn't the way I'm intended to go."

"None of us is, Jamie, but especially not you." With that, he nodded once more, passed by me, and started up the stairs to his room.

***

Fred Misurella

PART SIX:

SOMETHING YOU SOMEHOW DESERVE

XVI.

I spent the next week without seeing Thomas. I let my phone ring when he called, and on the days he passed me on the street and stopped to talk, I blew him off, telling him I had track practice to attend and too much schoolwork to catch up on. He flashed me his confident Tomaso grin, hunched up his shoulders, and stepped on the BMW's gas pedal, leaving a short track and the smell of burning rubber as he sped down the street toward the park.

"Never a policeman there when you need them," somebody grumbled beside me one day. I looked up and saw the dancer, Ciara, from the Cedars of Lebanon, smiling. "He a friend of yours?"

I waved my hand and started walking. Ciara took my elbow and pulled me back toward the Cedars entrance for a moment. "Come on in. Have a coffee or a sandwich. You look like you need to talk."

In fact, I didn't feel like talking, or eating, but she insisted, and I ended up having both because she made coffee and a sandwich without asking and then brought them to the table and sat down for a conversation. She didn't have to dance until that night, she told me.

"What happened to that nice guy you used to hang with—what's his name?"

"You mean Misha? I don't know, probably studying somewhere. He always does."

"Did you drop him? He seemed to really care about you."

I shrugged. I didn't know what to say about Misha and me at that time—certainly not anything that would make sense to a near stranger. I still hadn't figured out if we were family or something more complicated. His parents were always around, and the boyfriend-lover part seemed too cloudy—scary too—because of the lack of clear definition. There were times when I thought we ought to fuck just to see how disgusting it would feel, but then the risk of losing him as a friend forever because of sex always loomed. I had no idea if I could handle that.

Ciara tapped me on the wrist. "You know, Thomas—or Tomaso, as he sometimes calls himself—won't care for you that way," she said. Surprised that she knew his name, I looked up at her. "He comes in here with different girls all the time," she told me. "He's trying to get the boss to set up a hookah room for people to smoke in, and when they legalize his stuff, as he expects, well . . . you can guess the rest from there."

I laughed. "He'll make a million, I bet."

"He's a hustler," Ciara said, nodding. "No doubt about that. But don't get caught up in his plans. He thinks he's going to be rich, and he works at it. Always. You'll just be part of his famous ride to the top."

"It could be worse," I said. "He can be sweet."

"Oh, honey. Don't kid yourself. He's all out for himself and his wallet. I've seen it with the girls he brings in here, and with the way he talks to me and the boss. He thinks he's 'The Man.'"

I nodded. I could see she was probably right, just as I could see that Mr. Santa was right the night he talked to me about Thomas. What I couldn't see was

269

why none of that seemed to matter to me when I thought about us in the back of his shiny BMW—no matter how loud the tires screeched and squealed, and the engine smoked—inside me. "Well, I'm putting him off," I said, "for now."

Ciara nodded, reaching across the table to grab both my hands. "Keep doing it, honey. Go see your guy—Misha. Bring him in here some night for a meal. My treat. I'll dance for you too, if you want. If Tomaso sees him with you, he'll know you have other options."

"Tomaso, eh?" I nodded and said I would. Ciara let go of my wrists with a great big sigh. She leaned back in the chair and looked out the window to watch the traffic in the street. I felt glad for her interest, but I wasn't sure about anything at that moment—especially with Misha. At times like these, I really missed Mum and Dad. I could have talked to either of them about this situation—about Thomas and Misha, or anything else. They would have understood and probably would've given advice that I could trust and follow. But, of course, I wouldn't have had the problem if they were still here because Thomas would not be in my life, and Misha would just be a friendly, pretty good-looking high school boy—not a potential brother.

When I got home at Mr. Santa's that night, I texted Misha to ask how he was doing. After the usual meaningless chatter—"nothing," "homework," "when are we going to dance again?"—I told him that Ciara had invited us to the Cedars of Lebanon for a free dinner some night, and he stopped texting, calling immediately to talk about it. When I convinced him that the invitation was genuine, he agreed to go and suggested we do it on

the following Friday night. He would borrow his
mother's car, he said, and pick me up at Mr. Santa's
around six.

"Pick me up at the gym—earlier," I said. "I can
shower there. We can go to the Cedars from the gym and
maybe go dancing at the Y afterward." He thought that
was a good idea and said he would see me in two days,
after cross-country practice.

Two pretty happy days followed. No fights or
insults in school, decent practices with none of the guys
getting on my case when I kept up with them each day
and actually beat the whole team in a half mile sprint at
dusk on Friday (Time: 2:15; "Damn good," Mr. Span
said, and I was really happy he didn't add "for a girl.")

So I went to the locker room satisfied, took my
shower, and changed into a really nice black dress with a
short skirt—it showed off my legs and made my boobs
look as if they were a modest, but hidden treasure
beneath the fabric. Mrs. Alto had bought it for me about
a month before. She said I needed something basic and
attractive to go out in, and I was happy that its first
actual use came on a date with her son. Misha, as was his
usual habit, underdressed; he wore nothing fancy but
sported a very nice button-down ice blue shirt that
floated above his shiny chinos and showed off his sweet
bottom cheeks as if they were a ripe peach wrapped in
bright manila paper. He also had a blue blazer that I saw
as I got into the car—he had tossed neatly onto the back
seat.

"So," he said, "free dinner and then a dance.
Good deal. Thanks for inviting me. I'm looking forward
to it."

"Well, we know what the dinner will be like. I hope the dancing will be really special. I mean Ciara's, not ours."

Misha nodded, saying he was sure it would be fine. He started the car, heading toward Main Street and then turning left to get to Cedars. He parked across from the restaurant and actually came around to my side of the car to open the door and politely help me out, making me wonder if it was the dress he liked, the dinner we were about to eat, or something else. He actually held my hand as we crossed the street, and for a few steps I couldn't help but think of Mum and Dad and how they walked together—hands intertwined, whenever they went out. As you can imagine, at that moment Misha was more than just a friend, but of course I still didn't know what type of special he could be. Anyhow, for fun, I stepped close and let him feel the brush of my dress against his arm, a brush with no flesh in it—just cloth and the promise of a warmer something more. He looked at me and smiled.

We entered Cedars, took a seat near the window, and waited for Ciara to come out and greet us. Instead, the owner, Ahmad, came out of the kitchen in a white apron and gave us menus and a couple of special recommendations. I asked if Ciara was around, and he said she was in the back getting ready to do her number. "She invited us," I told him. "I hope we get a chance to talk after she dances."

Ahmad winked and nodded. "Don't worry. She'll come out. I encourage her to talk to all the diners."

The room was small and full right then—about fifteen tables with two or more people sitting at each one. There was a little space near the kitchen door with a couple of speakers on the wall behind it and a set of lights in the ceiling above. I had never seen a belly dancer before, except in a movie or two I probably saw with Mum and Dad, and so I was interested in what Ciara would do. Obviously sex had something to do with it because the dancers usually show a lot of skin, but I dimly remembered Mum telling me once that the belly dance was really about birth, not conception. "Women had to loosen themselves up, be ready to give birth— even while working in the fields. The belly moves are not about the penis. They're about celebrating— preparing to bring another human soul onto the earth."

That kind of talk struck me as a little scary when I was very young, but now it seemed kind of obvious and tame. Was it my maturity? I doubt it. More likely a year and more living alone inside a Pontiac in the woods made me a little harder—able to see more clearly that no matter how much we looked up to the stars, reality was pretty much tied to the ground we walked on, the soil we ultimately burrowed back into when all the stargazing finished.

Soon the music—which had remained in the background as Misha and I studied the menus and tried to remember what Ahmed had recommended—became louder, filling the room and taking our attention away from the food. It was some kind of loud, bowed-string instrument backed by a rapid, tapping drumbeat. As the music swelled, everyone looked toward the kitchen door. The space before it suddenly brightened with flashing multi-colored lights, and the door swung open as the music boomed—a moaning, searing groan and the drone

273

of the muffled staccato drumbeat seemed to urge everyone to hurry because time and life were fleeting.

It was strange, but also moving. Ciara glided out the door with hands and fingers snapping above her head, her bare legs and feet sliding along the floor, and her soft midriff undulating so that the glass jewel near her bellybutton shimmered like a ruby in the lights.

Misha and I laughed and clapped at the same time as the whole room seemed to fill with her presence. More than anything else, it seemed funny at first, and I had a hard time keeping a straight face. Ciara worked her way through and around all the tables, leaning close to the men, letting her haltered boobs brush the back of their heads and her arms and legs surround them as if they formed a web. She came to our table last, smiling at both of us and standing between us as she spun the net around Misha and wiggled her ass and thighs at me. Pretty silly stuff. I could smell sweat and perfume on her, and I felt a kind of shock at the overall tackiness of her movements, along with admiration that she could transform herself without embarrassment. She was nothing like the sisterly woman who had taken my arm on the street just a few days before, inviting me into Cedars for a sandwich and some talk.

She circled away from us after a few minutes, then danced back to the space by the kitchen door. The music sped up and just about gushed around us, forcing Ciara into a sort of earthy bump and grind that was not sexual at all—as if she were a tree or bush undulating in a fiercely dangerous whirlwind. Her hands and arms swept and swirled above her head, her legs bent and kicked as if she wanted to root herself, and yet her hips and stomach shimmied as if they wanted to shake themselves free. I had no idea what any of it meant, but I certainly saw how the dance could be about birth as well as sex and, maybe, something else—a moving attempt to bring together earth and sky. I looked at Misha and saw him staring as if this was totally new and very profound for him too. He grinned, shaking his head and clapping his hands along with the tiny cymbals on Ciara's fingers. Clearly, he was fully into it, and for a moment I thought he looked ready to get up and dance with her.

But then Ahmed slipped out the kitchen door and, with chef's hat and white kitchen jacket still on his thick body, danced along with her, grinning and snapping his fingers as the two of them circled each other and intertwined arms, legs, and hands. He was a lot older than her, I saw, probably in his forties or even fifties, but the music gave him energy and seemed to bring them closer, making them a pair. When it abruptly stopped and everyone in the room applauded at once, Ciara let out a yelp, wrapped her arms and legs around his middle, and planted a kiss on his smiling lips.

"I feel like we're at a wedding," Misha said, laughing. "That's a dad dancing with his daughter before giving her away."

"Kissing like that?"

I looked at them and shook my head, but at the same time I felt a very strange sensation—as if Misha was saying something about me rather than Ciara. For a long nanosecond I remembered this image of Coach and me in a motel room mirror, not with anything terribly raunchy going on, but the two of us wrapping arms and legs around each other and looking terribly in love. I remember wondering if he still embraced his wife with the same emotion and then decided he couldn't—not if he was doing it with me. But for the moment in the Cedars, I was back to wondering.

I tossed it away, however, looking at Misha and just shrugging my shoulders as we applauded. Ciara did a final shimmy shake with her bangles and, walking backwards, she and Ahmed bowed to the crowd before turning and entering the kitchen. We sat in silence for a few minutes—me thinking of Coach, Misha somewhere in Misha-land—both of us just glancing around the room and trying to find something cool to talk about. At least I was, but I must say nothing came. Most people were eating while two or three were studying menus, just as we were. Ahmed came out again and walked from table to table with a pad in his hand to ask what people wanted. A few minutes later, Ciara, out of her costume now, came to our table to take our orders. With a false smile I lied and told her that the dance was really cool, which I guess it was in an unusual way, though I felt cheap and even a little dirty saying it. Misha relieved me by commenting on the "classic" sound of the music and asking how much of their dance was traditional and how much was original.

"It's all improvisational," Ciara said, with a big smile on her face. "But it's all based on traditional tropes—woman wants; man wants woman; babies arrive."

She laughed, thanking us for coming, and then dropped a couple coupons on the table. Without another word, she took our orders and returned to the kitchen. It was a tough few minutes after that, I guess because I wanted to like her performance more. But I soon got over it because, as Misha and I stared at each other and waited for our food, the street door opened, and we saw Thomas walk in behind a very lovely young woman with long, flowing red hair. "Wow!" No one actually said that, but as the girl walked in, you could feel the collective breath being sucked right out of the room. She wore a tiny black dress, just like mine—believe it or not. But I'm pretty damn sure nobody looked when I walked in—they kept studying their menus. I have to admit Thomas's friend made it all look very different— fantastic, in fact. Suddenly, I felt awkward, as if I was a little child trying too hard to look womanly—a very sexy womanly—so I shrank down in my chair when I saw her, and tried to disappear.

"Hey, Legs," Thomas called. He came right up to our table, holding the redhead's hand. He smiled at Misha, then bent down to give me a friendly, brotherly kiss on the cheek. My uneasy silence turned to tension immediately because I pulled my head back in defense, and, though I didn't consider Misha or Thomas as fighting types, I sensed the beginning of some *mano a mano* conflict. I glanced at Misha and met his blank stare with as much of an apology in my eyes as I could muster. Luckily, Ciara came out of the kitchen with our food at that moment and, with a brief nod to Thomas, stepped in front of him to put down a couple of plates of falafel and salad along with long glasses of sweetened iced tea. "Let me know if you need anything else," she said, stepping in front of the redhead at that point, and excusing herself to us all.

Thomas shrugged and turned away. "Enjoy your meal. We have a party coming later for dinner." He winked at me, then knocked on the kitchen door and opened it, letting the redhead go in before him.

"Well, I guess he's somebody special," Misha said.

Embarrassed, I didn't know what to say, so, as usual, I said nothing. With Thomas, you could see he walked in a different ecosystem—one with a couple spots of oil to slip over and some pissy-colored vapor polluting the atmosphere. So, I shrugged and, to my relief, Misha didn't pursue the topic. He unfolded the napkin in his lap and started eating. We each stuffed the falafel into our pita pocket, piled on some salad and bit into it immediately. After a couple of chews, I dropped the sandwich onto my plate and drank some cold tea.

"You're not hungry?" Misha said.

"Not really. I ate here a few days ago. I think I'm more interested in the dancing."

He nodded, taking a huge bite of the falafel as the pita basically crumbled in his hands. Laughing, he held up his fingers, now dripping with sauce, as if the sandwich had disappeared. "I guess I'm more interested in the dancing too," he said. "But at the Y."

So, to be polite, we drank our teas and talked. We ordered some deep-fried ice cream for dessert, and after we ate that we decided to leave. Groups of gaudily dressed people—about fifteen couples in all—entered as we thanked Ciara and left a small tip. They went immediately to whatever event Thomas had set up in the back room, where Ciara would dance again in about thirty minutes, she told us. Neither of us wanted to see any more—especially among those who had just entered—so we left.

***

It was an awkward night in lots of ways. We drove to the Y, danced in the old gym there, and, after about ten or twelve numbers, we saw Thomas come into the room with one or two of the other couples from the Cedars. After paying an entrance fee for all of them, he immediately came over with the redhead trailing behind him and introduced her to me and Misha. Her name was Casey. She had just moved into town with her family and planned to tend bar while attending college in the next town over. Business Management, she said. Misha nodded, mentioned that his mother and father occasionally taught art classes there, and both Thomas and Casey said they would like to meet them. I offered nothing about my own life, of course, except that I attended the local high school and ran with the track team. And yes, as always in recent years, I felt a hole in my gut because I had no family or home to speak of. In many ways, I think I still lived in that Pontiac in the woods.

We danced to about a dozen more numbers, and then the DJ announced the final one for the night. Thomas proposed we drive to a club in the next town and dance a little longer—he said it was open until dawn. Misha and I looked at one another with an unspoken "no" in our eyes, and said we'd just go home. Thomas grinned, said we could do it another time, and took Casey's hand and left with the other couples. We went for pizza at Jimmy's—which we knew would be

open on a Friday night—and when we got there were
surprised to see Thomas and Casey there too. "Best pizza
in town," Thomas said, as we walked toward the counter
to order from Jimmy. "You guys have good taste."

Jimmy smiled. He was busily checking the crust
of a pie in the oven, but he turned around and gave us a
double thumbs up. "They have good taste, Tomaso—at
least I know this guy does." He high-fived Misha,
although to me Misha looked like he'd rather hide in the
corner than slap Jimmy's hand at that moment.

"The usual?" Jimmy asked. Misha nodded and
walked to the soda cooler to get us a drink. He pulled
out a couple Snapple bottles, and went to a table
completely across the room from Thomas and Casey. It
was up near the window at the front, just under the big
red "Jimmy's" neon sign. I followed him, and we sat
with our backs to the room, though it seemed to me
Misha would rather have left Jimmy's all together. "I
don't like that guy," he whispered to me. I told him I
didn't especially like him either, which I guess was sort
of a lie. But we decided to stay out of consideration for
Jimmy.

"How well do you know him?" Misha asked. He
gave me a disgusted kind of grin. "'Tomaso . . .' I don't
see him as your type of guy."

I shook my head. "He isn't." Which I guess
you'd say was another lie, though at the time it sure felt
like the honest truth. I told Misha I had danced with
Thomas a few times at some Y dances, but of course I
didn't go near those sessions in the back of his BMW.
Even now I can't explain them; I think I was just ready
to do some crazy stuff because I felt lonely and tired of

being scared. I couldn't see myself staying with Mr. Santa much longer, I didn't want to go back into foster care—with the Altos or anyone else—and for a few days I thought Thomas might be a decent substitute. I secretly batted that around in my head again that night until Jimmy told us our pie was done. I left the table and, using a pizza board Jimmy gave me, carried the pie along with some napkins back to our seats. As I did, I glanced over at Thomas and Casey and saw them eating a couple *calzoni* with knives and forks. Thomas winked at me, raised his fork, and called out *"Buon apetito"* with a terrible accent that I'm sure he thought was cool. Jimmy laughed and smiled with a resigned look on his face. "Hope you guys like it," he whispered across to us.

I set the pie down on the table and immediately began to tear apart the slices. We each took one and started to eat without talking. Then, in the middle of all that, I heard Thomas call out to us before walking across the room toward our table. He stopped beside Misha and patted him on the shoulder. To my surprise, Misha didn't budge—didn't even acknowledge the tap on his shoulder. Thomas sat on the chair next to him and basically put his face in front of Misha's. "Still have that hot SUV?" he said, without smiling. "What is it, a Nissan?"

Misha straightened his head as if surprised, pulled back, and, while looking at Thomas, chewed thoughtfully on the pizza. I was trying to figure what this was all about, when Thomas rapped his knuckles on the table and said, loud enough for the whole room, "I'll give you a half block head start and race you down Main—from here to the park, just before the police station. If I don't pass you, I'll pay for your pizza and drinks. Even if it's just a tie."

Misha looked out the window in wonder and shook his head. "You're serious?" he asked.

"Absolutely."

When he saw Thomas's determined look, he shook his head again. "It's not my car. It's my Mom's," he said.

Thomas waved his hand. "There's no traffic tonight. Nobody will get hurt. You're just racing—the car will be fine. How about a whole block lead?"

"Jesus, what's with you?" Misha said. "I'll pay for your meal, if you need the money."

Thomas reached into his pants pocket and pulled out a roll of bills. A big fat hundred lay on top. He winked at me, then opened the roll and counted some of the bills out. I saw at least a couple more hundreds, and a few other numbers I had never seen for real on a bill in my life.

"Money's not the point," Thomas said. "I want a challenge. I need one."

Misha took a big final bite of pizza and shook his head. "Sorry. I don't race, especially cars. And it's for sure I'm not going to race my mother's."

Thomas's grin broadened as he looked at me, then back to Misha. "Afraid, heh?"

Misha took a deep breath, dropped the crust onto his plate, and shook his head once more. "I don't race cars, so forget it."

Thomas stood and went back to his table without pushing in his chair. Misha turned to me with a dull look on his face. I put my hand on his arm to show him I was on his side, and then, without even thinking, I turned to Thomas, who stood at the counter, using that roll to pay Jimmy for food and drinks. Ours too, I heard him tell Jimmy.

"Hey, Tomaso. You want a challenge, so you can impress Casey? Guess what—I'll race you. I'll even give you a lead, if you want—a whole goddamn block."

He looked at me, put the roll of bills in his pants pocket, and—Oh, did I love the panic in his eyes!—tried to pretend he didn't understand. "You don't drive," he said. "Do you? For sure not that Pontiac."

"You know damn well I don't drive. I'm talking about feet and legs, mine against yours. Here to the police station, in the street or on the sidewalk. Whatever you prefer."

I could see him think, then squirm ever so slightly, especially when Jimmy and Casey started to look interested. Casey blurted, "Good idea!" just about the moment he shook his head.

"You're not afraid, are you?" I asked. "You said you wanted a challenge, so here it is—with me." I thumped my chest. "Yes—or no?"

"Go for it," Jimmy said. "You used to be a damn good runner. See what's left in the tank."

"You're in heels," Thomas said. "You're not getting far without your running shoes."

I shook my head, but I was ready for it. "I'll run barefoot. I don't care. I've done it before, and I can do it again. You can run in your fancy wingtips."

Misha took my arm and walked me a step away. "It's almost a mile down there, maybe more. Your feet will get torn up."

283

"I ran barefoot as a kid. I ran barefoot all last summer, in the streets and on the track. I'm pretty sure I can do it tonight. I'll pay for everybody if I don't finish."

"I don't know," Misha said, still holding my arm. "You're getting a little too serious. Why don't we just call it a night?"

"Right," Casey said. She gave Thomas and me a very level-headed stare. "Everybody's a little tired. Why don't we just go home?"

Misha nodded, as did Jimmy now, but I damn sure wasn't going to let Thomas off the hook. Let him squirm. "Well, if you're afraid a high school girl could beat you . . ."

I laughed and just let the words hang out there. Thomas looked from Casey to Jimmy and to me. Then he spoke to Misha.

"Well, if you're too scared, I guess, I'll just . . ."

"Great," I said, kicking off my heels. "Let's go."

I handed the shoes to Misha and started for the door. "Wait . . . wait . . ." That was Thomas. But he would not spit out the bait. He took off his jacket, loosened his tie, and started to untie his wingtips. I told him to leave them on unless he wanted me to give him a two-block lead. With a forced laugh, he straightened, rolled up his sleeves, and followed me to the door.

Outside, no moon shone; it was dark, cloudy, and a little humid. A warm breeze whistled around my thighs, making my legs feel loose and fairly lively. Thomas shook his head and stared at the sky, his face a funny mix of determination and doubt. Jimmy had stayed indoors because of a couple of take-out pizza orders he had to fill, but Casey and Misha were there, looking pretty much like a pair of reluctant adults somehow sucked into a childish game.

"Are you sure you want to do this?" Misha whispered. "You're going to tear up your feet. He'll probably beat you just because of that."

"No way he's going to beat me," I said. "I don't care about my feet."

"Even if they're bleeding? It's at least a mile. Who knows what kind of stuff you'll be stepping on?"

"Misha, I've done this before. I'll do it again."

Meanwhile, Thomas started to walk down the block in the direction of the police station. I told him to stop at the Cedars, if he wanted, just short of two blocks away. "I'll stop at a block and a half," he said, "but only because these shoes have pretty heavy soles."

"And the finish line is the police station's main door," I answered. "Misha will be there, waiting with his car. Right, Misha?"

Misha nodded, with a very reluctant frown on his face. He walked into Jimmy's parking lot and started his mother's car, driving off while Thomas continued in the direction of Cedars.

"Can you start us?" I asked Casey. She frowned at first, saying nothing to me as her date and his fancy shoes walked away.

Then she shook her head. "With what? I don't have a starting gun. I just have the keys to his car and his jacket."

"How about a whistle? That will do." I reached between my boobs just under my dress. I kept a whistle on a chain there from my year in the Pontiac. A nice cop who looked after me in those days said I could use it if I ever needed help. Casey took it, still frowning; and when she tried it out, Thomas said he could hear it easily from where he was, a short distance from the Cedars. "Then let's roll," I called.

I stood waiting at the neon "Jimmy's" sign, taking a few deep breaths—nose-in, mouth-out—to relax my muscles and get my heartbeat under better control. I looked down the road for Thomas, saw him nearing the Cedars now, and waited for a signal from him that he was ready to run. No signal came. He just sort of disappeared in the dark beyond the Cedars' dim lights, and I waited to see him emerge into the streetlight a half block farther on. "What's he doing?" I asked. "Where's he going?"—more to myself than Casey—but before she answered, she blew the whistle and waved. I stood there, puzzled for a couple seconds—stupid, really—but then Casey waved again and told me to get moving. I turned, saw nothing but the Cedars' lights, and took off down the street, stumbling when my big right toe found a sharp stone and caused me to slow down to a near stop.

At that moment, all my relaxation fled into the night, way ahead of my body and mind. I saw Thomas in the middle of the street about a block beyond the Cedars now, his fancy shoes flashing like quicksilver in the streetlights, his elbows pumping efficiently by his side. "The bastard can probably run," I whispered to myself. Taking a deep breath, I figured I'd never catch him, and, at a slow, frustrated trot for a second or two, I actually thought of stopping and letting him gloat when I talked of not having enough money to pay for everybody's food. But a car roared past, heading toward the police station as if it had important business there, and though it was probably some high school jock showing off to his girlfriend, I decided to sprint ahead in case there was some trouble for Misha, or maybe even Thomas, who had disappeared into dark shadows again. I lifted the hem of my dress, tucked it into the top of my underpants, and lengthened my strides while picking up my pace as if I were in a meet.

After another one or two minutes I saw Thomas's soles flashing in the lights again—this time much closer—and I let my own bare feet come down harder and quicker to the pavement. At that point each sharp slap of skin on sleight and cement felt joyful, rather than increasingly painful—which it was—as I began to see more and more of Thomas's legs and behind and realized I was actually closing in on him—fast. He was about three and a half blocks from the park at this time, with me one and a half behind. It would be tight, of course, but if I could catch him before he reached the main park entrance, I knew I could beat him to the station's principal door, which I could not quite make out yet, though I saw a car with shining headlights across the street from the station and figured was Misha.

Thomas glanced back and, I saw, knew I was getting closer. His hands and heels pumped higher, harder now, and for the first time I heard the slap of his shoes on the pavement. He swerved suddenly and leaped to the sidewalk beside the park. I ran on the police station side, with the macadam separating us now, so we could see each other clearly with a block or slightly more to the main park entrance. Now I saw Misha standing outside the car in the middle of the street. He was jumping up and down, cheering me on, and I realized

Thomas had just over a block to go. I'd like to say I turned on the after-burners to catch him and break into the lead at that point, but the truth is that Thomas went airborne at the precise moment I was giving up—his hands and feet suddenly swimming as though through violent ocean waves.

At first I thought he had dived to cross the finish line ahead of me, but then I realized he was way too early—about fifty yards too soon in fact. He landed head first, and I heard him bellow in surprise and pain. With hands and arms out front, he belly-flopped to the ground and then rolled over several times, right at the park entrance, where he smacked his head and stopped with his back against a tree.

I crossed the street, just missed by another passing car, and sprinted the fifty yards down the sidewalk toward him. Misha reached him just before I did, and we both called out to ask if he was hurt. Thomas did not respond. Misha squatted beside him, placed his hand on Thomas's shoulder, and gave him a little shake. "You all right, dude? Can you talk?" I squatted beside him too, laid my hand on Thomas's neck, and tried to feel his breathing. Absolutely no motion registered through his shirt.

"Jeez, we better call 911," Misha said. I shook my head, and ran across the street, into the police station instead. There, I spoke to the desk sergeant and told him someone was hurt across the street. The sergeant, who knew me pretty well, called several men from a back room and sent them with me to have a look. I guess I was in shock because I said nothing at first, couldn't talk in fact, just pointed to the park entrance where Misha still squatted and leaned over Thomas. "Call an ambulance," Misha shouted. "I'm not sure he's breathing."

One of the cops, a tall man with dark, very serious eyes, squatted beside them and placed two fingers on Thomas's neck. "Heart's beating," he said, then very carefully took Thomas's shoulders and slowly laid him flat on the ground.

"Fucking broke my leg," Thomas muttered, eyes still closed. "It's killing me."

"Which leg?" the other cop said. But then we all looked down and saw it right away—his left leg twisted out of its natural shape, bent from the knee down at a very extreme, unnatural angle. Blood stained his pant leg, about halfway between his knee and his very dirty left shoe. "Gotta get you to the hospital," the tall cop said. While he stood up and made the call, the other cop took down our names and Misha's account of what had happened, which was, of course, essentially nothing but a trip and a fall while running a stupid race for nothing but pride down the main street of our little town.

"How about you?" the cop said, looking from his notebook down at my feet. "Maybe you can use a doctor too. Did you fall?"

"No, I'm fine, I think." But then I looked down and up at him and Misha with a little squeal of surprise. My feet were bloody and bruised, and my toes— especially on my right foot— looked like they had been twisted out of their natural shape.

"I'll drive her to the hospital," Misha said. "She doesn't need an ambulance. Do you?" He looked at me.

289

The cops shrugged, and I shook my head, happy to have somebody take care of me. We telephoned Casey, waited about fifteen minutes for the medics to arrive, and after they rode off with Thomas laid out in a stretcher, got into Misha's car and went to pick up Casey before heading toward the county hospital just outside of town.

***

XVII.

In lots of ways, that's the end of the story I wanted to tell, but I know there are other important things people will want to know. Mum always told me that she liked stories that had loose ends because they allowed her to imagine how God could tie them all up. Dad liked them too, but mainly, he said, because that's the way life works. "Never a goddamn clear ending you can believe."

So, in lots of ways, I'd like to leave it all that way—Misha and I in a car, Thomas in the hospital, Jimmy at his pizza oven, and Mr. Santa and Coach each homebound because they want a family, and life has offered them all the family they'll ever have. Nothing much different from all that came about, but here are a couple of interesting rogue details:

Casey became a very good friend of Misha's, which, I suppose is no surprise because she's smart and beautiful and, most important, ready for the kind of life that Misha has always wanted. He's bright; so is she— and in fact within a year they were attending college together and sharing an off-campus apartment with two bedrooms, a kitchen, living room, and large dining area that immediately became a shared study. No, they didn't sleep together—at first—but I ended up living with them in my senior high school year, so I'll let you figure out how that particular game of musical beds worked out. Two single girls and a guy—Misha constantly studying and slipping out to work part-time at the hospital in the beginning; Casey spending her days at the university library, where she studied to be a physical trainer and partied pretty frequently (and soberly) during weekends; me sliding off the couch or out of bed to continue running with the cross-country guys and Coach each morning, attending college prep classes (actually doing my homework for a change), and, I don't know why, becoming much less of a code breaker in classrooms and hallways at school. And yes, I even received an award for self-improvement and personal growth at the end of my senior year.

Mr. Santa, my wonderful guide and godfather, acted incredibly proud of me at the awards ceremony, and when I walked down from the auditorium stage with the nice-sized plastic trophy in my hands, he stood up in the front row and led the applause. I almost tripped on my own feet when I saw him, but I looked up and found an auditorium full of students and teachers smiling and clapping for me. It was hard to resist my embarrassment and the impulse to run—yes, up the aisle and out the doors to the street—as I had so many times before. But the look on Mr. Santa's face held me in place—love, pure, obvious and simple, much like the emotional pull I received from Mum and Dad.

I placed the trophy on a table in the living room that night, and stared at the dark-haired ballerina (tutued and bowing, as if to thunderous applause) after I rose from bed next morning, as well as each day and night afterward while studying or preparing dinner. We invited Mr. Santa and Jake to eat with us the following weekend, and of course, that made an incredibly memorable evening for me and everyone else. As he left, Mr. Santa embraced me and, without the slightest hesitation told me I could visit and stay with him and Jake whenever I wanted. "It will be our pleasure," he said. "In fact, come and see us sometime this week."

I don't know what to tell you about Misha; in a strange way, we were never really close after the night I raced Thomas. Beautiful Casey reached him in ways I'm sure I never could—with calm, level-headed talk that, to him, I think, made her glow like a bright light from the sky on a murky ocean surface. I don't know if he felt turned-off by me, the stupid race, or the obvious bizarre relationship with Thomas, but our friendship changed— no more ragged-edged possible family ties, just the dullness of roommates who shared, but preferred having their own space. Sometimes I think he had heard whispers about me and Coach Span and felt disgusted. Sometimes I think his mother and father had something to do with the change, especially if they had heard the rumors too. Most of the time I think he just had had enough. Misha's always preferred things clear and simple. No tension; no personal baggage.

Whatever . . . Eventually, I stopped worrying about it and got on with my schoolwork and some kind of new attitude. At the end of my junior year, I had begun to think seriously about college and a career, and when I applied to college, I chose a double major— dance and physical education—and I pledged to try out for the women's track team. Occasionally, Thomas, with all his fancy self-importance as a man of respect and means, turned out to have a pretty generous heart. He and Mr. Santa bonded, strangely enough, and together, put up the money for my college application and then guaranteed the tuition for me. I worked as a barista at the Sugar Bowl from that point on, frothing up hot and cold drinks to pay for my portion of the rent and food. And Misha—dear, brotherly Misha—got a second job at the college library, shelving books, answering questions at the circulation desk, and carting heavy boxes of used volumes down to the basement so they could be cleaned up and made ready for the annual used-book sale, which was a pretty big event on our campus.

There's no boyfriend in sight for me now that I'm in college, but plenty of casual guys who I jog with on the track and occasionally go to movies with on weekends, or have over for study dates. Two or three girls I work with at the Sugar Bowl are, along with Casey and Ciara at the Cedars, potential BFF's, which for me will be a significant first. Finally, most importantly, I have a special little brother, Jake, who I make free sodas for at the Sugar Bowl and hang out with regularly until he walks home down Main Street or wends his way down school hallways in peace and comfort—because I'll always be there, along with his absolutely wonderful Dad. I give him support and advice as best I can—a big sister's take on how to grow up while being true to yourself as well as others; how to survive in a world where luck and happenstance mean as much, if not more, than individual talent and desire; and finally, how to stay strong and loving when you've lost it all—family, comfortable home, clear direction—and still have a long way to run in the race.

On the night I visited Mr. Santa during the week after winning my award, I was surprised to see a woman sitting across from him in the living room. She was slight, had wide, very intelligent eyes, set in a bony face that showed more skull than skin in the mellow light.

"I'd like you to meet a client of mine, Jamie," Mr. Santa said. "Leslie, this is one of my favorite young people in this town."

Leslie Russo was her name. She smiled, a little embarrassed, I thought, but she rose from the sofa, reached for my hand, and then basically fell into my arms and moaned. I held her, puzzled, looking over her head at Mr. Santa for help, but he just stood there and smiled. She leaned back and gazed into my face as if she wanted to read a story there, and in that instant I dropped my hands to my side and turned away.

"Jamie?—"

"Don't tell me," I said. I spun around to Mr. Santa. "What the fuck is wrong with you? I know who she is—I get it. But she shouldn't be here. She should be in jail. She threw me into a garbage dump—a baby!"

Leslie moaned louder when she heard that. Tears came streaming down her blotchy red face, the veins in her forehead turned blue and looked ready to pop. "No . . . No," she mumbled. "I didn't."

I could barely hold myself back from reaching for her throat, and in another second I would have punched her with all my strength if Mr. Santa hadn't stepped between us. "Easy, Jamie," he said. "This is a difficult time for everyone, including, ah . . . Leslie."

"I'm ashamed of you!" I shouted over his shoulder. "I've never known you, and yet I can't think of anyone in the world I would want to know less. Or hate more."

"Jamie . . ."

"Don't bother. I don't know what you think I'm supposed to feel right now, Mr. Santa, but it sure isn't love or thankfulness."

I turned and started for the front door. Just then Jake ran in from the kitchen, went straight to Leslie, and sobbing, wrapped his arms around her waist. My mouth dropped open. I stood at the door, hand on the doorknob, trying to sort things out. Mr. Santa stepped over and put his hand on my shoulder. "She's a client of mine, Jamie. Has been for several years. That's how I adopted Jake. She's had a very difficult life. But she's straight now, and she asked to meet you, though she knew it would be difficult. Give her a chance."

I turned the doorknob, started to yank open the door, but Mr. Santa put his hands on top of mine and, basically, made me stop. I dropped my arms to my side and leaned my forehead against the doorjamb. Jake came over, stood beside me, and looked up at my face. "Please, Jamie" he said. "You can forgive her. I have."

I looked at the woman's—Leslie's—tear-stained face and turned to Mr. Santa. He took my arm, led me to his chair, and let me sit in it. He and Jake went back to the sofa where Leslie had collapsed. She moaned miserably, and the only words I could make out sounded like sorrow and maybe, God's forgiveness. Or maybe, mine. At the time, I found it hard to believe she was actually who I knew she had to be.

"What do you want from me?" I shouted. "You throw me in the trash and then come back to my life years later as if it was a little mistake? I could have frozen; or been crushed in a garbage condenser. You have no idea how much I've thought about all the possibilities. And now you want me to forgive you? There's a place in hell for people like you!"

Leslie wailed; Jake sobbed louder than before; Mr. Santa sat with his arms around them both and shook his head. I went to the door and left, slamming it behind me to close off all the crying. Then I sprinted away, racing toward everything else in the world that might make me forget the very important things—and people—I had just left behind.

***

XVIII.

I had nowhere to go, really, except back to the apartment with Misha and Casey. But I didn't want to talk to, or see, anybody, so I ran to the gym, slipped through a secret side-door entrance and walked into the girls' locker room, where I lay on a bench for a while but found the moist, fluorescent atmosphere oppressive. I opened my locker, pulled out a sweat suit I kept stashed there, and put it on over my clothes. From there I headed down Main Street again, jogging toward the police station and the entrance to the park. In a matter of minutes, I was on the ground, leaning against a hickory tree, and staring at the empty space I used to live in. As you can imagine, it left a very large empty-pit-like feeling in my stomach.

It had been a couple years, but the shape of the Pontiac still scarred the ground, and the garden I had planted still showed loose, turned up soil along with small white and yellow flowers that somebody had sown or had grown there wildly. I looked through the limbs of the hickory to a fuzzy, clouded-over moon, and felt the joy of a breeze sweeping through the grass from the pond toward me. For a minute—oh, let's face it, for a much longer time, probably an hour—I just sat there and mourned the loss of my former houses—the Bonneville, the two-floor wood-frame where I lived with Mum and Dad, and then somehow, in a way that seemed perverted and weird that night, the trash heap in the alley behind the closed-down Mario's restaurant.

I stayed through the night, but didn't sleep much. Next day I went to Mr. Santa's office instead of school.

When I entered, he dropped his feet to the floor immediately, placed papers and pen on his desk, and positioned a chair for me to sit in next to him. I did not feel friendly, so I chose to stand in front of the desk instead.

"So, what's the story?" I said. "I mean with her, all of it."

Mr. Santa shrugged. "Not much to tell that you haven't figured out already."

"That woman is my true mother?"

"The biological one, as far as I can figure from what she's told me. Same with Jake. DNA checks out with him, but we haven't done that with you."

"Fuck DNA," I said.

Mr. Santa actually laughed. "We're going against trends," he said. "But I feel the same way, Jamie."

"I hate this," I shouted. "I fucking hate all of it!"

He rose, tried to put his arm around my shoulders, but I pushed him away, pretty roughly. He backed off to the side of the desk, but remained within a step or two of me. "She's not making any claims, Jamie. She gave Jake up to the county youth program. When they couldn't find a bed for him, I took him in. As you know, we got along, so . . ."

I was crying. I don't know why, exactly, but tears made a snotty river from my eyes and nose down my cheeks and neck to my shoulders and chest. "Fuck . . ." I said, as Mr. Santa pulled some tissues from the box on his desk. I wiped my face and blew my nose.

"What did she say about me?" I asked when he handed me another bunch of tissues.

"Nothing, at first. We just talked about Jake and why she felt she couldn't keep him. She doesn't trust herself anymore, if you want my opinion. In any case he's happy with me, so he's staying."

"Jesus Christ, what about me? What did she say about me?"

Mr. Santa shrugged. "Nothing at first—as I said. But then she started to talk to me about her wasted life, how much she regretted it, and what she'd done. And then she brought up a baby girl she had years ago . . ."

I put up both my hands and closed my eyes. "I don't want to hear this," I said, more to myself than Mr. Santa, but I opened my eyes and nodded to him. "This is where I come in, I gather."

He nodded. "Well, yes, but there's a little complication to the story."

"Complication? She threw me—"

"She didn't throw you away, Jamie. Your 'father,' if that's what you want to call him, knew someone who could get you adopted in another state— she thinks it was Florida—and get them some money in exchange. Jamie, this is sick stuff. Do you really want to know the whole story?"

I shook my head, but then I added, "It happened. So I should know about it. Go ahead."

"Well, he brought you to this guy; the guy wouldn't give him money without a fully-signed, guaranteed surrender for adoption letter; and so your 'father'—I'll flash the semaphores like your Dad did— waited a couple days, got some money through another drug deal, according to Leslie, and you ended up in the dumpster. They left town. Luckily, you cried out and were found—by your true mother—that very night."

"Wow, and she didn't give a shit . . . about the baby—me."

"She didn't know, she says. She had left and didn't find out about it until a few years later, after they signed away their rights to you. By then, you were living another life, or—"

"Or dead as far as they were concerned. I wonder which she preferred."

"You're being harsh, Jamie, as I guess you have a right to be. But she's changed. Been straight for a couple years, has a decent job, and just wants to know you're okay. Same with Jake."

"No thanks to her." I reached for another bunch of tissues because I had been bawling through the whole shitty story. I wiped my face, blew my nose again, and finally, laughing a little, sat on the chair Mr. Santa had pulled up for me.

"She wants to make amends," he said.

"She can't. What's more, I do not want to see her. My life has been miserable enough."

"It's your call, Jamie. She understands that. It's completely up to you."

"Oh, what power! Maybe I should throw her in the trash to show her what it's like."

"Easy," Mr. Santa said. He put a hand on each of my shoulders and looked at me. "Let it go. Give everything time. It will all work itself out in whatever way is best—for everyone."

With that, he returned to his chair, feet on the desk, and picked up a stack of folders. "People can reform, Jamie. Really. That's the basic message of forgiveness."

"Hmm . . . Yes. And that, too, is where I come in."

But I thanked him—with a big hug and a sloppy kiss on the cheek. Then I invited him and my little brother to have dinner with us that night. "Be warned," I said. "I'm doing all the cooking."

We both had a good laugh at that, but he agreed to come.

I left the office, took another run down to the park before circling it twice—checked out that empty parking spot as if it never existed—and headed back to the apartment. I had a meal to attend to—along with a soppy story to share with my new best friend, Casey, and my old best friend, Misha—no longer a possible older brother, I figured—just a guy I could outrun easily, but always have a problem catching up to.

ACKNOWLEDGEMENTS

I am grateful to the people at Pexels.com, the free photography internet site where we found the photograph by Anfiusa Eremina that so perfectly captures the spirit of Jamie's narrative. We have altered it slightly and printed over it to make the cover.

As always, thanks to Kim McKay, Alex Misurella, and Filipka Misurella who have filled this reluctant paterfamilias with a love and pride of family that he never thought was in him.

Thanks to Gary Will, the first reader of this story, who provided valuable comments on the writing.

And finally, thanks to longtime friends and fellow writers who have read my books through the years and said encouraging things about them. I am especially grateful to Milan Kundera, Stuart Dybek, Wayne Prophet, Joe Somoza, Hank Webb, and the late Kent Haruf, whom I dearly miss. He was a great writer and a wonderful friend.

Fred Misurella

ABOUT THE AUTHOR

A Pontiac in the Woods is the fourth in Fred Misurella's cycle of novels about the modern American family. The others are *Only Sons*, a saga of two competing Italian immigrant families in rural Pennsylvania, *Arrangement in Black and White*, the story of an interracial marriage in Connecticut, and *A Summer of Good-Byes*, about an American couple's attempt to restart their marriage on a visit to Provence in the face of past infertility and the wife's recent extramarital affair. Misurella has also written *Lies to Live By: Stories*, and *Short Time*, a novella about the Vietnam War. His literary journalism has appeared in *Partisan Review*, *Salmagundi*, *Voices in Italian Americana*, *Italian Americana*, *The Christian Science Monitor*, *The New York Times Book Review*, and other journals. His essays on Primo Levi appear in *The Legacy of Primo Levi* and *Answering Auschwitz*. He is the current book review editor for VIA (Voices in Italian Americana), a former Fulbright scholar in France, and a graduate of the University of Iowa Writers Workshop. He lives with his wife and children in East Stroudsburg, Pennsylvania.

Learn more: www.FredMisurella.com.

If you liked *A Pontiac in the Woods*, please help spread the word. Tell friends, review it on social media, mention it to your local library and bookstore. Thanks.

Fred Misurella